TEXAS TANGLE

After her cheating ex-husband stole her trust and her brother stole everything else, horse breeder Nikki Kimball is intent on reclaiming her independence. When her carefree neighbor Dillon Barnett and his enigmatic best friend Brett Anderson offer to help her out, both in the stable and the bedroom, Nikki relearns how to trust and discovers joy.

Ten years ago, the two friends fought a bitter battle for their high school crush. Although Brett longs to be the man in Nikki's life, he is forced to decide if he is willing to lose Dillons' friendship to gain her heart.

As their unusual relationship progresses, Nikki is faced with a conundrum she never expected to face. While her heart wants them both in her life, in her bed, society demands she choose between the two men. Now Nikki has to decide what price she is prepared to pay to keep the happiness and independence she's finally found.

TEXAS TANGLE

ALSO BY LEAH BRAEMEL

BARNETT SPRINGS

Texas Tangle

Tangled Past (historical)

Feeding the Flames

Texas Hook-Up

THE GRADY LEGACY

Slow Ride Home

No Accounting for Cowboys

Wrangling the Past

HAUBERK PROTECTION SERIES

First Night

Private Property

Personal Protection

Deliberate Deceptions

Perfect Proposal

Hidden Heat

STANDALONE STORIES

All I Need for Christmas

Unashamed

TEXAS TANGLE

LEAH BRAEMEL

Samarlane
Publishing

Cover art by covergirldesign.com

First print edition, 2023

ISBN (paperback) 978-0-9959429-5-0

CHAPTER I

"No, no, no!" With steam billowing from the hood of her truck, Nikki maneuvered blindly easing the vehicle to the side of the road, making sure the horse trailer she was towing wasn't blocking traffic. "You can't die here. We're so close to home."

With a sigh, she killed the engine, checked her phone even though she knew her battery was dead, climbed from the cab and kicked the front tire. "You couldn't have held on for another three miles, could you? No-o-o, you had to blow out the rad here, you piece of shit."

She waited in the inky black night for ten minutes before a vehicle crested the hill, its high beams blinding her until the driver dimmed the lights. She moved to the side, waving her arms for help. The Jeep zipped past, not even slowing. Over the next half hour, a half-dozen cars zoomed by without a single one slowing. She was starting to consider unloading her newest horse and riding him home when a familiar white pick-up slowed then parked in front of her truck.

First a long, booted leg, then the rest of the driver's body unfolded as he clambered down. Dillon Barnett jammed a dusty black cowboy hat on his head before he ambled over. "Hey, Nik. Need some help?"

"Yeah, my truck's overheated." Trying to ignore the ache that filled her every time she set eyes on her neighbor, Nikki reached for the hood release.

Dillon caught her wrist and stopped her. "Whoa, don't touch that yet. Let it cool down a while longer, or I'll be hauling you off to the burn unit."

Before she could stop herself, she leaned in and filled her lungs with his scent, detecting only a hint of the aftershave he'd used that morning behind a heaping of good honest sweat. Mostly he smelled of machine oil, sawdust and…mesquite? She scrunched up her nose and took another sniff. "You been at a barbecue?"

Dillon chuckled, a dark delicious sound that reminded her of humid summer evenings eating barbecued ribs and drinking cool beer. Of star-filled nights that promised long sessions of hot, sweaty sex.

Where had that come from? Maybe because she hadn't been with a guy and had hot, sweaty sex in a couple of years?

"We've been cuttin' down some mesquites out back of the old Pritchert place. New owners are plannin' on putting in a pool and hired me to do the landscaping around it. I figured I might as well get started in there with my machinery."

When he released her, she took a step back, stopping her sigh before it could escape. *Stop with the fantasies, Nik. If Dillon was interested in you, he'd have made some move after Wade moved out.* Oh, he was always over checking on her, helping her fix the fences the horses or weather knocked down, but not once had he given her any indication he was interested in her.

No, Dillon just did those things because he'd been raised to be a good neighbor, willing to help the struggling divorcee with the measly forty acres of scrub behind his spread of two hundred and fifty. Still, a girl could fantasize.

Oh. My. The fantasies she'd been having about him lately.

But had she imagined the way he'd held her after pulling her against him? Or the way his hand stroked the small of her back? That couldn't have been accidental. Could it?

The sigh she'd been holding back escaped. "You know, your hat's the wrong color."

Frowning, he took off his Stetson and examined it, checking it both inside and out. "What d'ya mean? It looks fine to me."

"It's black. It should be white." *Lame, Nikki. Real lame.*

"Why—oh, white hat. Good guy. I gotcha." His puzzled expression remained. "Why am I a good guy? Because I stopped? Heck, I couldn't have just driven by. What type of a person would that make me?"

"Like the half-dozen other drivers who left me standing here?"

After knocking the dust off his hat on his thigh, he resettled it on his head, covering the thick black hair she'd been fantasizing running her fingers through. The shadows thrown by the brim hid the liquid-chocolate eyes that turned her knees into putty. "Pretty girl standing all alone at the side of the road at night? You're safer that they didn't stop."

Her heart thumped a little harder against her ribs. Pretty girl. How pretty could she be, considering she'd been in a truck all day? Still, it was nice to hear.

He grimaced at the still-steaming engine. "You call a tow truck?"

She shook her head. "My phone died and I forgot my charger."

He pulled out his own cell. "Hey, Gloria, it's Dillon Barnett. Nikki Kimball's truck's overheated. Looks like she's going to need a tow." There was a pause then he frowned. "Shoot, you sure he can't be here any quicker?"

At Nikki's anxious look, he shook his head. "Yeah, okay, guess there's not much choice. We'll leave the truck here, and I'll take Nikki home." He paused, listening. "We're on Tower Hill Road, 'bout a half mile south of my place, right before it meets up with Alvarado. Oh, and Glor? Have Ernie call her when he knows what's wrong and how much it's gonna cost to fix it, will you?"

He ended the call and pocketed the phone with a frown. "There's a big pile-up on the interstate keepin' all the trucks busy, so the soonest Ernie can get a truck out here is an hour, maybe even an hour and a half. I'll take you home, and he'll pick up your truck soon as he can."

"What about Bashir?" Nikki waved to the horse trailer she'd been hauling. "I can't leave him here."

"How about we unhook the trailer, and I'll tow him home." He peered in the back of the trailer. "Bashir, huh? That's a rotten name to stick on a horse. You should rename him Buddy or Bucky or some good Texan name."

"Buddy?" She laughed. "Considering he's from Arabian bloodlines, I think Bashir suits him just fine."

The dark shadows accentuated the bright white of his grin. "Seems to me, one of your beloved Blues is named Daisy. Can't say it's a particularly Arabian name now, is it?"

She rolled her eyes. Figured he'd point out her lapse. "Daisy came to me already named. I could hardly change it since she'd gotten used to it, any more than I'll change Bashir's name."

Twenty minutes later, the trailer successfully unhitched from her truck and hooked up to Dillon's, Nikki found herself sitting beside Dillon in the cab of his truck. While he started the truck, she fiddled with one of the vents, turning it so the stream of cool air blasted her. The A/C in her truck had stopped working months ago. The trip back in the damned Texas heat had just about had her melting into the vinyl seats of her truck.

"Where'd you pick this one up?" Dillon checked his mirror and eased onto the road.

"Muncie."

"Indiana?" He whistled through his teeth. "That's quite a haul to do by yourself. You do it all in one shot, or you stop over somewhere in between?"

"I didn't want to give Bashir's owners a chance to change their mind, so once I closed the deal, I loaded him up and headed straight back." She closed her eyes and fought the exhaustion swamping her.

"Shit, woman, that drive's a good fifteen, sixteen hours one way even if you're not hauling a trailer. You shoulda stopped somewhere in between. You coulda fallen asleep at the wheel."

Without opening her eyes, she lifted one shoulder in a half-hearted shrug. "Thanks for stopping tonight. I appreciate it."

"As I said, I wouldn't be much of a neighbor if I hadn't offered a hand." A strong hand dropped over hers, his thumb stroking hers. She didn't dare open her eyes. If she did, he might stop.

He was always touching her. Nothing sexual, just little things. Massaging her shoulders when they were repairing the fences, or keeping his hand wrapped around hers after he'd helped her off her horse at the end of her last endurance ride. But after not having been held by a man for several years as her marriage fell apart, every nerve ending fired each place Dillon touched her. Tonight, being so close to him in the dark cab, her imagination inundated her with images. Images of him slipping his hand beneath her top, of him cupping her breasts, bending his head down to take her nipple in his mouth.

Her body heated, softened, imagining his hard thighs pressing hers apart, or holding her up against a wall as he plunged into her. The taut muscles in his forearms planted on either side of her head while he pumped into her. Thick shoulder muscles rippling beneath her palms, except in her imagination, instead of hoisting himself on one of his horses, it was her he rode.

Dillon, bless his soul, didn't say a word for the next ten

minutes, allowing her to indulge her fantasies. The truck slowed, the steady click-click of his turn signal announced they were turning onto the boundary road. Five minutes later, he turned right again. The truck bounced over the washed-out spots the spring rains had worn away, forcing her to grab the door handle and pray Dillon's truck didn't break a spring.

"Damn, Nik, you need to get a road grader in here to smooth these ruts out right soon. You're not going to be able to get the truck out one day."

"Graders cost money." Money she didn't have. Not that type of money, anyway. Not unless she got a couple more horses to board.

"You didn't happen to notice I've got one as part of my business?" He snorted. "I'll send one of my guys over to fix this up tomorrow morning."

When she started to protest about how much it would cost, he narrowed his eyes at her. "No arguments. It won't cost me a thing."

Except paying the guy who ran the grader, or the gas both for the machinery and for the truck to haul it over. But she knew if she argued those points, she'd hurt his pride.

Once he'd backed the trailer up beside the barn, she reached for the door handle, only to hear him say again. "What's your hurry? I'll get it for you."

She settled back and waited, half amused at the idea of a man opening her door and half sad. It had been so long since anyone had bothered to worry about manners around her. Wade had never bothered with such niceties. And her brother Phil? The temperature in Hell would have to reach the negative numbers before he ever got off his ass to do something for someone else.

Dillon hopped out, walked around the front of the truck and opened her door, holding his hand out to help her down. The moment their palms touched, a spark of electricity pulsed between them. Nikki stared at their joined hands then looked up to find Dillon watching her, desire bright in his eyes. His thumb swept over the pad at the base of her thumb. The spark between them shot straight up her arm and spread out like fork lightning to every part of her body. "Why don't I help you get Bashir settled in?" *I'd rather you helped me settle in for the night.*

Flustered at how her body softened just from imagining cuddling up to him, Nikki nodded and slid out from the truck. Instead of letting go of her once her feet were on the ground, he slammed the door shut and walked with her to the back of the trailer, her hand still in his.

Once there, he had to release her so she could unlock the door. She backed her newest acquisition out the trailer and led him toward the barn, concentrating on where she was putting her feet along the rutted path.

A two-pitched bray started up from the pasture and a donkey trotted out from the ink-black night and butted his nose into Nikki's stomach.

"Hey, Merlin, you miss me?" Chuckling, she stopped to scratch behind his ears.

"He acts like he hasn't seen you in a couple weeks." Dillon reached out and scratched the other side of the donkey's neck. "Heya, buddy. How you doin'?"

Merlin quickly abandoned Nikki, switching his attention to Dillon.

"Traitor," she muttered.

Throwing the latch on the barn, she opened the door and was nearly knocked over by her part-mastiff, part German shepherd. The huge dog barked and ran circles around her before haring off across the fields. "Rascal? What were you doing locked in the barn?"

Shaking her head, she led Bashir into the barn and switched on the light. "Oh, shit! Phil, you lazy ass."

"Mmm, shit is about right." Dillon gestured to her oldest

mare Witness's stall. "Looks like no one's cleaned out for a couple of days."

She led Bashir into an empty stall and tethered him. Swearing under her breath, she grabbed a halter and slid it over Witness's head. "Come on, girl, let's get you out of there."

Dillon frowned as the mare at first balked then limped from the stall. "From the way she's movin', I'm bettin' he hasn't given the poor old girl her meds today."

Cursing her brother, Nikki tied up the mare by the door and checked the other horses. "Crap. None of them have any water. All the buckets are dry."

A check of the feed room had her swearing even harder. "Damn it, there are as many feed bags as when I left." She wheeled back to face Dillon and found him watching her again. His eyes swept down her in a slow glide. The track of his gaze branded every inch it touched as if he were staking a claim.

"I-I must have told him a dozen times he needed to check the troughs and make sure they had enough water." She wasn't imagining the look he'd just given her, not this time. She forced herself to concentrate instead of indulging in the fantasy Dillon Barnett might actually be interested— sexually—in her. As if he would be thinking about sex in the heat and the stench of the barn. "It looks like he hasn't done anything since I left."

He grabbed a pitchfork leaning against the wall. "Then we'd better get to it, hadn't we?"

Between the two of them, they cleaned out Witness's stall. Dillon disposed of the soiled bedding and replaced it with fresh straw while Nikki filled first the water bucket, then stuffed a hay bag and hung it in the corner. Once the mare was back in place and munching on the fresh hay, Nikki checked the horse's swollen joints. "I swear some days I want to just hit that lazy brother of mine up the back of the head. You'd think he'd be glad to be living with me instead of in a halfway house with a bunch of strangers."

"Yeah, well, Phil doesn't seem to like getting off his keister unless someone's prodding his sorry ass with a pitchfork. I say we march up to the house and make him come down and muck out while we watch."

Straightening, Nikki turned her attention from the mare and watched Dillon, who was working on the next stall. The barn still held the day's heat, so he'd ditched his shirt. The muscles of his back rippled as he dug into the soiled bedding with the pitchfork then hefted it into a wheelbarrow. The overhead light glistened off a bead of sweat at the top of his neck. Nikki forced air into her lungs as the bead trickled down over his spine, disappearing into his jeans.

He glanced over his shoulder with a puzzled expression, then straightened and leaned on the pitchfork. "Nik? I'm serious. What d'you say I go up and march Phil down here to help out?"

She frowned. "His car wasn't out front, so he must have gone out."

He was probably drinking down at the Boot-T Bar. Figured. If he got stopped for a DUI, he could spend the night in jail. There was no way she was bailing his ass out this time. Let him explain it to his parole officer.

"Hey, it's all right, Nik." Dillon laid a hand on her shoulder, rubbing it lightly. "At least you weren't away any longer, and from the looks of it, the horses are all okay. It won't take us long to get it cleaned up."

"Yeah, it just pisses me off. All his life Phil has gotten away with this type of shit while I've been left cleaning up after him. I wish just once he'd do something without me having to push him every step of the way."

"He's twenty-four years old. It's time you push him out to find his own way, damn the consequences. I just can't figure out why he couldn't live at your parents.'"

"It's part of the court stipulations. He had to live within

Barnett County until the remainder of his sentence is served. Since Mom and Dad moved back to Michigan…"

"You didn't feel like you could turn your back on your family. I get that. But why couldn't Phil have gotten an apartment of his own?"

"He can't afford it without a job. And a guy with a record isn't exactly the type most employers are looking for." She wasn't about to explain how her mother had played the guilt card, or how she'd not felt she could say no. Besides, she was the only one living in the house now, not to mention she'd thought Phil would help out. "If it was one of your brothers, wouldn't you have taken them in?"

"Yeah, I guess I would. But they would have been out here doin' their chores instead of parkin' their keisters on the couch all day."

There wasn't much she could say to that, so Nikki returned her attention to her chores. They worked in a companionable silence, though she'd never been so aware of having another person in the barn with her. When she reached for a bag of grain, Dillon took it from her as if it were no heavier than a bag of sugar. "I got it."

His stomach muscles taut, he carried it to the spot between Bashir's and Witness's stall doors before dropping it. He bent over to rip it open, his jeans pulling tight over his ass. Paying so much attention to the delectable sight instead of where she was walking, Nikki stumbled over an empty bucket she'd left on the ground.

"Whoa, watch out there." Dillon grabbed her, his arm whipping around her waist.

She landed against him with an oomph, aware of how his thigh muscle pressed against hers, his arms banded around her waist, his muscular chest mashed into her breasts. She could have blamed the heat flooding her on the sultry August evening, but she had no explanation for the electricity arcing between them.

His breath whispered out of him, a soft caress over her cheek. The brim of his cowboy hat brushed the top of her head as he closed the distance between them, skimming his lips over hers.

Holy crap, he was kissing her. In real life, not in one of her fantasies.

She tilted her head, her hands clutching his arms half afraid he might disappear if she let go. While beneath her hand, his heart pounded in a steady beat, her own pulse spiked as fast as a hummingbird's.

The tip of his tongue brushed the seam of her mouth; she parted her lips, allowing him entrance. He didn't plunder, but he didn't let her escape either. A hint of burnt coffee and spicy male teased her taste buds. Her breath hitched when he shifted positions, pressing the hard length of his erection into the cradle of her hips. Savoring the taste of him, her mind swirled into fantasies of getting naked with him, his hot flesh sliding over her, into her.

One of his hands slid under her tee and splayed over the small of her back. A shiver zigzagged along her spine, following the path of his calloused fingers and palm as they rasped her skin. She made a tiny whimper as she ground against him, urging him on. Taking the sound as encouragement, he deepened the kiss, took more from her. Demanded more. She gave everything he asked of her, but took equally from him. Her body pulsed with need by the time he finally ended the kiss, the stiff stubble of his beard abrading her cheek as he withdrew.

His gaze traced down her in a long slow path. "How long you been on the road?"

Huh? Was that a backhanded way of saying she looked tired? Or that she needed a bath? She glanced down at her now dusty jeans and scuffed-up boots. *You are* so *not sexy, Nik.* Here she'd been fantasizing about them taking the leap from friends to lovers for months, and he'd chosen to kiss her socks off the night she resembled Rascal after he'd fought a knock-down-drag-out with the local raccoon.

"I left Muncie last night as soon as we closed the deal." The heat of the kiss bled away, replaced with the frustration she'd felt at seeing the conditions Bashir had endured. "You should have seen the place, Dillon. It was a disaster waiting to happen. There were old junkers and car parts in the middle of the pasture, and their horses were so freaking thin they wouldn't have scored more than four on the Hennecke scale. I've a good mind to report them to the sheriff. I wished I could have taken all their horses."

"Hey, there's only so much you can do." He lifted his hand as if to cup her face but dropped it again. Yeah, he was already regretting kissing her.

"I guess."

"You've been on the road a long time. You must be exhausted."

Not too exhausted for you. "I'm ready for bed, if that's what you mean."

She wanted him to be in her bed beside her. On top of her. Inside her.

She headed out of the barn, waiting for him before she closed the gate. "Do you want to come in? Have a beer or a soda or something?" *Me?*

"You're not too tired?" His eyes were hidden in the shadow of the brim of his hat, but his voice made promises that had her pussy throbbing.

"Come on in for a while." *Stay tonight. Tomorrow. As long as you want. Ride me until I'm too exhausted to move, to think.*

He covered the distance between them before she could blink. His hand cradling the back of her head, he stared down at her. "You're sure about this, Nik?"

He had to ask? "I'm sure."

He strengthened his hold on her hair, tilting her head so he could feather kisses down her neck. At the same time his free hand cupped her ass as he ground his erection into her. She hooked one leg around his hip, and rocked against him, the pressure against her clit setting off a firestorm of sensation.

"Not here, baby. Inside. Where we can take our time."

Despite her frustration at having to delay her gratification, she nodded.

Lacing his fingers with hers, they walked toward the house, Dillon catching her when she stumbled over a rut. "Sure is dark back here. You need to install a motion-sensor light to cover this area."

"I have one. Phil must have turned it off." She stopped and stared at the house, scanned the yard. That's what was wrong. There were no lights on. Phil never turned off the lights. Even if he had, there'd be the flicker of the television on the walls since he usually fell asleep in front of it, leaving it running all night. So why was the hair on the back of her neck prickling?

"What's the matter?"

She slowly shook her head. "I don't know. It's silly. You'll probably think me nuts. Phil's car's gone, which means he's out. He's probably just turned off the lights, or maybe we've blown a fuse, but something just doesn't feel right, you know?"

His grip on her tightened as he guided her back to the cab of the truck. He retrieved a shotgun from behind the seat. "Gimme your keys. I'll make sure there's no one inside."

She rummaged in her bag and flipped through her keys, separating the front door key from the rest.

He jammed it in his front pocket then tightened his grip on the gun. "Stay here."

She reached out, grabbed his hand before he could leave her. "Dillon, be careful."

With a smile, he covered her hand with his in a comforting

gesture. "It's probably nothing, but it doesn't hurt to be careful. Right?"

With that, he released her and slipped through the shadows to the front of the house. A minute later, light flooded out the living room window, spilling across the yard. She expected to see more lights turn on; instead, he reappeared, hurrying toward her, his cell phone to his ear.

Once he'd shoved his phone in his pocket, he wrenched open the truck door and growled, "Get in the truck."

"What's wrong?" Her seatbelt had barely clicked into place before he'd started the engine and they were halfway down the lane. "Was someone there?"

"I didn't want to wait to find out." His jaw tightened. "Sorry, Nik, but you've been robbed."

CHAPTER 2

Even in the dark of the cab, he couldn't mistake the way Nikki's shoulders drew up danged near her ears, nor the way she hugged herself. Thank God her truck had died where it did.

He hadn't been lying when he said he would have pulled over to help no matter who had been standing there, but her comment about him wearing a black hat rankled. Here she thought he was being a nice guy driving her home, not realizing the whole time all he'd been thinking about was how to get in her pants. Not that he didn't often fantasize about getting her under him, but he hadn't wanted to push her before she was ready. Now she'd had some time to recover from the wounds left by her divorce, he'd decided to press his case a little stronger.

The kiss had been totally unplanned, but once he'd started it and from the way she'd responded, he'd been unable to pull back. If his dick had any say, they'd have been doing one helluva lot more than kissing once he'd gotten her inside. Hell, if wishes were horses, he'd have been riding her all night long.

Taking one hand off the wheel, he rubbed her shoulder, hoping to soothe her, but the tenseness of her muscles didn't subside. "Hey, it'll be all right. It's just things. At least you weren't there when they broke in."

Though he had a damned good idea that the person who'd taken her stuff hadn't needed to break in.

She didn't turn to look at him, just continued staring back up at her house. The dim green glow from the dashboard highlighted her throat as she swallowed. "So why'd we take off like that? If everything's gone, then they're gone too. There were no other cars or trucks there, so it should have been safe. Shouldn't it?"

Once they reached the main road, he parked the truck so it wouldn't block the driveway, but left the engine running. "I didn't want to take the chance that whoever took your stuff might come back and find us there."

Or might have still been lying in wait, expecting her to come home alone. What if Phil hadn't taken her stuff? What if she'd arrived earlier, while the bastards were still there? She could have been hurt. Raped. He clutched the steering wheel.

Ten long minutes passed before they heard sirens wailing in the distance. Once the first patrol car pulled up beside the truck, Scowling, Dillon lowered his window. Damn it, why the hell wasn't it Brett responding? This was his territory. "Hey, Tiny. Where's Brett?"

The deputy sheriff shrugged. "There's a big pile-up on the interstate tying up most of the station. It'll be a while from the sounds of the mess. So what we got here?"

"Nik's been robbed."

"She okay? They rough her up at all? She need an ambulance?"

"No. She wasn't there when they took her stuff." Thank God for small miracles.

"Then she's been burgled, not robbed."

If he hadn't been in the truck and Tiny in his car, he might have popped the deputy in the jaw. "Jesus H. Christ, Tiny.

Robbed, burgled. Nik's stuff is gone. What the fuck difference does it make?"

"'Cause one's right, and the other ain't." Tiny put his car into gear again. "You two stay here until I make sure the scene's secure, ya hear?"

His car had disappeared over the ridge just as two more units turned off the road. Their lights caromed off the trees and rocks as the cars muscled their way over the washed-out driveway. Less than five minutes later, one of Barnett County's newest officers cruised back down the lane and stopped at the entrance, blocking anyone else from accessing the place. He swaggered over to Dillon's side of the truck. "Tiny says for you to bring Ms. Kimball up to the house now."

Dillon turned the truck around and headed back up the laneway, parking beside the police cars. Lights blazed from every room in the house. Tiny stood on the porch, talking to two of his officers. "It's all clear, folks. From the looks of the stuff they dumped out of the fridge, whoever did it is long gone."

Dillon didn't know if he was pleased they'd missed them or pissed off that he didn't have a chance to show the scumbuckets a little Texas justice.

Tiny held up a hand to stop them once they reached the top step of the porch. "Ms. Kimball, before you go in, I need to ask you a few questions."

Dillon took her hand in his. The little squeeze she gave him in return wound its way into his chest and around his heart. Thank God he'd been running late and had been the one to stop to help her.

Tiny flipped the page on his notebook. "When were you last here?"

"I left just after seven on Wednesday morning."

"You mind tellin' me where you went and why?"

Though Dillon could sense her impatience, Nikki answered

the questions about her trip to Indiana and about the horse she'd rescued. How they'd gotten him settled and cleaned out the barn before checking the house. About how she'd left Phil to look after the place. And how Phil's car wasn't parked out back in its usual spot. "We didn't realize anything was wrong until I noticed all the lights were off. That's when Dillon checked the house and discovered I'd been robbed—I mean burgled."

Tiny hmmed but didn't say anything more, just continued jotting down notes.

"When can I check my stuff? See what they've taken?"

Tiny shot Dillon a why-the-fuck-do-I-have-to-be-the-one-to-break-the-bad-news, thanks-a-lot-dipshit look. "I've only got a few more questions, then we'll be through. Did you lock the door when you left? 'Cause there's no sign of any damage to the lock or the door."

"Yes, but Phil was still here when I left. Maybe he left the door unlocked."

"The door was unlocked and partially open when I checked it," Dillon added, pissed off he might be giving Phil a possible get-out-of-jail-free card.

With a grunt, Tiny scratched something into his notebook. "D'you know where your brother is right now, Ms. Kimball?"

Her shoulders slumped. "No."

"He got a cell phone you can call him on?"

Dillon pulled out his phone and dialed the number Nikki dictated. A half minute later, he shoved it back in his pocket. "No answer. Can you track it?"

"Could, I suppose." Tiny looked doubtful. "I'll check with the judge but you'd probably have more success if you keep phoning— somebody'll probably answer at some point." He used his notebook to tilt his hat back. "Your brother been workin' anywhere recently, Ms. Kimball?"

"No, not many people are willing to hire a man with a

record." Plus Phil was a lazy-ass bastard who was content to let his sister do all the work while he sat on his butt.

"If he left here, you have any idea where he might head? Maybe to your parents' or some girlfriend's or something?"

"I don't know. If he went home, it would be in violation of his parole."

Tiny hmmed again. "He got any friends with a truck who might've helped him?"

"You think Phil did this? No." She took a step backward. "No. Phil wouldn't steal from me. I'm his sister. I took him in after…"

She trailed off. Dillon could practically see the moment she did the math and realized X equaled her brother.

"All right, you can go in now. We're going to need you to tell us what's missing."

Her grip tightened around Dillon's fingers at her first glimpse of her living room. The only sign there'd been any furniture in the room were the dents in the carpet. A silk flower arrangement she'd had on the coffee table had been flung into one corner. In the far corner, framed photos from the shelf unit now lay scattered over the floor, the glass smashed where someone had swept them off their shelves then stomped on them.

The choked gasp that escaped her was like a dagger in Dillon's chest. Though she hadn't said much about it to him directly, he'd heard a lot of talk in town about how Wade had fought to take everything from her during the divorce. What few belongings she had left were hard earned. Now even they were gone.

Right then and there he vowed if he ever saw Phil—he had no doubt it was her brother who had taken her belongings— he'd stuff her brother's nuts in the mulcher and use them as fertilizer.

Tiny tagged along behind them as they toured the house, writing furiously in his notebook as Nikki cataloged what was missing. The television, a DVD player, the sofa, love seat, coffee tables. The dining room table and chairs. Gaps accentuated where the fridge and stove should be standing, the contents of the fridge dumped on the counter, the vegetables from the crisper already wilted and flies buzzing over them.

When they got to the tiny spare bedroom she used as an office, she cursed, her fingernails digging into Dillon's hand. The woman sure had a good grip. He'd have to make sure his brother Matt never challenged her to an arm wrestling match. That boy's ego would take a hit to be beaten by a woman, but he'd sure as shooting lose to Nikki as worked up as she was right now.

"Look at this." She waved a hand over the paper-covered floor. "He must have dumped everything out of my desk and the file cabinets. Do you know how long it'll take me to sort this out?"

Nikki freed herself from his hand. He and Tiny stayed in the doorway while she walked into her bedroom, her boots echoing over the scarred plank floor. She pivoted in place then stomped to the closet and wrenched open the door. "He even took my clothes. Why the fuck would he need them? Most of them are old anyway."

Instead of the bereft look he expected to see, anger blazed from her. Even Tiny retreated a half step at her fury. "He stole everything. He's cleaned me out."

Letting out a screech of frustration, she pushed past them and raced down the hall, her arms wrapped around her waist. Moments later, the front door slammed, rattling the windows. Dillon started to go after her, but Tiny caught his arm before he'd taken two steps. "If I were you, I'd let her get a head start. She needs to get it out of her system. You step in now, you'll likely find yourself with a fat lip or a broken nose."

Deciding to heed Tiny's advice, he stayed where he was. But five minutes was all he'd give her. Then he was going after her.

"How sure are you that it was Phil? Maybe she's right. Maybe he took off, and someone else cleaned her out."

It was a rhetorical question. He'd bet dollars to donuts Phil had taken her stuff, but he had to have something to tell her.

"It's possible, but I'm betting my money on her brother." Tiny took off his hat and scratched his receding hairline. "I'm also betting he didn't do this alone. For the amount of stuff he's taken and the size, he would have needed a truck and another strong back or two. You wouldn't happen to know any of his friends, would you?"

"Phil and I aren't exactly close." Though they lived on neighboring farms, he doubted they'd exchanged more than five words to each other. Mainly because Phil was always planted in front of the television, while Nikki bore the burden of the chores. "You'd have to check with Nikki."

He glanced out the window where Nikki paced the front lawn, her lips moving as if she were cursing out an invisible opponent.

Tiny followed his gaze and grunted. "I'll give her some more time to calm down. She didn't happen to mention anything about where her brother hangs out, did she?"

"Nik complained a while back that he's always down at the titty bar out on the loop. You could try there."

"The Boot-T Bar?" Tiny made a disparaging sound in the back of his throat. "I'll go talk to the bartender, ask if they've seen him around."

Brett had mentioned the type of clientele who frequented the bar as well as some of the fights, a few involving weapons scarier than a broken beer bottle. "What if Phil lost a bet to the wrong type of person, and they wanted more than just Nikki's stuff to pay off the debt? Do you think Phil's not here because he was part of the payment?"

"You mean they've decided to use him to fertilize some field right now?"

Dillon nodded.

"It's possible. But considering he's already out on probation for breaking and entering, and possession of stolen goods, I'm betting he cleared the place out as soon as she left and has a two-day head start. He could be halfway to the coast by now." Tiny hitched up his pants and glanced around again. "We'll be putting a *Be on the Look Out* for him as a person of interest either way. If we hear anything, I'll let you know. I would recommend you don't mention that little theory to your girlfriend there. She's got enough to worry about."

Shit, what if they came back looking for more money from Nikki? There was no way he could leave her alone now.

"Anything I can tell Nik in the meantime? What are the chances of getting any of her stuff back?"

Tiny scratched his arm with the edge of his notebook. "Slim to none? I have more hopes we'll find her brother before we find her belongings. That boy's a trouble magnet. It'll only be a matter of time before he winds up in the slammer. If he's lucky, it'll be in some other county."

With a nod, Tiny left him. Dillon heard him telling his men they could wrap up and head home. So much for fingerprinting and all the forensic crap they showed on TV. Still, if Phil wound up in the local jail, Tiny'd make sure he'd wind up eating a bellyful of knuckle sandwiches. If Brett didn't get to him first.

BRETT ANDERSON SWITCHED off the strobe lights and parked his squad car beside the others. The three units parked in front of Nikki's, lights still flashing, highlighted the trim figure striding back and forth across the lawn, her arms wrapped about herself. Where the hell was Dillon, and why had he left Nikki alone?

He got out of the car and headed straight for her, ignoring

the house for the moment. When he'd recognized the address blasted over the police radio, it had been all he could do not to abandon the accident site out on the highway. At least Tiny had been the first responder on scene and had kept him in the loop.

"Hey, Nik."

Nikki's head snapped up. "Brett!"

She launched herself at him, wrapping her arms about his waist. The fear that had caught him since he'd first heard the call relaxed as he closed his arms around her. "You okay, sweetie?"

"Yeah, it's just…" She buried her face against his neck, her chest heaving as she struggled to maintain control. If he knew her, it wasn't an effort to hold back tears but to contain her anger. "Everything I've got is gone."

"I know, Nik. But it's just stuff. At least you're safe." Tucking her head under his chin, he stroked her back, enjoying the feel of her in his arms. Despite the number of visits he'd made to her place over the years, only in his fantasies had he been able to hold her like this again.

They stood wrapped together for a few minutes, her breathing gradually calming down, her body softening against his. Brett memorized how she fit perfectly against him, taking the time to notice the tinier details like how her braid dangled halfway down her back. He fantasized about removing the elastic holding it in place and running his fingers through her hair, freeing it from its bindings. What would it be like to lie beneath her, to feel her hair cascade over his chest?

"Tiny thinks Phil did it." She tilted her head back to look at him, reminding him of the last time he'd held her in his arms. What would it be like to kiss her the way he had then?

Not now. Not yet. She's been victimized. If you make your move now, you'll never know if she's turned to you because you represent safety or if she's hot for you.

"I heard." When he'd heard Tiny broadcast the *B.O.L.O.* on

Phil, the tow truck drivers had saluted the curse he'd uttered. "We'll find him. Don't worry."

"I don't understand any of it." She shook her head in confusion and looked toward the house.

Goddamn that lazy bastard. How they could be related was beyond his imagination. Then again, of all people, he knew how genes didn't carry the best—or the worst—traits between family members. Thank God for small mercies. "Honey, there were no marks on the lock to show someone had broken in. There were no broken windows—"

"No," she interrupted. "I understand why they think it was him, but what I don't get is how he could have done this to me, his own sister. I took him in instead of making him live in a halfway house, or somewhere with strangers. There must be some other explanation."

He cupped her cheek until she looked at him. "It's not about you. To Phil, it's about satisfying himself, no matter who he hurts."

She leaned her cheek into his palm, her eyes closing. "What would I do without friends like you?"

Friends? Yeah, he'd tried to stay her friend. After he'd come back from college, it had hurt to see her in town with her husband, to be reminded of what he'd lost. A couple months later, he'd joined the Barnett County police and had discovered her husband receiving a blow job from town slut Patsy Schrader in the grocery store parking lot. It had just about killed him not to warn her that her husband was cheating. Same with the next time, when he'd caught them *in flagrante dilecto* in the back seat of Patsy's van. Or the next.

Right after she'd finally kicked the sorry bastard out the year before, he figured he'd have another chance. But every time he'd checked on her since, she'd been oblivious to why he was visiting. Instead she'd announced she was determined to make it on her own and spurned all his help.

Maybe now they could pick up where they'd left off ten years before. He moved a half step closer, and she didn't step away. Instead she continued to look up at him, her lips slightly parted. Inviting him to kiss her. He bent his head until the brim of his hat brushed the top of her head.

A throat cleared on the porch. "Hey, Anderson, you get that accident scene cleared up?"

Stifling a sigh, Brett pulled back. On the porch, Tiny rocked on his heels, one eyebrow raised. *Shit.* There went the professional rating on his next review. Then he saw Dillon standing in the shadows, arms folded across his chest. *Shitfuck.*

When Dillon stepped into the light, he couldn't miss his friend's narrowed eyes. Nor could he miss the heat in them when they turned on Nikki. *Shitfuckdamn.*

You've been down this road before. Remember that fiasco? It's Dillon's chance with Nikki this time. Not that either of them had ended up with her back in high school, but he wasn't prepared to lose Dillon or the Barnetts. Not again.

He dropped his arms from Nikki, and stepped back. "Hey, Dill. Nik, I gotta go help Tiny here. I'll talk to you later, okay?"

CHAPTER 3

From the dark look on Brett's face as he stomped into the house, Dillon could tell if Brett found Phil in some dark alley, Phil could expect to be dickless and nutless pretty damned fast. For her part, Nikki had calmed down. Looked like Tiny's advice had paid off.

He stepped off the porch and captured her hand in his. "Tiny says there's nothing more he needs from you. Come on, you can sleep at my place tonight."

And the next night, and the night after that, and for every night after if he had a say.

It didn't surprise him when she shook her head. "No, I'll be fine. I can stay here."

"Come on, Nik, there's not even a pillow left for you to sleep on."

"I'll sleep in the horse trailer. It's got a bunk I can use. I don't want to put you out."

Of course she wouldn't want to put him out. Nikki was all about keeping everyone else happy.

"I'm not leavin' you here when I've got a perfectly good

bedroom you can use. Besides, that tin can of yours will be a hundred degrees inside."

"But I have to lock up after the police leave."

"Brett will look after everything. Don't worry." Taking her hesitation as agreement, Dillon handed Tiny the key she'd given him earlier then led her to his truck.

As he opened the door, she tried one last time. "Really, Dillon, I can sleep in the trailer. I'll be fine."

"Nikki," he spoke through his teeth, "humor me on this, will ya?"

"I don't want to be a burden."

"Don't you worry about that. Think of it as me being neighborly. You'd help me out if I had an emergency, so don't try to stop me from helping you."

Her shoulders slumped, and she nodded. "Since you put it that way." Her fingers glanced over his arm, sending a blast of sheer need straight to his cock. "Thank you, Dillon. For everything you've done tonight."

One of the spaghetti straps holding her top up had slipped off her shoulder, leaving the thin cotton top to gape open. He didn't mean to look, swear to God he didn't, but damned if he could help noticing she'd gone braless, and he could see clear down to her pebbled cinnamon nipple. What he'd give to play with that pretty peak. She had no idea how close he'd been to shoving her up against the barn wall and fuckin' her brains out earlier. Even now, it was only the pale exhausted look in her eyes that stopped him from yanking her top down and tasting those sweet breasts.

After helping her into his truck, Dillon climbed into the driver's side and slammed his door, cursing Phil under his breath. Especially after noticing the way Nikki's eyes could barely stay open as she sagged in the seat beside him.

Before he could act on his impulses, he shoved the truck into gear and concentrated on driving down the cart path she called her driveway. Once his tires hit the smooth pavement, her chin bounced gently on her chest. By the time he turned into his own place ten minutes later, Nikki was fast asleep. She'd hiked one leg up beneath her and lay half curled sideways into the seat, her lashes long on her cheek.

Oh, baby, you have no idea how long I've wanted to sleep with you, but this sure isn't the way I wanted it to be. He fingered the end of her long ginger braid. He hadn't seen her hair loose since they were back in high school and wondered what it would be like freed, hanging like a curtain on either side of her face as she rode him.

Down, boy. You don't hit on women who can't say no.

Leaving her sleeping, he climbed out and opened her door. After undoing her seatbelt, he slid his hand beneath her legs and behind her back and drew her toward him. She murmured softly and settled against his chest. Her warm breath feathering over his skin had his cock hardening against his zipper.

Later, buddy, he told his dick. Tonight she's too exhausted. But tomorrow. Tomorrow all bets would be off, and he'd be hard-pressed to keep his hands off of her.

He carried her inside and up the stairs. His step faltered just outside the spare bedroom.

Begin as you mean to go on, his mother always told him. He meant to have Nikki in his bed, permanently. He continued to the end of the hall and laid her on his bed. As soon as her head hit the pillow, she sighed and rolled on her side, tucking her hand beneath her head and murmuring something unintelligible.

He smoothed the long bangs that had fallen in her face. So soft. Yet from the work she'd done in the barn, the load she was carrying running her farm by herself, she'd proven herself anything but soft. A primitive surge of protectiveness filled him. Goddamn, she worked herself too hard while her brother lounged around on his ass and her ex-husband had let her have dick-all in the divorce.

"You're not alone anymore, Nik. Never again."

Dillon wrestled off her boots and dropped them on the floor. What next?

The thin cotton top she was wearing could probably stay on, but there was no way he could leave her in those jeans, not after mucking out the barn. He shook her lightly. "Nik? Wake up, hon. You need to get undressed."

Not opening her eyes, she unzipped her jeans and shimmied them down off her hips, hooking her panties at the same time.

He should turn away. He should at least stop staring, but holy shit, she was even prettier than he'd imagined. It took all his restraint not to part her legs and bury his face in the narrow triangle of ginger curls guarding her pussy, not to lick the sweet pink lips and find out if she tasted the way he'd imagined.

His balls ached, needing a release he wasn't going to find in his bed tonight. The only way he'd get it would be by his own hand. With a last lingering glance at Nikki's body, he settled the sheet over her and headed for the shower.

When he came out twenty minutes later, a towel wrapped around his hips, she hadn't moved. He flipped off the overhead light. "I'll go sleep in the guest room. If you need anything, just holler."

He froze in the doorway when he heard her murmur, "That's silly." Her eyes didn't even open as she patted the pillow beside her. "S'your bed, you should sleep here."

"Are you sure?"

Her head bobbed up and down once.

Thank you, sweet baby Jesus.

He dropped the towel and slipped between the sheets, wishing the light was still on so he could look at her a little longer.

As he lay beside her, his brain starting churning over how

she hadn't completely opened her eyes and looked at him. How she'd behaved mechanically, unaware of what she was doing. What if she forgot she undressed herself and woke up here beside him and freaked out, thought he'd stripped her, maybe copped a feel? Or more.

Maybe he should just go sleep in the guest bedroom.

She chose that moment to turn on her side, throw her arm across his belly and snuggle against him. Nikki stretched in his arms with a sigh of satisfaction. She reminded him of a Siamese cat Gramma Barnett had once had. Elegant and lithe, yet with an underlying strength that was easy to misjudge.

His balls drew up into his body, and his cock hoisted the goddamned sheet like a circus tent. There was no fucking way he was leaving now, even if he could. He doubted he'd get much sleep with her naked beside him, not with the hard-on he was sporting.

SLOWLY SWIMMING TO CONSCIOUSNESS, Nikki didn't have to open her eyes to know she wasn't on the hard bunk in her trailer. Not only was the mattress she was lying on comfortable, but the light was all wrong. The morning sun wouldn't have been hitting her right in the face the way it was now. Or had she parked it in a different spot? Come to think of it, where had she parked it?

What the hell was she using for a pillow? Whatever it was had hair that was tickling her nose. And was warm. And breathing.

She opened her eyes and gasped when she recognized the familiar face so close to hers.

Not only was she in bed with Dillon Barnett, but she was

plastered against him, one arm draped over his waist. *Oh, man, is this a dream?* Because when Dillon had said she was going to be spending the night at his place, she sure as heck hadn't figured he meant in his bed.

Hmm, that wasn't entirely true. After their kiss in the barn and he'd invited himself inside, she'd figured they would be taking things to the next level, but she figured she'd at least be awake for part of it. She'd also figured she would have had the privilege of watching him—heck, helping him—get naked.

Was he naked?

Taking a chance that he was in a deep sleep, she lifted the sheet and peeked underneath. Whoa momma, the man was nekkid as the day he was born.

As she watched, his cock twitched and rose to half-mast. She dropped the sheet and glanced at his face only to find his eyes still closed.

She'd finally connected with Dillon Barnett. Yet what had she done? She'd slept the whole night through and missed out on what could have been the best sex she'd had in her life.

Slowly tilting her head, she watched him sleep. The straight black brows that had drawn together when he'd questioned her about the house were now relaxed. His eyes were closed, his dark lashes resting on angular cheeks. A heavy early-morning stubble covered his sharp jaw. In the barn he'd been impressive, but here, with them both in bed, he seemed bigger. More imposing.

Maybe it was an illusion, a figment of imagination because she was nearly naked.

Her confidence returning, she splayed her hand on his belly and waited to see if he'd react in some way. His chest rose and fell in the same slow pattern he'd had when she'd first woken up; his eyes stayed closed.

On its own volition, her hand roamed up over the taut skin

of his chest where his hair thickened. Her thumb brushed over one of his nipples that beaded under her touch. She abandoned the exploration of his chest and moved lower, stopping only when the tips of her fingers brushed the satiny soft skin at the head of his cock. Slowly releasing her breath, she closed her fingers around his shaft. Dear Lord, if the man was primed and ready while he was asleep, what would he be like wide awake?

She started to pull back, but his hand circled her wrist. Her gaze shot up to find his lids only half covering his dark pupils.

"Don't stop now, Nik."

His quiet rumble settled in her chest, sent a vibration clear down to her pussy until his words penetrated her still sleepy brain. Oh, God, what was she doing? If he'd felt her up while she was sleeping the way she had, she'd accuse him of sexual assault. She freed her hand, sliding from beneath the sheet and grabbing the clothes scattered on the floor.

"Sorry. I've gotta—" She held her pants against her backside, clutched her T-shirt to her breasts and made a mad dash into the bathroom, slamming the door behind her.

Oh God, oh God, oh God. Could she be more of a spazzed-out perv?

Less than two seconds later, Dillon rapped on the door. "Nik? You okay?"

"Yeah, I'm fine, I just have to...I'll be right out." With a groan she slumped onto the toilet. *Great, now either he thinks you're so desperate you can only get a guy when he's sleeping, or that you're a total slut.*

Wait a minute. She lifted her head and stared at the door. How did she know he hadn't felt her up while she was sleeping? Who would have been there to stop him from copping a feel or two? Or six?

Yeah, right. Dillon Barnett would have drawn the line at taking advantage of a sleeping woman. Not a chance would he lay a finger on a woman without her permission.

"Nik?" His voice was soft through the door. "Don't put your clothes on until we've had a chance to wash 'em, okay?" He paused. "They sorta still smell like the barn."

She frowned and lifted her clothes to her face, then grimaced as the stench hit her. *Gak.* She probably didn't smell much better. A quick sniff under her arms confirmed her suspicions. *Real sexy there, Nik.* It was a wonder he hadn't left her to sleep on the couch instead of taking the chance of ruining his mattress and linen for life. And here she'd been worried about morning breath.

"I'm leaving a clean shirt and a pair of sweats for you to wear just outside the door," Dillon continued without waiting for her to answer. "There's a new toothbrush in the drawer on the right you can use. There should be clean towels in the cupboard over the toilet if you want to take a shower."

Oh man, why hadn't she dated him in high school instead of Wade? Because Wade had asked and Dillon hadn't. Then thanks to that goddamned broken condom, she'd discovered she was pregnant just as she had been considering breaking up with Wade. "Thanks, Dillon. I'll be out in a minute."

He rapped on the door twice. "Take your time. I'll wait for you in the kitchen."

Seconds later, she heard the bedroom door close.

Brett snorted when he rotated the handle on Dillon's front door. How many times did he have to remind him to lock the damned thing? Apparently once more. Didn't he realize how many nutjobs were out there? Especially after Nikki's place had been cleaned out.

He stepped from the damned Texas heat into the cool foyer as Dillon appeared at the top of the stairs, wearing a wrinkled work tee along with a pair of blue jeans, the top button undone. From the way his dark hair stood up on end on one side and was flat on the other, he'd just gotten out of bed.

"Hey Dill, you wanna come down and watch this?"

Once Dillon stood beside him, Brett made a show of closing the door and flipping the deadbolt. "See? Up means unlocked, sideways means locked. Always make sure you keep it locked when you're here. And when you leave, what do you do?"

Dillon's snort filled the foyer. "You're sounding more and more like Dad every day."

"I can't think of a better compliment." A pity Dillon didn't have the cautious nature of his father. Then again Dillon wasn't responsible for protecting a family. Oh, Dillon would pound the shit out of anyone who threatened his sister. But as a landscaper he was more used to working with plants than with deadbeats who would shoot you as soon as look at you.

Dillon padded down the hall, calling over his shoulder, "You want some breakfast?"

"As long as it comes with coffee." Having been up half the night combing through Tiny's notes and calling in favors with the county's pawn shops, his body craved caffeine. He followed Dillon into the kitchen and leaned against the counter as his friend dug around in the fridge.

Dillon pulled out the carton of eggs before glancing at him. "So you find anything out about Nik's scumball brother?"

"Not much. Tiny let me listen in on his call to her parents, just in case Phil shows up at their place." Brett leaned against the counter. "Man, they are a piece of work. Her mom didn't once ask if Nik was all right, just railed about how everyone misunderstood her little boy."

Dillon's snort echoed the disgust Brett felt. "So what happens now?"

"We've got an alert out on him, but basically we're in wait-and-see mode." He waited for Dillon's nod. "I need to ask Nikki if she has a list of serial numbers for things like the DVD or television or anything else Phil took. Those would be a big help tracking things with the pawn shops."

"You can ask her when she comes down." Dillon broke an egg into the frying pan.

"Be gentle with her, okay? Wade could be a piece of work, you know what I mean? She's probably still dealing with baggage from all his shit."

A hardness Brett rarely saw filled Dillon's eyes, and the eggshell crumbled in Dillon's fist. "He hit her?"

"Not that she'd admit. If he had, I could have hauled him off to jail. Look, I probably shouldn't be telling you this, but old lady Patterson sent us out there a couple times complaining she could hear Wade yelling and throwing things clear down at her place."

It hadn't happened a lot but enough that he'd stopped waiting for the calls and made it a habit to drop in unannounced. He'd told himself it was just to make sure Nikki was all right. He'd told himself that a lot. Taking a deep breath, he forced himself to relax his hands. "I walked in on them one day while he was calling her all sorts of names, told her she was useless and stupid." Dillon swore. "Fuck that poem about sticks and stones. Words can leave scars that hurt worse and linger longer than any bruise."

The good Lord knew he had plenty of scars both inside and out to prove it, thanks to his father.

"I never figured out why she didn't leave him sooner."

"If her parents' reaction to what happened tonight was typical, she probably felt she had nowhere to go. You hear you're stupid and no one else will want you often enough, you start to believe it." Look how long it had taken for the Barnetts to convince him his father was wrong. "Especially if it's someone you care for. Someone you respect."

Or someone you're told you're supposed to respect.

Someone you're told you're supposed to love. Who knows where he'd be now if Dillon's parents hadn't taken him in. Probably living in the bottom of a bottle, just like his old man. Or in jail for murdering the bastard.

Dillon snorted again. "Respect? Wade didn't deserve one damned bit of respect. He was a fuckin' trouser snake. Nikki's better off without him."

"I'm not talking about Wade. Her mom was feeding her the same crap, and her dad wasn't much better. That's why she stayed with Wade for so long, because her parents threatened to cut her off if she divorced him. I dropped in one day when her folks were visiting. The damned fools told Nik she was a failure if she let a man like Wade get away. That she wasn't a good wife, wasn't woman enough, if Wade had to go to other women for satisfaction."

Dillon swore. "I do not get how people can treat their kids like that."

That's because your *parents always believed the sun revolved around their children.*

"Nik get any sleep?" He regretted the question as soon as the words were out.

That damned smug smile of Dillon's just widened. "Yeah. I tell you, you should have seen her while she was sleeping. It was like watching an angel."

Knots formed in Brett's gut. Jealousy ripped its way from deep in his gut and up his esophagus, the rising bile burning his throat.

"Except she's not an angel exactly. She's got a bit of devil in her too. This morning...hmm, yeah, just forget I mentioned it."

Oh Christ, it had gone further, faster between them than he'd thought. Dillon was already sleeping with her. He grabbed the carafe from the coffee maker and went through the motions of making a fresh pot. The routine, from counting out the scoops of frozen beans into the grinder to filling the pot, gave him time to regain control. And firm up his resolve to stay out of Dillon's love life.

CHAPTER 4

TEN MINUTES AND A GOOD HARD SCRUB LATER, NIKKI STOPPED IN the kitchen doorway. Dillon wasn't alone. While Dillon poked at the frying pan, Brett Anderson was pouring coffee into a mug.

It had been a common joke in school that if you wanted to find one, you hollered the other's name, and they'd both show up. A lot of people even thought them brothers, though Dillon was dark haired and darker complexioned, compared to Brett's strawberry blond hair and freckles. Except they weren't brothers. Not brothers by blood anyway.

Though both men were the same height, Dillon was longer in the leg while Brett was longer in the body. Dillon had pulled on a faded and wrinkled DB Landscaping tee, the top button of his blue jeans undone. The relaxed dress was a direct contradiction to Brett's dun-colored uniform. Even though it looked like he'd just gotten off duty, he radiated confidence, demanded respect. Hinted of danger. Damn, there was something about a man in uniform that she found attractive.

She couldn't remember making a sound but two pairs of

eyes, one set chocolate brown, the other sky blue, turned to her at exactly the same time.

"Good morning, Nikki." Brett nodded.

He grabbed a mug from the cabinet and filled it with coffee, then added a single spoonful of sugar. When he held it out for her, she couldn't contain her surprise. She'd lived with Wade nine years, and he'd never remembered how she took her coffee.

Dillon fixed her with a predatory look. "I'm fixin' some steak and eggs. Want some?"

To her embarrassment her stomach gave a loud rumble. Dillon chuckled. "I'll take that as a yes."

Feeling a blush working its way up her throat and into her cheeks, Nikki ducked her head. "I should call Mom and Dad. Let them know about Phil."

She didn't miss the sideways glance Dillon gave Brett. Nor did she miss the sympathy lacing Brett's answer. "They already know. Tiny phoned your folks last night."

"Oh." Her stomach knotted imagining that conversation. Her mother had probably ranted about how everyone was out to get Phil, and how he was such a good boy who didn't deserve the trouble the police gave him. Still, they were her parents, and since she'd promised them she'd look after Phil... "I should phone them anyway. At least to let them know where I'm staying."

The two men shared another long glance before Dillon slowly nodded. "You can use the phone in my office if you want privacy."

The half-dozen steps to the room off the kitchen he set up as an office might as well have been a mile, from the way her feet dragged with every step. Taking a deep breath to steel herself for the upcoming conversation, she lifted the receiver and dialed.

Her father's voice echoed down the line before it had rung twice.

"Hi, Dad."

Before she could say another word, he interrupted her. "What type of woman sets the police on her own brother? I'm disappointed in you, Nicole." When was he not?

"Nicole?" Her mother came on the line. "Where are you staying? This isn't your number."

Her mother must have been listening in on an extension. Wonderful. They were tag-teaming her. "Since I didn't have a bed left to sleep on, I stayed with a friend last night, Mom."

"You're not shacked up with some man, are you?" Without waiting for Nikki to answer, her mother quoted scripture about the evils of fornication outside of marriage. "Don't you know the shame you've already brought upon this family?"

How could she forget? Her mother mentioned it in every conversation they'd had since she'd told them she was pregnant. Her divorce from Wade had only cemented her mother's opinion.

The scent of eggs and steak drifted in from the kitchen. When she'd been upstairs, her stomach had growled in anticipation. Now it threatened to heave the way it often did during a conversation with her parents.

"Why did you set the police on your brother?" her father interrupted, repeating his earlier question. "You should never have involved them in a family matter."

"I didn't know Phil had been involved when I discovered I'd been robbed." How had she become the bad guy in this? She was the one who had lost everything. "I thought someone else had done it."

"Of course it was someone else," her mother insisted. "Now you call those awful police and tell them to look for the real thieves instead of targeting poor Phil."

Poor Phil. How many times had she heard that refrain? "Phil is supposed to check in with his parole officer on Monday, so hopefully we'll know more then."

A soft knock had her swiveling in her seat to find Dillon standing at the doorway, a sympathetic look on his face.

"You want me to talk to them?" he asked quietly.

His quiet unwavering support eased the knots forming in her stomach. How strange that a neighbor, a friend, could be more supportive than her own family. Not just last night and this morning, but this whole year. Helping out with the fences and all the myriad other ways he'd been there when she needed a hand. Brett had been the same. Where her parents offered little else than constant judgment, both men were there, willing to help out without being asked.

She shook her head and turned her attention back to the phone. "Mom, Dad, I have to go. I'll call you when I hear more, all right?"

"Fine," her mother answered, "but I want you to phone me as soon as you hear from Phil and let me know he's all right. And you phone from your own place, you hear? I don't want to hear any gossip about you whoring around again."

All right, so maybe her stomach wasn't quite settled after all. She pressed a hand against her belly as she hung up.

Dillon pulled her into his arms. "Hey, you okay?"

No. But she would be. Especially with friends like him and Brett supporting her. "I'm fine."

His eyes searched her face. "They give you grief because I called the cops on Phil?"

She shook her head.

He hmmed, his tone telling her he didn't believe her, but thankfully he didn't call her on it. "You still up for breakfast?"

Once she'd nodded, he led her back to the kitchen and seated her on the bench at the table.

Brett sat on the chair opposite her. "You all right?"

"Fine." It was starting to become her mantra. Maybe if she said it enough, she'd start to believe it.

His examination of her was as thorough as Dillon's. "Why don't you let me handle calling them from here on in? I can do it in an official capacity."

"Thanks, but they're my parents. I can deal with them."

"Just because you can doesn't mean you should have to," Dillon noted. "Not if they're going to give you grief because of me."

He plated the food and placed it in front of her, his other hand brushing the tops of hers. He set up two more plates and set them down, one beside her and one in front of Brett. "Dig in, buddy."

The whole time they were eating, Dillon found ways to touch her. He slid beside her on the bench, close enough that his thigh touched hers. Their hands grazed again when they both reached for the salt shaker at the same time. When he refilled her coffee, she couldn't help notice how he'd drawn out releasing the mug, dragging his fingers over hers. When he returned to sit beside her, his bare foot slid over her arch. When he reached for the steak sauce, his other hand splayed over the small of her back, creeping under the fabric.

By the time she'd finished her food, every inch of her body was aware of him. Aware of the damp tendrils of dark hair tucked behind the curve of his ear betraying that he'd found someplace else to shower, and the clean scent of his soap. Especially aware of the rough calluses of his hands as they rasped over her skin. She couldn't help but imagine the bulging strength of his forearms holding him over her. His thick thigh muscles flexing between her legs as she wrapped herself around him, pulling him deep into her.

The fantasy shattered when Brett stood. If his expression had been sympathetic when she'd come out of Dillon's office, now he looked more relaxed. Except that while his lips smiled, the smile didn't reach his eyes. Maybe it was a mask he'd learned to wear for his job, a way to conceal his emotions. But what would he need to conceal from her?

"I'm gonna go check in, see if they've got any leads on Phil yet." The sarcastic way he said her brother's name had her breathing a sigh of relief. He was pissed off at Phil, not her. "You two have fun."

He carried his plate to the dishwasher, then headed down the front hall without looking back.

Nikki rubbed her hands on her thighs. "I should see if I can catch Brett and get a lift into town. I need to start replacing everything I lost. " A new mattress for a start. She couldn't keep relying on other people's charity, even Dillon's. "And I should talk to Ernie, see how much it's going to cost to fix my truck."

Instead of moving out of her way as she'd expected, Dillon stayed in place. "There's no hurry for you to do that. The cops might get some of your stuff back, and then you'll have wasted your money. As for your truck, Ernie'll phone you with an estimate soon enough."

"Okay, I guess. But you let me know if I get underfoot or anything, all right?"

"It's not under my foot where I want you." He cupped his fingers under her chin and lifted her face so she would look at him. Before she realized it, he was kissing her again. It didn't start out with the heat she'd remembered from the night before; this one was soft, gentle. An exploration. But soon it strengthened as he took charge of the kiss, his tongue plundering her mouth.

By the time they broke off, they were both breathing heavily.

"You didn't have to stop." The huskiness in her voice surprised her. Fighting the fear skittering beneath her skin, she lifted his hand and placed it on her breast.

Even as his thumb stroked her nipple through the thin fabric of her tee, Dillon's eyes searched hers. "I don't want to push you. If you want to date for a while, I'm fine with that."

Date? It was the reasonable thing to do. The proper thing. What society would expect. But they were both adults and damn it, who knew if she'd have another chance?

"Why don't we just say all those times we worked on the fences or went riding together were dates? Besides, we both know what we were talking about when I invited you into my place last night." She stroked a finger up his jaw and around the shell of his ear. When his breath hitched, she knew she'd won her point.

He tugged her closer, resuming their kiss. His hand slipped beneath her tee and cupped her breast; she was surprised to hear a moan filling the kitchen and realized it was her own.

It had been years since anyone—Wade—had touched her there. She shifted, pressing herself into his palm. Her breasts grew heavier as he played with her nipples. It was as if there was a direct connection between her breasts and her core, her pussy aching for attention, to be filled.

She slid one hand around his waist. The table thwarted her attempts to straddle him. Dillon shifted on the bench, pulling his hand back.

"Shit!" He broke off the kiss and clutched the elbow he'd just rammed into the edge of the table. "Goddamn, there's not enough room here."

With an impatient movement, he used his foot to push the table away. She squeaked when he lifted her to straddle his lap, and then stood. His growl and strengthened grip on her were his answer as he strode down the hall.

Wade had never carried her once in all the time they'd dated; not that she was too heavy, but he'd always been more of a wham-bam type of guy. Oh, she'd been thrilled the first time they'd made love. He'd made her feel so feminine. Pretty, even. He'd changed his stripes once they'd gotten married though, blaming her for everything that went wrong in his life. Like she was responsible for the plant closing and him getting laid off. Then again she had lost his baby. Not that he'd wanted it in the first place.

"Nik? Where'd you go?"

Dillon's quiet question roused her from her memories and made her aware he'd stopped walking. She lifted her head from where she'd buried it against his neck and realized they were now in the middle of his bedroom.

Was she nuts? She was thinking about Wade when she had Dillon right here?

He relaxed his hold on her, letting her feet slide to the floor. "We don't have to do this if you don't want. I can wait."

God, how many other guys would walk away without calling her a cock tease? Which made her decision to continue that much easier. She put her hands on either side of his head and tugged him down to her. "I want this. I want it a lot."

She kissed him, her lips pressing hard against his, her tongue pushing into his mouth, tasting the coffee he'd just finished. Oh, she wanted it all right. She wanted it all.

For one second, maybe two, Dillon was still. She'd shocked him perhaps. Then he wrapped his hands in a length of her hair and took control of the kiss. They were both panting by the time they broke off. He grabbed the bottom of her tee and lifted it over her head in one swift movement. Her sweats pooled around her ankles seconds later.

She didn't waste any time pulling his clothes from him either. Dillon's work on the job hauling dirt and equipment had hardened and defined his muscles.

Dark hair covered his chest, thinning at his belly button to arrow down to his groin. As if she needed a roadmap to the bulge in his pants, thank you very much. She played with his nipples that puckered into hard little buds, then moved south and dragged his jeans from his hips. His cock sprang free, the head bulbous and heavy, a thick nest of black hair at its base. Before she could wrap her hand around his shaft, he backed her up until her legs hit the mattress. She lay back, allowing her legs to splay open on either side of his thighs.

His gaze trailed down her breasts, then stopped on her groin. "Oh, baby, your pretty pussy is glistening. You're ready for me, aren't you?"

DILLON SLID one finger between her labia, then lifted it to his own mouth and sucked it deep into his mouth. Damned if she didn't taste as sweet as she smelled. She stared up at him, her pupils full and dark, her lips swollen from kissing him. Down in the kitchen, he'd been tempted to sweep the dishes off the table and take her right there, but he hadn't wanted to do that for their first time. That would be a fantasy he'd fulfill later. And oh, man, what a fantasy she'd become.

He dipped his head and caught her lips beneath his again, grinding his erection into her belly. Her hips wriggled against him, and she repeated the deep moan she'd made earlier that rumbled all the way through his chest and down to his dick.

She showed no hint of modesty, not trying to cover herself. In fact, her own gaze raked his length, devouring him.

His cock hardened more if it was possible. Her breasts were fuller than they had been last night, heavy in their arousal. Her hips curved the way he liked—he never did care for the feel of hip bones jutting into him like rocks.

He straddled her and played with her breasts, molding them with his palms. Indulging himself, he bent over, taking a nipple into his mouth. As he did, his cock rubbed along the silken skin of her belly. Damn. If he didn't get control of himself, he was going to come all over her like a randy teenager.

Resting most of his weight on one elbow, he covered her body with his. Her breasts felt so fantastic mashed against his chest, her body cradling his cock like God had designed her just for him. When she tilted her head seeking his lips, he felt like he'd conquered the world.

Her hands moved over his chest, then slid to his back, cupping his ass, her hips grinding against him. The need she'd aroused when he'd woken up to find her playing with his dick reared its head and demanded he take action. Now.

His dick slid through her folds. He couldn't wait to go down on her, taste her pussy again. But for now he needed to bury himself deep in her.

She whimpered, her body quivering beneath his as he rubbed the length of his shaft over her clit. "Condom?"

Shit, how had he forgotten protection? Murmuring for her to wait, he rolled off her and reached for the night table for a condom. She'd pushed herself up on her elbows, watching him tear open the package and roll the condom over his dick.

Realizing the moment was lost, he decided to indulge his earlier fantasy. He positioned her so her pussy was at the edge of the bed, then knelt between her thighs. Watching her face, he lowered his mouth to her folds, parting them with his tongue. Her essence burst over his tongue like a ripe peach, everything he'd imagined for the past year. He circled her clit, lapping on either side of it. Her eyes fluttered closed, her breathing hitching with each stroke he took.

When he captured the swollen bud with his mouth, her head fell back, exposing her long neck. Such a pity he couldn't be up there as well, kissing its length, playing with her breasts at the same time.

He inserted two fingers into her pussy as he lashed her clit with his tongue. Her thighs trembled and clamped around his head as her body sucked his fingers deeper, her muscles milking them. He slipped a third finger beside the other two and stretched her tissues as he lightly bit at her quivering flesh. He drove her up to the edge, making her whimper as she begged for him to let her come. Easing off, he let her simmer for a while.

He filled his lungs with the lingering scent of his soap on her skin, combined with the musky smell of her arousal. He'd never be able to use that soap again without thinking of her spread out in front of him like this.

She made a breathy purr, reminding him once more of a cat, and her body heated beneath him. "You like me eating you, don't you?"

Her inner muscles squeezed his fingers. So she liked him talking dirty, did she? "I love how slick you get for me, how your cunt gets all slippery. Once I'm done eating you, I'm going to fuck you hard and fast." Her fingers dug into the bedding as she writhed beneath his mouth. "You're so fucking tight. I can't wait to get my dick inside you."

His cock and balls aching, he tipped her over the precipice.

She cried out as her orgasm overtook her, her body arching up off the bed, her hips bucking against him. *Shit, she is beautiful.* He lapped at the juices that coated his fingers and dripped from her pussy in a slippery rush. Before her muscles stopped rippling, he withdrew his fingers and placed the head of his cock at her entrance.

Stabbing his arms into the mattress on either side of her body, he thrust into her, grunting as she squeezed and convulsed around him. A flame from within the sweetest body, the tightest pussy ever to singe him. Holding still, he stared at her face, at her unfocused eyes, her hair loosened from its braid, floating in wild streams over the sheet. If he never made love to her again, he'd remember her like this for the rest of his life.

Unable to hold off any longer, he pulled back then drove into her again. Her hands clutched the bedding, and with each stroke he pounded her further up the bed. Her body pulsed around him, her muscles gripping him tight against each withdrawal. Needing to give her the same pleasure he felt, he surged back in. She groaned, not in pain, but passion, her body shaking as her orgasm built again.

He slipped a hand between them. Finding her sensitive bud, he flicked it as he surged into her. She lifted her hips, wrapping her legs around his waist so his cock could stab even deeper into her body. Muscles, honed from years of riding, tightened around him. His cock felt like it was in heaven.

If he could have dragged in enough breath to speak, he would have whispered some pretty words he knew women liked to hear. Nik deserved more than the dirty words he'd given her. She deserved much more. And he was just the man to give her whatever she desired.

He pistoned his hips, unable to prevent himself from shouting as fire speared from the base of his spine, through his balls, and out of his cock. His shout changed to a roar as his balls emptied into the sweet tissues convulsing around him.

CHAPTER 5

NIKKI COULDN'T STOP THE SIGH SLIPPING FROM HER AS DILLON parked his truck in front of her home. Her now-empty home. She couldn't help comparing Dillon's cleanly painted and shuttered house to hers, with its faded paint and sagging porch. The straight lines of Dillon's bright red barn with its white trim only highlighted the way her battered and weather-worn metal shed leaned. From this angle, it looked like it was being held up by the rusted shell of a pickup Wade had abandoned beside it. While the Barnetts had never made her feel like white trash, right now she felt it more acutely than ever.

Why the hell was Dillon Barnett interested in her? Though he hadn't said so, she had a feeling their lovemaking earlier had been just that. She hadn't been a quick fuck to him; he'd made love to her. She couldn't say why she thought that, but she did. Yet even if she'd misinterpreted him, if he dumped her tomorrow, she wouldn't regret having slept with him.

Joy sang through her veins; her head spun in a thousand directions until she felt like a school girl experiencing her first crush. She would treasure the memory of the passion he'd shown her forever. Her brother may have ruined so much for her, yet in robbing her, he'd given her the greatest gift she could have received. He'd pushed her from behind the barriers she'd built and had given her a chance to find love.

Love. *Whoa. Slow down. Dillon hasn't said he loved you. And while you've known him for half your life, and he's great, what do you know about love?*

Another sigh slipped past her lips.

Dillon covered her hand with his. "Hey, it'll be okay. The hock shops in the area have been alerted to look out for your stuff. And your insurance should cover whatever they can't get back."

"I don't have any content insurance." Staring at the ground, she scuffed the toe of her boot against a rock. Despite what Tiny had said the night before, she still wasn't convinced it had been Phil. It could have been one of his friends. Maybe he'd been bragging about how he had the place alone to himself and they'd seized the opportunity to rob her while he was at the bar.

Except if it hadn't been him, then where was he?

No, Phil had taken everything not nailed down. There was no use pretending he hadn't.

Not wanting to think about it anymore, she turned her back on the house and headed to the barn. Merlin greeted them with his musical hee-haw as he trotted toward her.

With Dillon helping her, the work was finished faster than usual. Which was what she had hoped would happen when she'd agreed to let Phil come live with her. Instead of lightening her load, Phil had tripled it.

While Dillon finished filling the final water trough, she checked over the horses for any injuries they might have received while she was away, leaving Bashir to the end. "Hey, boy, how you doing?"

Slipping him a carrot she'd grabbed from Dillon's fridge, she rubbed his velvety nose.

Dillon wrapped his arms around her from behind. "All done. Everyone's fed, watered and out to pasture."

"Thanks for the help."

One of his hands stroked up the length of her side, stopping to cup the underside of her breast. She leaned against him and closed her eyes. Even though it was less than two hours since they'd last made love, her body needed him again. Her oversensitive breasts ached, not with pain but with pleasure. When he tugged on her nipple, she swore it was a switch to start her pussy pulsing.

Was there a place in the barn they could do it without getting straw in their butts?

Much to her body's regret, he stopped and went back to simply holding her. "Brett phoned while I was cleaning the troughs."

Wow. He could think straight. Given the erection pressing into her behind, she figured he'd be focused on only one thing, the way she was right now. Guess not.

"He says he forgot to remind you this morning to phone the credit bureaus and put a hold on your credit in case Phil tries anything. Oh, and he wants to know if you had a power-on password on your computer. If you did any online banking..."

Brett. Back in high school she'd been more interested in Brett than Dillon. There was something dark about him, some hidden secret that intrigued her. Her and half the girls in their class. So when he'd centered her out at Tater's New Year's Eve party, and they'd spent an entire evening necking, it had shocked the heck out of her.

She leaned into Dillon's embrace. "I kissed him once, you know. Back in high school."

Dillon stiffened. Crap, her and her big mouth. What had made her admit that? What guy likes to hear about another guy kissing his lover? "It happened ten years ago, Dillon.

No, they'd done more than kissing. They hadn't gone all the

way that night but it had been a close thing. Then the next day Brett had disappeared, and when he'd returned he'd kept his distance from her and left her confused. Disappointed. Certain he'd led her one and once he'd learned her limits had dumped her. Which might explain why she'd accepted Wade's attentions. Boy, had that been a mistake. "There's nothing between us anymore."

"It doesn't bother me."

She rotated in his arms and flattened her hands on his chest. "No? Then why'd you tense up?"

His eyelids lowered as his gaze dropped to her chest. "Because you pressed your butt against me, and now I want you again." He cupped her breast, thumbed her nipple. "Hell, Nik, all I've been able to think about this whole time is how I want to make love to you again."

Really? He'd been thinking about her that whole time too? Her hand acted without consulting her brain by fumbling with Dillon's zipper.

His eyebrows quirked up as she withdrew his cock from his pants. When her fingers curled around his shaft, his shoulders half fell against the wall and his hat fell to his feet.

Damn, he was so big, so ready for her. She sank onto her knees and buried her face in the thick nest of hair at its base. He hissed when her tongue darted out and licked it from bottom to top, swirling around the thick head.

"Baby, we can go up to your house, or in the truck if you want," Dillon murmured, his voice rough. He batted Bashir away when the horse poked its head over the stall's door and tried to eat his hair. "You don't have to do this here in the barn."

"I want you. Here. Now." She didn't want to give him the chance to rethink being with her. She didn't want to rethink it herself. Her pussy ached, needing to be filled, so she shifted until her cleft rode her heel. Watching his expression carefully, wanting to learn what pleased him, she took the tip into her mouth and sucked lightly.

Staring down at her, he burrowed his hands into her hair, clamping them about her skull. "Take all of me, Nik. Suck it down."

His voice deepened, betraying his need. She obeyed him, sliding her lips down the length of his shaft until her nose once again nestled against his groin, the head of his cock bumping the back of her throat. He held her in place while pulling his hips back, withdrawing halfway, then he shoved in again.

The heady scent of him—of musky male, of heat and desire—surrounded her. While he set the rhythm, she used her tongue and her teeth on his shaft, reveling in feeling him shake, in hearing his groans as she sucked him down. His cock swelled in her mouth, his grip in her hair tightened.

"Shit, that feels so fucking good."

Sucking him down here where someone could walk into the barn and find them made what she was doing that much hotter. Wondering if he felt the same way, she glanced up at him, but he'd closed his eyes.

He groaned from deep in his gut as she slid him out until only the plump head of his cock was trapped by her lips. She slowly worked her way down to the root again. Another deep male groan filled the barn. Being in control of him, knowing she could make him come—or not—pleased her in ways she'd never thought possible.

One of the barn cats wrapped itself around her, its tail tickling the underside of her jaw. She abandoned Dillon's cock long enough to push it away, then swallowed him again, her cheeks hollowing as she sucked him deep.

"Yeah, baby, suck it deep and hard, just like that." Dillon groaned so low it sounded like a growl. Primal.

Her nipples rasped against his thighs, the pressure in her pussy intolerable since she knew she wouldn't find her own release. His hands dug into her scalp, and she found herself unable to move again. She couldn't complain; she loved that she'd driven him to such a frenzy as he fucked her mouth. His penis swelled against her tongue, and his hot salty musk coated her tongue before it splashed against the back of her throat.

WHEN HIS BODY finally stopped pumping into Nikki's hot mouth, Dillon peered down at the wanton figure at his feet. A bright flush coloring her cheeks, her green eyes stared back at up him, brighter than he'd ever seen them before.

He untangled his fingers from her hair and stroked one side of her face as he withdrew his cock from between her swollen lips. "You are so beautiful."

After he wiped a drop of his come from her lip, her tongue darted out to lick it off his thumb, her eyes closing as if she savored the taste.

He contemplated the barn, trying to figure out where he could lay her down and bury his face into her sweet pussy again. Here in the barn was out—too much straw floating around. Feed room? Same problem, as with the tack room. Not to mention the danged barn cat winding around them, and the horse sticking his head over the stall.

"Come on." He zipped up his pants, then led her out to his truck and stood her on the running board.

Damn, she was sexy, especially the smoldering look in her eyes, half hidden by heavy lids. Unable to resist her parted lips, he plundered her mouth.

When he finally pulled away, she stared at him with a dazed expression while he unbuttoned her jeans and shoved them down around her knees. He couldn't stop the smile from spreading across his face when he remembered she hadn't had any underwear to put on that morning. "Lie back on the seat, baby. Spread your legs for me."

The color that had started to fade from her face flared up again as she realized what he was going to do. "Out here? Now?"

"Right here. Now." He couldn't resist mimicking her earlier command and was pleased to see the recognition flare in her eyes. "Don't worry. You're safe with me, baby."

She settled back, then sprang up off the seat. "Yow, it's hot."

"Not as hot as I'm gonna make you in a couple minutes." He stripped off his shirt and spread it beneath her. "Set your sweet little tush down. Now."

Once she'd obeyed him, he palmed her thighs apart, admiring how her labia glistened in the sunlight. "You're so pretty."

He feathered a kiss to her cleft, then blew lightly on her engorged clit. Despite the heat of the day, goosebumps formed on her skin beneath his fingers. Not just pretty but responsive too. "Pull your shirt up, baby. All the way up."

Her gaze darted out the cab window, then behind him. Her shyness intrigued him. Had she and Wade never done the nasty outside? "Relax, Nik."

Supporting herself on one elbow, she hauled her shirt up and held it beneath her chin. Even sprawled as she was, her breasts were round and full. Her nipples were drawn up into tight spheres, puckered, begging to be suckled.

He leaned into the cab, supporting himself by leaning one hand beside her head, and captured one taut peak between his teeth. A whimper escaped her when he nipped it lightly then soothed the sting with his tongue. With his free hand, he found her narrow channel, sliding his fingers up and down her labia, teasing the skin to either side of her clit as his tongue teased her breast.

"Dillon." Her hips rotated in an attempt to force his fingers to make contact with the swollen nerve endings. Her arousal drenched his palm as she undulated, her muscles clamping around him.

He'd planned on going down on her first, but his dick had other ideas. The hell with her fucking his fingers. In two seconds flat, he'd undone his fly, freed his dick, dug a condom from his back pocket and sheathed himself. He closed his eyes to feel her body closing around him, her muscles rippling along his length until he damned near lost his breath at the sensation.

When he opened his eyes, the half-lidded sultry look she gave him had him fighting the need to take her hard and fast. She deserved better than to be taken out here in his truck. She deserved tenderness and pampering.

Despite his efforts, the angle of him standing on the running board didn't give him proper access to her sweet pussy. He had her move over, then took her place on the seat and dragged her to straddle his lap. Holding her hips, he lowered her onto his shaft. "Ride me, baby. Take me however you want."

She lifted herself up until only the head of his cock remained in her passage, then dropped down to cover him again.

"Shit, yeah!"

As her hips lifted and lowered, her breasts jiggled their lovely berries in front of his face. On one of the upward trips, he captured a nipple. Her inner passage rippled in response to his sucking. He sucked harder, lashing the nipple with his tongue, tormenting it until her body fisted his cock in its moist heat.

The musky scent of their lovemaking filled the cab. If he was lucky it would permeate the seats, and he'd be able to smell this moment for days to come. Although it might be hard to explain to his men why he kept sporting a hard-on every time he climbed out of his truck.

All thoughts fled when she held onto his shoulders, her head falling back as her breathing roughened. His way eased by the sweat building between them, he slipped a hand between them and found her clit. He teased it until she was frantic, her pussy clamping down on him, milking his cock, her entire body shuddering her release.

All he could do was hang on for the ride until her body wound down. Then when she finally sank back, he grasped her hips and powered deeply, shouting as he emptied his balls into her.

He had no idea how long they sat in the truck, their bodies quivering with the last of their release before she finally had the energy to crawl off of him.

CHAPTER 6

The metal napkin container shook in a slow progression across the table, bouncing to the beat of whatever damned heavy metal song the DJ was playing. Brett leaned so close to Tiny that he was afraid he'd get razor burn and still could barely hear what the deputy was asking the large man opposite them. Hell, it was so loud in this fucking joint, he'd probably lost a part of his hearing permanently.

"So I said, sure he could borrow it, so long as he got it back to me Friday night, 'cause I needed it yesterday." Their informant picked up the long neck beer bottle and sucked back the last half. He slammed it on the table to join the four empties he'd already lined up. "See, I'd already promised my cousin he could use the damned truck to help his brother pick up a flat-screen. But fuck-it-all if that lowlife Kimball never brought the damned truck back." He pointed a thick finger at Tiny. "You find that sumbitch, you let me know. I'll teach him a lesson about how a man honors his word."

You'd think after living in Texas for the last fourteen years, Nikki's brother would have learned not to get between a man and his truck. Phil better hope the cops found him before Bubba here did. From the size of Bubba's arms, picking up a vehicle all by himself wouldn't have him working up a sweat. Heck, he made Tiny look...*tiny*.

Bubba called over the waitress and yacked with her about everything under the sun before Tiny finally grew impatient. "Do you know if he had any friends to help him move the stuff?"

The chair groaned in complaint as Bubba raised himself half out of his chair and yelled to the three men clustered at the end of the stripper's runway. "Hey, Billy, getcher skinny ass over here."

The shortest one of the bunch stuck a bill into the dancer's G-string before ambling over. "Whatcha want? I was just gettin' me some action."

"Action." Bubba snorted. "Dream on, B-man. You ain't seen action since your momma changed your diaper and cleaned your little willy."

He hooked at thumb toward Tiny and Brett. "These here fellas are asking about that skinny punk who stole my truck. Tell him what the sumbitch told you."

An hour later and no further ahead than before he'd lost his hearing, Brett followed Tiny from the raucous bar into the only slightly less noisy parking lot. He ignored the couple going at it in the cab of the pick-up three trucks down and stopped in front of Tiny's squad car.

"I'll add the truck's description and license to the B.O.L.O., see if it's shown up anywhere, but I wouldn't hold up much hope that you'll find Ms. Kimball's belongings." Tiny climbed into his car, but left the door open and one foot on the ground. "She still stayin' out at Barnett's place?"

"Yup."

"You were sayin' earlier that you're stayin' out there too."

"Yup. Dillon's worried Phil might come back with some buddies, hoping to score more cash." Not to mention Dillon wasn't about to give Nik a shot at slipping out from under him.

Literally. "Figured she'd be safer over at his place. I'm stayin' over just to make sure no one comes round when Dillon's at work."

That earned him a slow nod. "Considering what he did to you back in high school, I'm surprised he asked you. Or that you agreed."

"Yeah, well, that was a long time ago. And he apologized." He shoved his hands in his pockets and frowned at the college boy stumbling down the stairs from the bar. Looked like they'd have to break out the breathalyzer if that dumbass tried to get behind a wheel tonight. Once the kid finished puking, that is.

Shooting him a knowing look, Tiny unwrapped a stick of gum. "So how come you ain't asking her out? If I remember the story rightly, you were the one she was kissin' at Tater O'Neill's party. Not Golden Boy Barnett."

"Hey, back off. Dillon's a good guy."

"You weren't sayin' that ten years ago. Which is why I don't understand why you're letting him chase after a woman you've had your eye on all these years. It don't make no sense."

"It does to me."

CAREFUL NOT TO DISTURB THE softly snoring Dillon, Nikki rolled out of bed. She padded downstairs, not bothering to turn on any lights, and found her way to the kitchen. It wasn't until she opened the fridge door that she noticed Brett sitting at the table, nursing a beer, watching her. As soon as he realized she'd seen him, his beer bottle became his object of interest.

"Hey," she said softly. "I didn't hear you come in."

"Got in about an hour ago," he told the bottle.

An hour ago. She winced. No wonder she hadn't heard him

—she and Dillon had been making love about then. Dillon had been particularly vigorous. And particularly loud.

Heat spreading across her cheeks, she ducked her head and looked into the fridge. Poor Brett, having to listen to them. She made a vow to try to be quieter next time.

Once she'd poured herself a glass of milk, she slid onto the bench across from him. He was still in his uniform, though his hat lay on the table between them. She took a sip of her milk. When she raised her eyes again, she caught him looking at her again. As soon as their gazes met, his skittered away. Yeah, he'd heard them.

After a few minutes she broke the silence. "Tough shift?"

One shoulder hitched up, then slowly dropped. "Same old, same old."

She reached out and touched his hand, stroking the backs of his fingers. "Dillon told me you're going to be staying here for a while."

His fingers curled as he pulled away from her. "That's what friends are for."

"How'd I get so lucky?"

"What?"

"Having such good friends. You. Dillon. I keep trying to figure out what I did to deserve you guys."

"Me? Nah, it's all Dillon's idea. He's the one you deserve." He lapsed back into silence. The stillness in the room was broken only by the crickets chirping outside and the tick of the wall clock's pendulum. Each time she took a sip of her milk, his eyes would flick up to watch her. Then once she lowered the glass, he'd drop his gaze and resume his examination of his now empty beer bottle.

Is that why he'd walked away from her in high school? Was his sudden disinterest not that he'd played her but that he was keeping to some sort of guy code between him and Dillon? "You know, back in high school, I don't remember you saying you wanted to be a cop. I thought you and Dillon had talked about going into the landscaping business together."

His brows drew together, focusing harder on the bottle's label. "Yeah, well, plans changed. I realized landscaping wasn't for me."

While he picked at the label, she thought about the night she and Dillon had discovered Phil had taken everything she owned. And how Brett had held her. How right she felt in his arms. If he'd asked her, would she have gone to his place that night? Would he have asked? If he'd asked, she would have gone with him. She drummed her fingers on the table debating whether to ask him outright what had happened back in high school. Nah. None of them were in high school anymore.. If he was interested in her, he could get off his ass and tell her outright and she could make a decision between the two of them. Her decision, not theirs. Still…maybe he felt locked in to some sort of bro code thing?

Sensing that once he removed the label, he'd leave, she took a deep breath. "You know, the last couple months when you'd drop in? I know you said it was to check on Phil, but I got the impression that maybe…"

"Maybe what?" His gaze shot up and held hers for the first time that evening. Did she detect panic in his voice? It couldn't be. Of everyone she knew, Brett was the most even tempered.

"Every once in a while, I got the impression that maybe you wanted to ask me out." So much for not getting into this tonight.

His gaze slipped to the door as if he were gauging the distance. Then his lips compressed into a thin line, and he dropped his eyes again. "I was there to check on Phil. Just like I said."

She replayed all their conversations—all his visits while she was married to Wade, and afterward. Each time she circled right back to how he'd held her the other night, the way his head had dipped down toward her. "So the other night back at my place, when you were holding me out on the lawn, you weren't going to kiss me?"

"Nope." He kicked his chair back and stood. With a jerky movement, he snatched the bottle and walked to the bin Dillon kept under the sink, depositing it there.

What was going on?

"So you aren't upset with me for coming home with Dillon?" Instead of you?

Without turning to look at her, he shook his head. "No." The word snapped through the air like a whip.

He took a deep breath and ran his hands through his hair. "Don't mind me. You're right, it was a tough shift. I guess I let it get to me more than I realized."

He started to head out of the kitchen, pausing when he got to the hallway door to say over his shoulder, "Dillon's a great guy, Nik. You two belong together, and you deserve everything he can give you. I think it's great that you two have finally gotten together."

With that, he left her alone with his hat and the pile of label he'd shredded.

CHAPTER 7

Dillon positioned the chainsaw in the shade of the barn, where he could watch Nikki working one of her colts. She moved with a grace, yet handled the long line with a confidence borne over years of handling her precious Blues. No one else would know the smile she shot him was a hint of the sensual being she kept carefully hidden from others. She lifted her hand in a wave before returning her focus to the colt.

Just last night, he'd been the focus of her attention on the porch swing. Man, that had been a sweet evening. Lying with her on top of him as the sun set, the breeze keeping them both cool. She'd had her hands all over him. And he'd returned the favor, discovering all her ticklish spots. It had been good to see her laughing. To feel her throaty moan reverberating through his chest when he'd gone down on her.

Even now the fruity scent of her shampoo filled his head, and the skin on his chest tingled everywhere she'd touched. A hint of her strawberry-flavored lip gloss lingered on his tongue from when she'd kissed him earlier.

She called an instruction to the pony, her voice strong and confident. Different from the soft, breathless pleas she'd whispered when he'd woken her that morning. The juxtaposition of strength and softness fascinated him.

"You gonna work on that chainsaw, or you planning on oglin' me all morning?"

He laughed. "I plan on doin' both, darlin'. You sure are a prettier sight than the inside of my workshed."

She stuck her tongue out at him before clicking to the colt, wheeling him in the opposite direction.

Dillon dropped to his knees and rummaged through his toolbox, searching for a screwdriver. As he unscrewed the saw's air filter housing, his father's old Ford pulled into the yard.

His father resettled his Stetson and joined Dillon in the shade. "Hot one today."

"Yup. Gonna reach one hundred again." Had probably reached it already. Which made him worry about Nikki working out in the sun.

"Your mom was disappointed you missed Sunday dinner." His dad hunkered down and poked through his toolbox. "You know how important it is to your momma to have her family together at least once a week. Especially with Griff working up north and Ethan away at college."

"Sorry. We were over at Nikki's place helping her clean up the mess Phil left, and I lost track of time." He sat back on his heels watching her pull a water bottle from her pocket and take a long swig. Even from this distance, he could see the long, smooth column of her throat move as she swallowed. He released a breath as he remembered touching it when she'd gone down on him in the shower. Damned if he didn't get hard just at the memory.

"You running her back and forth to her place to do her chores every day?"

He shifted, easing the tightness in his jeans. "Nah. Brett thought it best if we brought her horses over here, just in case

Phil realized how much they were worth and decided to come back for them."

"That must have taken you a while, shipping all those horses in her little trailer. You could have borrowed my big rig if you'd needed."

Dillon shot him a smug grin. "I just cut a hole in the fence between our places and led them through."

"Smart." Easier than trying to load up the horses into the trailer and make the trip to Dillon's place. A half dozen times.

"I've fixed the hole so Phil can't come back and steal them too, but we can discuss putting a gate in there once the whole Phil business is dealt with."

"Why would you need a gate?"

"In case we combine the two spreads," he answered with an easy grin.

"She moving in with you permanently, son?"

He could only hope but he shook his head, warned by the hint of disapproval in his father's tone. "Brett and I have worked out our hours so there's always someone here to keep an eye on her, just in case Phil does try something though."

"Speaking of Brett, where is your brother? He around?" His dad picked up a socket wrench and spun it around in his fingers, making it whir. Geez, sometimes he could be as big a kid as Dillon's youngest brother, Matt.

"Brett's run into Dallas on police business."

Nikki had the colt switch directions, rewarding him with a click when he obeyed. Dillon found it hard to believe the horse had never worn a halter a month before. Then again, he'd wear a halter if it meant she'd pay attention to him, reward him with treats the way she did the colt. Or better yet, he'd like to use some leather bindings on her. Tie her up to his bed and spend the day pleasuring her.

"Thought he was off on today."

Dillon grabbed the rag from his pocket and wiped his face.

Fantasizing about tying up your girlfriend when your father was a couple feet away definitely breached the weirdness boundaries.

"Shoulda been but Tiny O'Brien called this morning, saying they had a lead on her brother. They traced Nik's cell phone to Dallas. Brett figured they might get further with the boys in blue there if they had to deal with an actual person, instead of a voice on a phone."

"When he gets back, tell him to drop by, will you? Your sister wants to ask him about living in Boston. Figured he'd be able to tell her what it was like from when he went to school there."

Why would Lily want to know about Boston? "She doing a school project or something?"

His father grunted as he replaced the wrench and picked up a file. "She's trying to decide where to apply for college. She got some wild hair about going to school up east like Brett did, instead of going to Aggie like the rest of you boys. Your mom's hoping Brett will dissuade her, but I'm not so sure. The boy stayed there even on his breaks, especially that first year."

Dillon couldn't look at his father; they both knew why Brett hadn't come home. Dillon swore as he stripped the threading on the screw. Jeezus, that had been a shitty year. One neither of them had talked about since he'd finally gotten his head out of his ass and apologized to Brett.

"By the way, have your girlfriend call your mom, will ya? Your mother and grandmother are planning on having some sort of fundraiser over at the church for her, but they need to know what she needs the most."

Dillon's chest swelled with pride. Trust Mom to come up with some way to help out. He just hoped Nikki would accept whatever help they came up with. "Might be better if I call Mom and see what we can come up with. Nikki might be embarrassed and try to turn them down."

"You know what your grandmother would say about that."

The two men grinned at each other and recited, "Pride's all well and good, but there's a difference between a hand-out and a hand-up."

A donkey's bray interrupted them. Dillon laughed as Merlin raced across the field to where Nikki had led the colt to set him free, the training session over. The donkey's musical hee-hawing ended as he head-butted Nikki. "That donkey's in love with her. He does that whenever he sees her."

His father made a sound in the back of his throat. "From the way you've not stopped looking at that girl the whole time I've been here, I'm guessing he's not the only one in love. Or is it more lust at this stage?"

The tips of his ears burned at the thought he'd been that obvious. "I'm just trying to be a good neighbor. I could hardly leave her to sleep on the floor at her place, could I?"

"Uh huh." His father sounded doubtful. "So she's staying in the guest room, and Brett's sleepin' on the couch, is he?"

Busted. He ducked his head, hoping the brim of his hat hid the color rising into his cheeks. Shit. He hadn't blushed since he was in Bible camp and Tommy Snider had pantsed him in front of the entire camp.

His father scowled, stared at him a long moment. "You know your momma's buying wedding magazines already. Talking swatches and color schemes and all those things women love."

Shit. Rolling his shoulders, he pretended to examine the chainsaw's air filter. This was going in a direction he'd not wanted. Not yet, anyway. "Talk about jumping the gun. We've only just started dating. Besides, Nik's first marriage wasn't great, so I doubt she's ready to tie herself down any time soon."

"Glad to hear it."

That got him staring at his father, his fingers clamping over the screwdriver. "You don't think Nikki's good enough for me?"

His father held up his hands. "Now, don't go puttin' words in my mouth. All I meant is that marriage can be hard work. It ain't all about the fun you have in the bedroom. Especially once you've got kids. So it's not something you should rush into."

"Shit on a stick, Dad. I'm not the one who mentioned marriage here."

"Maybe not, but you do have a tendency to rush into situations, thinking you know everything there is to know. Look at that fight you and Brett had senior year of high school. If you'd just taken the time to—"

"I know." He tossed the screwdriver back in the toolbox. Christ on a crutch. How had a perfectly nice afternoon gone downhill so freaking fast? "I know I should have checked out Wade and Dave's story and made sure it really was Brett's condom. It was Brett who'd taken my Camaro to Tater's party; how was I to know Dave and his girlfriend had snuck into the backseat and f—made out in my car, huh?"

"You should have trusted Brett. Brett had already told you what happened and yet you believed those other boys over him even though you knew Brett wouldn't have lied to you."

"I know, all right?" He took a breath and forced his shoulders down when his father raised an eyebrow at his sharp tone. "I apologized when I realized what had happened."

Of course, that had taken over a year.

"That's what I'm saying, son. Apologies sometimes aren't enough to patch things up. Not in a marriage. Some things a body just can't get past. Lack of trust is a big one."

"You think I won't be able to trust Nik?"

"I'm not saying that. I'm more worried about your impulsiveness. I hate to see you hurt by jumping into a relationship with a woman you barely know, only to end up hurt in the end. Or doin' anything else you might regret."

"I'm not eighteen anymore, Dad." He sure as shit sounded like a surly teenager. "I own my own business and make decisions that affect my clients and my employees every day."

"I know, and your mother and I are as proud as peacocks

about how things have worked out for you. I'm just sayin' take your time. Get to know her and make sure she's what you want before you get in any deeper. Hellfire, son, you had her move in before you even started dating." His father stood with a groan and dusted off his jeans. "For all you know, you're her rebound affair. Once she's worked out her issues with you, scratched whatever itch she's got, she may want to move on."

Rebound affair? Was that what he was to Nikki? His guts sure didn't like the thought that she might be using him to work out any issues.

"Ah, who knows? For all I know, I could be talkin' out my hat." As he passed Dillon, his father tapped Dillon's brim, a habit that had started when Dillon was a kid and got his first Stetson. Normally he liked the ritual. Today however, it bugged the bejeebers out of him. "I gotta go. Don't forget to tell Brett to call your mother when he gets back."

The dust left by his father's truck had long since dissipated before Dillon roused himself. He tossed the chainsaw into the back of the truck, not caring that he'd cracked the casing.

Rebound affair ringing in his ears, he stomped into his workshed and slammed the door behind him. His father had to be wrong. This thing with Nikki was more than an itch to be scratched. He was in it for the long haul. But was she?

CHAPTER 8

Nikki fumbled with her purse as Brett parked his car in front of Ernie's Motors and turned off the ignition, then hopped out to open her door.

"You don't have to stay." She took the hand he held out to help her from the car. "I'll just pay the bill."

"It's okay. I'll wait to make sure you get home safely."

Shaking her head at how different he was from Phil, who would have driven her as far as the nearest bar and told her to find her own way, she headed into the cramped garage office. "Hey, Gloria, I'm here to settle up."

"Hey, Nik." Gloria shuffled through a dozen forms in a metal tray and selected one, then slid it across the counter so Nikki could read it. She ticked off the list of things they'd had to repair. "By the way, Ernie says your brakes are going to need fixing soon."

Fantastic. It was starting to get to the point where the truck was costing her as much in maintenance as it would to pay a loan on a new one. She handed over her credit card, tilting her head toward the fan when it blew her way. "I don't know how you work in an office without air conditioning, Gloria."

"Not as if I have much choice. With the economy the way it is, we can't afford to replace the old unit." Gloria ran the card through the machine, and Nikki dutifully punched the buttons.

A few moments later, Gloria frowned. "Sorry, Nik, but the transaction's been declined. You got another card you want to try?"

Nikki took the card back and stared at it. There should have been enough money to cover the repairs. "What? That can't be right." Oh shit. They'd had her cancel her credit cards, no wonder it had been declined.

She didn't like to admit that Phil had stolen her stuff, even though everyone in town had probably heard about it already. She dug out her debit card. Luckily the repairs were just below her daily limit. "Can I use my debit card?"

"Sure." Gloria tapped some buttons and gestured to the machine. "Try it now."

She tapped the buttons indicating they were to take the money from her checking account. Declined. *WTF?* She tried her savings account with the same result. The acids in her stomach burnt the back of her mouth. She'd definitely had enough to cover the bill in her savings. There had to be—she'd been saving to pay for her next tax bill. If that money was gone.... No. This couldn't be happening. Phil couldn't have cleaned out her bank accounts too.

The bell over the door jingled as Brett stepped into the tiny space. She hadn't thought of him as large until he stood beside her. "There a problem?"

"The bank declined the transaction," Nikki explained, hoping neither he nor Gloria heard the desperation in her voice.

He flipped open his billfold, selected a Gold Card and held it out. "Put it on my card."

Before Gloria could take it from him, Nikki grabbed it and shoved it back at him. "I can't take your money."

"If you don't, you won't get your truck back."

Damn it, but he was right. If she didn't have her truck, she'd be reliant on him or Dillon to drive her anywhere she wanted to go. Either way, she was going to owe him big time. More than she already did. "All right, but I'm paying you back."

Despite the smile on his lips, there was a shadow to his expression. "If you want to pay me back that's fine, but it wouldn't kill you to accept a gift when it's offered."

Once the bill was paid and she had her ignition key in hand, Brett walked her to her truck. He waited as she unlocked it, then reached past her and opened the door for her. Instead of closing it once she'd climbed in, he stood there, his forehead wrinkled as he stared at her purse. "You thought there should have been enough money in the account to cover the bill, didn't you?"

She bit her bottom lip and stared at his hand resting on the door. Damn Phil for taking every shred of dignity from her. She shouldn't have to answer questions about how much money she had, even though Brett didn't mean it as an insult. "Yeah. There should have been enough."

"Thought so. Look, do yourself a favor and go to the bank. Make sure Phil hasn't found a way to get into your accounts."

She huffed in exasperation. "I've already called the credit card companies—"

"I know." His tone was gentle, but firm. "But maybe he found a way to get an extra ATM card or something."

Shit. It pissed her off to admit it, but he was right. "All right. I'll go to the bank to check into what happened, and then I've got a couple other things to pick up. I'll meet you back at Dillon's in a while." She put her hand on his shoulder and leaned over, pressing a light kiss on his cheek. "And thanks for the loan, Brett. You're a real good friend, you know that?"

"Anything for you, Nik." He waited until she'd started the engine before rounding the front of her truck and heading to his own car.

Anything for you, Nik. Was it her imagination, or had there been an undercurrent to his phrase? Almost a longing.

Nah, you're imagining things. Same as you'd thought he was going to kiss you a couple nights before.

Focus. She needed to get shampoo and conditioner, and a couple other things at the drugstore, but Brett was right. First she'd need to get her bank account figured out.

When she got to the front of the line at the bank, she swiped her card into the machine, tapped in her pin then explained her problem. "So there should be enough money to cover the bill."

The teller typed something into the computer. "Sorry, Ms. Kimball, but it says here there's nothing in that account. Looks like there was a cash withdrawal for the balance on Monday morning."

"What?" Everyone in the bank stared at her, so she lowered her voice. "I didn't take any money out, and I'm the only one with a card to access it."

"Can I help?" The assistant bank manager appeared at the teller's side. Wouldn't you know, it was Dillon's aunt, Missy. Was there anyone not related to the Barnetts in this town?

Missy listened with pursed lips as Nikki explained about the missing money. "Why don't you come with me, and we'll see what we can find out?"

Nikki followed her into the manager's office. Like the teller had minutes earlier, Missy tapped her account number into her computer. And like the teller, her forehead wrinkled into a myriad of lines. "I see you've put a hold on any future credit."

Nikki explained about Brett's warning about freezing her credit.

The manager pursed her lips. "It says here there are two cards authorized to access those accounts. Who has the other one?"

"Two? No. I'm the only one with a card." She'd made sure of that when she and Wade split.

Missy leaned back in her chair and tapped her nails on the edge of the keyboard. "Did Phil have access to your computer?"

"When I wasn't in the house, I guess. I'd turn it on in the morning and leave it on all day—check my horse loops and email and stuff." Oh, dear God, what else had Phil done online under her name? "How could he have gotten it without my authorization?"

She closed her eyes. If he'd found the book she kept her passwords and PIN numbers in, it would have been easy.

What an idiot she was for not thinking of it sooner. Especially after Brett had told her to check.

"Well, someone did. The transaction was an ATM in Dallas."

Dallas? She clutched her purse tight to her side. "Could you write down the details so I can give it the police for their investigation?"

"Of course." Missy hit a button; seconds later, her printer whirred to life, and a sheet of paper rolled out of it.

Once she'd tucked the printout in her purse, she steeled herself and asked, "Can you tell how much is on my credit card?"

"Which one?"

Nikki shook her head in confusion. "I only have one."

The lines on Missy's forehead deepened even further. "According to your credit report you've got—" Missy ran her finger down the screen, her lips moving silently as she counted, "—nine credit accounts you owe money on right now."

"Nine!" Oh God, how much money was she going to be on the line for?

"You didn't know about them?"

"No. Isn't this covered by insurance? Can I get my money back?"

"Well, maybe. As long as you can prove you didn't know about them."

"How do I prove that? And how did my brother get access to my credit account anyway?"

Missy steepled her fingers and tapped them together twice before speaking. "Did your brother have access to your regular mail?"

She nodded. "Sure, he went out and got it from the box for me every day." It was one of the few things Phil had done for her without being pestered.

"It's possible it's something as simple as taking the blank applications companies sent out in mass market mailings and forging your name. Then he'd just have to make sure he got to the mail box before you did and collected the new cards."

"How long...when did he..." Her questions stuck in her throat.

Missy must have understood because she clicked her mouse a few times then said, "According to the records, it looks like you started applying for more credit about seven months ago."

A couple weeks after Phil had come to live with her. He'd been stealing from her this whole time? She clutched the arms of the chair and took several deep breaths. With the anger surging through her at the moment, Phil would be lucky if the police would pick him up before she found him, because right now she had an urge to throttle him.

"Since you've already frozen your credit with the bureaus, that'll stop him from getting any more cards or credit, but you'll have to notify each of them that the account was opened fraudulently. They're also going to want to make sure fraud charges are laid against him which means you'll need to file a report with the sheriff. And you will have to convince the various creditors you didn't know about the fraudulent cards because if they think you knowingly allowed it to continue, you may never see your money back and you'll be held liable for his expenses."

Twenty minutes later, Nicole stumbled from Missy's office

and nearly ran into another customer. The woman grabbed her arm and steadied her. "Hey, hon, you all right?"

Nikki stared blankly at her for a second before her brain clicked in on the woman's identity. Oh, great, this was *so* not the way she wanted to meet Dillon's mother, Faith. "I'm fine, thanks."

"I hope you don't take this the wrong way, but you don't look fine. Should I call Dillon for you?"

"No, it's all right. Really." *Once I get my hands around Phillip's neck and watch his eyes bulge out of his frickin' head.*

Dillon's mom linked her arm with Nikki's. "Well, now, you come with me, hon, and let me buy you a cup of coffee. I've been wanting to talk with you anyway."

Crap. "Dillon told me you were thinking of having something up at the church to help out. You really don't need to go to all the bother. I'll be fine."

"That's what he told me you'd say." Mrs. Barnett squeezed Nikki's arm. "But that's not what I want to talk with you about."

Aw, crap. *Let the floor open up and swallow me whole. My boyfriend's mother wants to talk with me.* Last time that happened, Wade's mother had offered her a check to say the baby she was carrying wasn't her grandchild— with a little something extra, as she'd put it, so she wouldn't hold Wade back by forcing him to marry her. "Honest, I'm fine. I should be getting out of your hair."

Mrs. Barnett fixed her with a stern look. Wow, how did Dillon manage to get away with half the stuff he'd told her about with a mother who could give that look?

"Now, hon, I am not going to let you get in a car and drive right now. You look like a hummingbird could knock you down."

Sensing it would be easier to stand against a rampaging bull than stand up to the other woman, Nikki allowed herself to be towed out of the bank and along the main street toward the

Twisted Tabby's diner. She found herself seated at a table and a coffee placed in front of her before she knew it.

"Honestly, I'm fine, Mrs. Barnett," Nikki repeated. "You didn't have to go through all this bother."

"Nonsense. And call me Faith—there are so many Mrs. Barnetts around these parts, you're likely to have six women in this diner alone thinking you're talkin' to them." Faith reached over and patted her hand. "I'm so glad to have run into you. I've been hoping for a chance to get to talk with you away from Dillon."

Oh, shit. Here came the "you're not good enough for my son, how much will it take to make you go away" speech.

"I was hoping I'd see y'all for Sunday dinner, but I understand you weren't up to socializing."

She didn't need a mirror to know that a blush was spreading over her face. Once he'd returned from whatever errand his grandmother wanted him to do, she and Dillon had spent most of Sunday afternoon in his bed. "I didn't know Dillon was expected for dinner. He never mentioned anything about it to me."

"He said something about you being outside working your horses when he phoned to tell me he wasn't comin' over." The glint in Faith's eyes and the twitch at the end of her lips told Nikki she knew exactly what they'd been doing. "I hope the three of you will come over next Sunday. I do love to have my family all together—they're growin' up so fast. With Dillon and Brett out of the house, and Griffin away—first at school, then doin' his training, I want to enjoy my family bein' together as often as I can."

"I'm sure I'll be back in my own place by next Sunday, but I'll make sure to remind Dillon and Brett not to disappoint you."

A shadow flickered across Faith's face but disappeared so quickly, Nikki questioned whether she'd seen it at all. "How are they getting along? With Brett staying out there?"

"Fine. Why?"

Faith pursed her lips then picked up her coffee and took a sip, as if she needed to consider her answer. "I'm being an over-protective mother, don't mind me. I just wanted to make sure they didn't butt heads—they're both stubborn boys."

Although she had the feeling she was missing a large part of the picture, Nikki didn't feel comfortable asking Faith anything more. She could always collar Dillon about it later. Or Brett.

Faith put down her coffee and checked her watch, then grimaced. "I lost all sense of time. I'm sorry, hon, but I've gotta get goin'. I gotta pick Lilly up at school and drive her into town for a dentist appointment." She stood up and tucked her purse beneath her elbow. "You make sure you come over on Sunday. If you're back in your place, just drive on over. And if that truck of yours gives you any problems and Dillon or Brett aren't around, you just holler, and I'll send Jackson or Griffin over to fetch you."

NIKKI OPENED the door to Dillon's place and stood in the hall. *How are they getting along? With Brett staying out there?*

What was it Mrs. Barnett had been worried about? Weren't Dillon and Brett best friends? Or did Mrs Barnett suspect Nikki was tagteaming her sons?

"Hey, Nik. Did you get everything straightened out at the bank?" Brett called from the top of the stairs, interrupting her musing.

She glanced up, and all thoughts of Mrs. Barnett evaporated. Brett must have been in the middle of changing into his uniform, but only gotten the bottom half of it on before she'd come home.

Man, he looked good without a shirt. He could have been

Mr. July in one of those beefcake calendars. Maybe she should suggest it as a fundraiser next time the police benefit people called for a donation.

Not an ounce of flesh jiggled when he walked down the stairs. It didn't take a uniform to command her attention. Brett was all man, hinting at a barely controlled passion as he prowled across the front hall toward her. "Nik? Did you have any problems with the truck?"

"Uh, no. It works fine." She closed her mouth and swallowed. *Stop looking at his chest. Look at his face.* Maybe Mrs. Barnett wasn't too far off the mark with her worries because having both Dillon and Brett in her bed was starting to sound like a freaking fantasy.

"Nikki? Is everything all right"

"Oh, um, yeah, I talked with Dillon's aunt. You know, she's the bank manager."

He nodded, his lips crooking up slightly as if he were trying not to smile. "Yeah, I know Missy."

Of course he'd know Dillon's aunt is the bank manager, you dumb-ass. He'd practically been adopted by the Barnetts, after all.

Shit, he smelled wonderful, all clean soap and an understated cologne. He was more like a big brother, not her lover. So why was her pulse spiking into triple digits as she imagined Brett holding her, kissing her? Especially considering the number of times she'd had sex with Dillon in the past couple of days. It's not like she was starved for sex or anything.

Dillon. She closed her eyes and let the image of him, of how he'd managed to make her laugh, of his quiet assurance, remind her that he was the one she wanted. Not Brett.

"You were saying something about Missy?"

"Um, yes." *Geez, Nicole, what is going on with you?* "Missy says Phil must have ordered a duplicate bank card somehow and cleaned out my accounts. And he's taken out nine credit cards in my name. So it was a good thing you made sure I put a freeze on my credit."

The latent passion toward Brett leeched away as what Phil had done to her snaked back. Phil had been living with her, eating her food, sleeping in her spare bedroom, and the whole time he'd been stealing from her. His own sister. How could he have done that? Didn't he have any sort of a conscience?

But was she any better? She was sleeping with Dillon— she was fairly certain she'd fallen head-over-teakettle for him—yet here she was, lusting after Brett at the same time. The Kimball genes had to be really screwed up. "I'm sorry."

Brett wrapped his arms around her, cupping her head until her cheek rested on his chest. "Hey, it's all right."

Not wanting to admit to her failings, yet unable to pull away, Nikki leaned into him, her arms snaking around his waist. "I know, it's just..."

The whole week, from the length of the trip up to Muncie and seeing the horrific conditions Bashir had been living in, to the truck breaking down, to arriving home and discovering Phil had ripped her off for everything she owned, to the bank, to being torn between loving Dillon and thinking there might be something between her and Brett...it all came crashing down on her. Her breathing uneven, she struggled not to give in to the tears that threatened to spill.

"He took things my grandma had given me that can never be replaced." She lost her fight as tears cascaded down her cheeks. "They're gone, Brett. Everything's gone."

"Oh, honey." Brett's arms tightened around her. He rocked her, murmuring soft words that didn't penetrate the sobs that clawed their way out until she couldn't draw a full breath. He bent down and placed an arm beneath her knees, lifting her into his arms. As if she weighed nothing at all, he carried her to the couch, settling down with her on his lap.

She buried her face in his chest, wanting to crawl into him, to cover herself with his strength like it was a blanket. "I'm sorry. I'm being a wuss. They're just things, I know."

"It's all right, Nik, you don't have to explain."

And she didn't. She knew Brett understood she wasn't just crying about her belongings, she was crying about everything. Her failed marriage, the baby she'd lost. Her hopes and her dreams that had died with it. The family she should have been able to trust, to count on, but couldn't. Without her having to say a word, he understood.

She lifted her head and found his expression filled with compassion. As she watched, something dark filled his eyes. A smoldering heat, a promise of danger, and unrivalled passion.

He lowered his head until his lips were inches from hers, then stilled, hovering so close his breath tickled her face.

What were they doing? What was she doing? Despite her earlier fantasy of being with them both, she couldn't do this. But she wanted him. As much as she wanted Dillon.

Choose. You have to choose between Dillon or Brett.

But hadn't she already chosen? Hadn't she woken up in Dillon's bed this morning? With a shake of her head, she pressed her hands against his chest. "I can't do this. It's not like Dillon and I have any sort of agreement or anything. We're not officially dating or anything but this—" she circled a finger between herself and Brett "—doesn't feel right."

The heat in his eyes disappeared. His mouth opened a couple times before he loosened his arms from around her with a, "Yeah. I gotta go."

Half shoving her off his lap, he stood and dashed out of the room. His footsteps thudded up the stairs, then moments later down again. She found him in the hallway, shrugging on his shirt, belt slung over his shoulder, his holster thumping against his chest. He yanked open the door and was out on the porch before he turned around.

"I gotta go," he repeated.

"Brett? Wait!" She raced toward the door as he jumped off the porch. By the time she reached the porch, his car was gunning down the drive, leaving a plume of dust in its wake.

She sat down on the top step of the porch with a thump. Of course Brett wouldn't poach on another man's girlfriend, especially if that man was Dillon. But he'd almost kissed her, and she'd almost kissed him. So despite him declaring he wasn't interested in her the night before, he was.

Wasn't he?

CHAPTER 9

Nikki brushed the strand of hair that had fallen into Dillon's eyes from when he'd laid his head on her lap. Hoping she didn't rouse him, she pushed the porch swing with her feet.

The way Brett had lowered his head, not only this afternoon but back that first night, niggled at the back of her mind. She couldn't deny it made her all squidgy inside to think that *maybe* he'd been tempted to kiss her.

So why was she gnawing on her thumbnail down to the quick?

Because they both meant so much to her. Brett, for his quiet support and friendship over the years, and Dillon...because he was Dillon. He was just as supportive as Brett, but he made her laugh. Where she was a glass-half empty person, Dillon's glass was full to the brim. Being around him made everything seem possible.

If Dillon thought Brett was attracted to her too, wouldn't he be jealous? It could tear them apart. They may not be related by blood, but they were as close as any brothers she'd ever known. Who was she to destroy that friendship, that bond, because of an overactive imagination? Even if they didn't blame her, their family would lay the blame at her feet.

After all, Dillon was a Barnett. Of the Barnett County Barnetts. As in Barnett Lumber, and Barnett Pharmacy. Barnett Auto, Barnett Real Estate. Heck, Doc Barnett, her horses' veterinarian, was Dillon's uncle. Then there was Mayor Barnett, a second cousin twice removed. His family even had a state senator in their family tree.

They had oil and cattle. They had money. Old money. Well, not Dillon's particular branch, but they still had connections. His family was better off than her family had ever been.

You? What have you got to show for yourself? An empty house, thanks to Phil, on a piddling forty acres with a hefty mortgage compared to Dillon's two-fifty or his family's seventeen hundred.

They'd have heard the trash talk Wade's family spread around about her. Heaven knows all the gossip at school had spread fast enough. About how she'd trapped Wade into marriage by deliberately getting pregnant in senior year. Neither Wade nor her in-laws had ever once acknowledged it had been an accident, thanks to a broken condom.

Surely the Barnetts would expect Dillon to carry on the Barnett name. Something she'd not be able to offer considering she'd probably be unable to carry any more babies to full term, even if she could get pregnant. Which meant they wouldn't want her to be part of his future.

God, it was going to be so tough to have to live next to him, watch him dating someone else. Because sooner or later, that's what she'd have to do.

Dillon lifted his arm and peered out from under it. "You're thinkin' so hard I can hear the gears grinding."

She forced a smile and rolled her head back to face him. "It's nothing."

A couple moments passed as he considered her. He shifted

until he was sitting, then cupped her cheek with his palm, his thumb stroking her jaw. "Are you regretting being with me? Did I push you too fast? Because if I did, we can slow things down."

Did he want to slow things down? Her grip on the swing tightened. "You didn't push me, Dillon. I like being here with you. Did you want to slow things down?"

"Nope, I like things just the way they are. I'm kicking myself that I took so long to ask you out."

A warm glow started in her belly while knots grew in her throat. She blinked several times, trying to ignore the feeling. "You've been a good friend to me, Dillon. I don't want to lose that."

"You won't lose me. Not now. Not later. I promise. You mean something to me, Nik. You always have." His voice dropped a half octave on the last word. As if to seal the promise, he dipped his head and brushed his lips over hers, his breath a warm whisper across her cheek, an unseen caress. When she relaxed her jaw and parted her lips, his kiss grew stronger, his tongue softly sweeping into her mouth, exploring, testing.

His hand traced down her side, then slipped between her thighs, beneath her skirt. He slid one calloused finger between her labia, parting them, sliding beside her clit, but not touching it.

Wanting him to feel the same heat, she slid her hand between them and unzipped his jeans. The barrier between them removed, she wrapped her hand around his cock.

His hand closed around hers, stilling her. "You're playin' with fire, you know, Nik."

"I thought I was playin' with you."

"This isn't playin' we're doing, Nik. I'm dead serious here. I want to know everything about you. From what you're thinking about right now to what drives you crazy with need, even what makes you make that soft little moan you do right before you come."

Geez, the man had a way of crawling into her chest and into her heart. If she stayed with him much longer, she'd lose it completely. "So how come I can't explore you?"

"Oh, you'll have your chance, but right now it's my turn."

"What? Are you going to tie me up if I touch you?"

His grin slowly widened, and his eyes sparkled with humor. "If I have to."

A thrill shot through her. Why did her heart do this little flip every time he grinned?

"Hmph, as if." She wrapped her fingers around his shaft and teased his bulging head with her thumb.

Before she knew it, she found herself over his shoulder, the air jarred out of her lungs with every step he took through the kitchen and up the stairs. "What are you doing?"

"Teaching you not to doubt me." He lowered her onto his bed. "Be a good girl, get your clothes off, then lie back and grab the headboard."

Rolling her eyes, she did as he asked, watching him open a dresser drawer. Her heart did that little flippy thing again when he pulled out two ties and dangled them over her chest.

"You're not really going to tie me up, are you?" Holy shit, why was her body reacting as if it was a good thing? Oh, yeah, because it had long been a fantasy to be tied to Dillon's bed and at his mercy.

HE HADN'T PLANNED on tying her down, but now that she was on his bed, her legs sprawled open, he couldn't resist. If nothing else, he'd find some way of distracting her from whatever had been bothering her downstairs. Something had happened. Maybe her parents had called again and given her grief for still being in his house instead of moving back to hers? Whatever it was, he had to find some way to make her relax.

He twirled the end of the tie over her nipple, watching it bead. "I've been thinking about this for a while now. I sorta have a hankering to use your reins to tie you up, but for now we can use these."

"My reins?"

"Yup. Something about seeing you in leather makes me hard as a rock."

Her gaze dropped to his groin. When she saw proof of his words her breath stuttered, and the artery beneath her ear betrayed how her heart raced. Not out of fear, he was sure.

"What do you think? Do you want to try a little bondage?"

"Yes. I'm willing to try anything with you, Dillon." As if the husky quality to her voice didn't betray her desire, she held up her left wrist and allowed him to bind her.

If this might distract her, he was willing to give it a shot. He wrapped the silk around her left, and then around one of the cannonballs of the headboard, then did the same with her right wrist.

He stood back and frowned. Was he doing this right? "Too tight?"

"No." Her eyes were wide, her pupils enlarged and her breathing had quickened. Wow, she was as turned on as he was. He'd been afraid she might think him a pervert.

Satisfied he could proceed uninterrupted, Dillon dipped his head to one pale nipple and tongued it, then blew on it until it was a hard point. "Let yourself go, Nik. Feel what I'm doing to you."

He settled between her thighs, spreading them wide. Using his thumb to part her labia, he bent his head and swiped his tongue around her the hard bud of her clit. Her body shook beneath him, her hips lifting to meet his mouth. Dipping his head, he spent a long time licking her, enjoying her taste, watching her reactions so he could increase her pleasure. Once she was writhing beneath him, straining against her bonds, he inserted two fingers into her pussy and stroked deep inside. Her hips rotated with each stroke, and the little purr signaling she was about to come grew louder. She wasn't going to last long if he kept this up, so he slowed his rhythm.

Hell, *he* wasn't going to last long if he kept this up. His blood pounded in his ears, a primitive drumbeat forcing him on.

Her body tightening around his invading fingers, he pulled back to nuzzle her damp curls. The musky fragrance of her juices clinging to his chin and his upper lip were a heady elixir. He dragged his beard over the sensitive skin of her inner thigh, marking her as his.

He returned to her swollen cleft, lapping her sweet honey, keeping her on the knife edge of orgasm.

"Dillon, please." She lifted her head to stare down at him, her hair a corona of fire spreading across his pillow. Her hands clenched around the ties binding her to the headboard.

"All in good time."

She arched up again, thrusting the taut bud into his mouth. He cupped her quivering pussy, her juices drenching him. His hips ground his cock into the mattress, his mind fighting his body's need to bury himself deep inside her again.

"Dillon." A demand, not a plea.

He captured her clit between his lips, lashing the swollen tissue with his tongue. He lifted his gaze from the beautiful dark pink folds to watch her as he thrust a third finger deep inside her tight channel. "Come for me, baby."

He swiped his thumb across her pulsing clit. That's all it took to force her to climax. Her voice sounded like she was about to cry, but then her body shuddered. The headboard creaked from the strain as she pulled on her bonds, and a look of bliss filled her eyes. Sensuous, uninhibited. His.

Before her orgasm died off, he'd wrapped his cock in a

condom and sheathed himself to the balls in her slick pussy, the heated passage still rippling the remains of her orgasm.

She writhed beneath him, her hands wrapped around the ties binding her to the bed, pleading for him to take her hard and fast. While he missed having her hands on him, digging into his shoulders, clutching his ass, something dark inside roused, some cavemanlike instinct that reveled in being in control of her, being completely in charge of her pleasure.

The way her fingers dug into the silk bindings, the desperation in her voice, set his instincts aflame. He dipped his head to the curve of her neck and licked the salty taste of her sweat, her skin.

He withdrew slowly, then pressed in just as slowly. His eyes closed in ecstasy from the pressure as he buried himself in her to the hilt.

Another slow withdrawal, followed by a slow return. He felt the familiar warning at the base of his spine. He wasn't going to last much longer, whether he went fast or slow.

"Dillon, please." Desperation filled her voice. "I need you."

How long had he wanted to hear her say that? Every day since he'd bought the land adjoining hers and had seen her riding along their shared fenceline. Longer. Since high school. Before she'd started dating that sorry-assed husband of hers. He'd let her get away once. Not again. If he had to leave her tied to his bed until she agreed, or wrap her in cotton wool to protect her, he'd do it.

"You want this?" His voice was gruff as he thrust into her and held still. Her body trembled around him, her pussy clenching and releasing. She was so close to coming, taking him with her, and him not moving a damned muscle. "You want me?"

"Yes. Please, Dillon. Move, damn it!"

He stole her breath by catching her bottom lip between his.

Her eyes fluttered closed as he withdrew and thrust in again, filling her completely.

The sound of their flesh smacking together, of Nikki's moans and his grunts each time his cock hit the end of her tight channel, filled the room. Everything else faded; his world reduced to the sensation of her pussy squeezing his cock, the feel of his sweat-covered body slipping over her soft skin, her gasps, his harsh breath. With a roar, he buried himself twice more before his balls completely tightened, and he pumped his release for what seemed like forever. He gently untied her, and held her until she drifted to sleep. Something had spooked her earlier. What? Maybe Brett knew.

He slid off the bed and padded down to the room Brett had been using. Empty. He wasn't downstairs either and his car wasn't out in the yard. What the hell? Dillon checked his phone for messages. A single "going to my place" message from Brett, with no explanation. Which made him suspect something had happened between the two of them.

Midnight had long since come and gone when Brett let himself into his apartment. His shoulders loosened, as did the knot that had formed in his gut. It was stupid. He'd already driven by the Double Bar and saw Dillon's truck parked out front and knew there'd be no one here. Yet he'd expected to find Dillon waiting for him, even braced himself to have a knock-down-drag-out.

Not that he'd done anything wrong. Yet. He hadn't kissed Nikki, though he'd been less than a nanosecond away from giving in to temptation. So Dillon had no reason to beat him up again. But, shit, he'd come so close.

It damned near killed him trying to pretend he didn't want to drag Nikki up to his room and make love to her night after night. To pretend he didn't need her cuddling him in the darkest hours of the night when the nightmares hit.

He diverted to the kitchen and grabbed a beer, then padded into the living room. Stretched out on the couch, he pillowed his head with his arm and settled back with a sigh, using the television as his nightlight. He flipped around the channels, but gave up on finding anything good, so he switched to the streaming service and played the first thing on the list.

Instead of paying attention to whatever the hell crap movie was playing, his mind drifted back to his *situation*. He'd almost blown it today. Considering Nikki was very definitely in a relationship with Dillon this time, if he'd moved that half inch, if he'd given in to his fantasy, he'd have found himself cast from the Barnett family permanently. After Dillon had kicked his ass from here to kingdom come.

He pounded his fist into the couch. What the hell had he been thinking, agreeing to stay at Dillon's while Nik was there? Why the hell had he thought he could pretend he wasn't still attracted to her?

He'd paved the goddamned road to hell with all his good intentions, hadn't he?

The light from the television flickered over the ceiling as he stared at it. No matter how many times he replayed the afternoon, it still came back to him losing control, to him losing everything he cherished. His friendship with Dillon. His family.

He flung his hand over his eyes. While it shut out the light, it couldn't stop the feeling of failure flooding him. He hadn't even had the balls to stick around until Dillon had come home. No, he'd run off and left Nik all by herself.

Come on, if you'd stayed, you'd have had her naked and horizontal in another five minutes.

No. That would never have happened. She'd told him no. She wasn't the type to fool around. She'd proven that all those years she was married to Wade. What made him think he could have changed her mind?

Stop your whimpering, you fuckin' little bastard.

He tried to protect himself from the coming blow, but he couldn't move one of his arms. Had he been tied up again? Pain exploded in his head as his father's fist connected with his face. He hadn't done anything wrong, he wanted to argue. He'd gotten home from school on time, just like he'd been told. He'd kept quiet. He'd done his homework.

Think you're so fuckin' good, don't you, boy? Just like your mother.

A blow to his stomach drove his breath from him. He gave up trying to stand and huddled in a ball on the floor, his working arm flung over his head trying to protect himself, like he'd done a hundred times before. Humming to himself didn't drown out his father's curses. Pretending he was at the rodeo on a bucking bronc didn't ease the pain when his father hit him again and again and again.

I'll show you who's the man around here, you little shit.

The toe of his father's boot pounded into his side, the pain excruciating, the crack of bone telling him he'd broken at least one rib. Another kick, another crack. *So hard to breathe. Hurt so bad.*

Brett opened his eyes to blackness, his breath ragged in his throat, afraid to shout and draw more of his father's ire. Yet afraid if he didn't call out, he'd be left in that darkness forever. Forgotten. Alone. *I'll be good, papa. I promise.*

Wait, it was soft beneath him. The couch, not wooden planks. His apartment, not the shed.

Releasing a shaky breath, Brett sank back against the couch pillows. Sweat dripped down his forehead; his shirt clung to him in damp patches. Damn, it had been so long since he'd had one of those nightmares.

He grabbed the remote and switched to one of the late night talk shows. At least this one had a good musical guest for once.

In a futile attempt to distract himself from the memories, he turned up the sound hoping the godawful racket would drown out his dreams. His memories.

Surrendering to another night's lost sleep, Brett headed back to the kitchen. He was just finishing the last of his second beer when someone pounded on his apartment door.

Dillon. It had to be. Who the fuck else would be awake at five-fucking-thirty in the fucking morning? The door rattled on its hinges as a fist pounded it again. ShitFuckDamn.

"Come on, buddy, open up." Yup. Dillon.

He walked to the door, but before his hand touched the lock, he hesitated and rested his head on the jamb. All hope for happiness drained from him, as if someone had pulled a plug.

Get it over with.

"Brett, open the door, will ya? Your car's out in the parking lot, so I know you're here."

He flipped the lock and, bracing himself, opened the door.

Dillon pushed past him and glanced around the apartment, as if he'd never been there before.

Not for the first time, he wondered why he couldn't have been the one to drive past her that first night. To have bought the place bordering hers. Sometimes fate was a black-hearted bitch. "What do you want, Dill?"

Dillon took off his hat and banged it against his thigh a couple times before he faced Brett. "I want you to explain what the fuck you're doing sleeping here. You're supposed to be stayin' at my place."

Brett rubbed his hands over his face. "I felt like sleeping in my own bed, all right?"

He realized too late that he'd left the bedroom door open, and Dillon could see for himself he'd not slept in the bed.

Dillon tilted his head to one side, his eyes glittering obsidian in the dim light. "You look like shit."

"Fuck you too."

"Nikki was antsy earlier too. And now you're here instead of at my place. So you want to tell me what the fuck's going on? Did you two fight or something?"

Few other men would have heard the challenge in Dillon's voice. So Nikki wasn't just a casual fling to Dillon. There went that fantasy. "No, we didn't fight. Didn't you ask her?"

"Yeah, she wouldn't say anything. When you didn't come home, I figured something may have gone on between you two. So what happened?"

There was the opening. He should just admit he had a thing for Nikki still and get it over with. "She tell you about what she found out at the bank?"

"About Phil cleanin' out her bank accounts? Yup."

"Yeah, well, she was crying about losing all her stuff, and I—"

Before he could get any further, Dillon interrupted him.

"She was crying?"

"Yeah."

"Shit!" Dillon ran his hand through his hair, spiking it in a half-dozen directions. "She's not once cried around me."

"She's trying to be strong, Dill. She thinks she has to prove something. That she has to handle things all by herself, or she's failed or something." She'd felt comfortable enough to cry on his chest but not on Dillon's? Did that mean something?

Shaking his head, Dillon tossed his hat on the chair and paced across the room. "Why would she think that? She has me to lean on." He waved a hand in Brett's direction. "She's got you too. She doesn't have to do everything all by herself."

"She thinks she does."

Was she more comfortable with him than with Dillon? Why would she feel she had to put on a front with someone she trusted? Or did she feel Dillon had taken control and she was back into a situation with Wade? He shook off the questions that assailed him, setting them aside to dwell on the meaning later. When Dillon wasn't standing in front of him.

Maybe I should have kissed her. But I didn't kiss her, he argued with himself. She pushed me away. "Outward she's comes across confident, but inside? She's probably hearing everything her parents said to her, about her being stupid and such. She's hurtin' still, Dillon."

"Yeah, I know. That's why I want you to come back."

So I can act on my impulses when she was pretty damned clear she didn't want to kiss me this afternoon? No fucking way. "You don't need me there anymore. You didn't before. Phil isn't coming back. I'm the third wheel. I'm in your way."

"You're just going to walk away? Leave her to do the morning chores all by herself. Just like Phil." It was a low blow, but maybe he deserved it.

"Ask Matt to help her out in the mornings, before he heads to school. I got things to do. Besides, my shift switches to mornings next week anyway." He walked to the door and opened it again. "I'll let you know if I hear anything more about Nik's stuff."

Dillon rocked on his heels for a moment. "What about your responsibilities to Nik?"

"I've done what I can. It's time to get back to a normal routine. To get on with life." *It's too dangerous for me to go back there again. It hurts too much.*

"Huh." The black Stetson banged against denim with a sharp snap before Dillon placed it back on his head and walked to the door. "Never figured you'd walk away from a promise. Your word used to be good for something."

Well, shit. Whoever said words couldn't hurt didn't know jack shit. Because he felt like he'd just been stabbed with a fucking bowie knife right in the chest.

"Tell Nik…" *Tell her I love her.* "Tell her I'll call you if anything new comes up on her stuff."

CHAPTER 10

Brett reached for Dillon's front door then stopped. Why couldn't Dillon have been home? At least that way he knew he could control himself. Even though he'd stayed away a full month, he still hadn't gotten Nikki out from under his skin. *Get it over with. Give her the news, then stay far away.*

He lifted his hand and after a moment's hesitation, knocked on the door. Maybe he'd get lucky, and she wouldn't be here. Maybe she'd gone into town with Dillon.

The door creaked open, and there she was, wearing one of the white shirts he'd left behind, a pair of cut-offs beneath. She'd left the top three buttons undone, giving him a tantalizing view of her cleavage. His cock punched against his zipper at the thought of unbuttoning the rest of the buttons, of spreading the fabric wide and tasting her nipples.

Why didn't he just cut off his balls and hand them to Dillon on a plate?

"Brett?" She looked startled to see him. "Come on in."

He followed her into the kitchen, watched her fiddle with the coffee maker. Nikki never fiddled and, more importantly, she wasn't looking at him. He made her nervous. Did she worry he might try something on her again?

His fists clenched at the thought that he might have scared her, made her think he might take what she wasn't willing to give.

"I didn't mean to drive you away." She made a gesture of impatience. "I've missed you."

The heated blood racing through his veins headed south when she smoothed her hands down her front, tightening the fabric over her breasts, accentuating that she wasn't wearing a bra.

Did she realize how beautiful she was with the color high in her cheeks when she blushed? Longing spun his senses until he felt like he'd been caught in a twister, especially when she turned those soulful eyes on him. The lost tone in her voice cut right through him, pierced defenses he didn't know he'd erected. *Shitdamnfuck, get control of yourself, Anderson.*

He closed his eyes and tried not to focus on the memory of how she'd softened in his arms, how right she'd felt cuddled up to him.

I've missed you too. "Sorry, I've been busy. With work and stuff."

"Dillon's missed you too," she continued. Her head tilted to the side, and a strange look flickered over her face. "Are you deliberately avoiding us? Did we do something to upset you?"

"No. There's just been a lot going on. At work." *It was easier for me, less tempting to take you in my arms again.* Though the ache in his chest that had formed as he'd driven away hadn't eased at all.

"At work," she repeated, a hint of doubt—or suspicion? —in her voice. She took a deep breath and stared out the back door. "I take it since you're here that you've got news about Phil?"

Thank God she'd given him a way out. "Yeah, the truck Phil used to transport your stuff turned up. Apparently, he sold it to a guy who didn't realize it was stolen and tried to change the ownership with the DPS. He said he bought the truck at a swap meet after Phil had sold everything in it."

Her shoulders slumped, and the light in her eyes faded. "Oh. I was hoping…"

Her voice was so small, so heartbroken, that before he thought twice about it, he'd wrapped his arms around her, tucking her head under his chin. "I'm sorry, Nik, but I doubt you'll get anything back unless you start haunting yard sales."

She breathed an even quieter "Oh" into his chest.

How had he ended up with her in his arms again after vowing to stay away from her? What type of bastard was he that his cock was demanding to be buried in her when she needed to be comforted? *You stupid fucking prick, you're going to destroy everything you've got.*

"Have you talked to your parents about Phil? Have they offered to help you replace any of your stuff?" Are you thinking of moving back to your own place?

"Dad got laid off again a couple weeks ago, so they don't have any money to spare. Besides, they're still angry that the cops were called. They think I should have kept it quiet, not said anything to anyone. When I told them the bank and the credit companies were planning on laying fraud charges against him, they…well, they haven't called me since, and they're not picking up when I phone them."

Her body trembled against his, the effort at not crying evident in the way she was gulping air. Her hair tickled his cheek when he pressed it against her head and ran his hands along her spine in a futile attempt to soothe her. "It's all right, baby. You didn't do anything wrong. Everyone knows that. I'm here for you."

He was here for her? Where had he been the last month? He'd been off licking his own wounded ego when he should have put her first.

A board squeaked on the porch; Dillon stared at them through the screen door, his jaw jutting to one side.

Shit.

Brett pulled his arms from around Nikki and placed them on her shoulders, drawing her away. "Sorry to bail on you, Nik, but I have to get back to work."

He stiffened when she stood on her toes and kissed him, her lips brushing over his as soft as a butterfly's wings. "Thanks, Brett. I'll never be able to make it up to you."

Aware of Dillon watching them, he swallowed and nodded, wanting to tell Dillon that her kiss meant nothing, that he felt nothing but friendship for her. But he didn't. He couldn't.

"I'd better be going." Stepping around Dillon with a nod, he hurried down the stairs and around the house to where he'd parked his car. A hailstorm of gravel flew out from behind the car as he spun it out of the driveway.

Five miles later, he slowed for a stop sign at the edge of town. *Shitfuckdamn.* Why the fuck had he walked away? There was no ring on her finger. As far as he knew, Dillon had never once said he loved her. Why should Dillon get Nikki? Didn't he deserve a shot?

Because if you try to get between them, it'll be senior year all over again. No, it would be worse, because the rest of the Barnetts would have to side with Dillon this time. And he'd lose them too.

Which was exactly why he had to keep pretending watching Dillon with Nikki didn't rip his guts out.

DILLON TOOK off his hat and slapped it against his thigh to dislodge as much dust as he could before he came in the house. Holy hell in a bucket, there had to be something wrong with him. Who else would get a hard-on from watching Brett holding Nikki like that? If it had been anyone else with their arms anywhere near her, he would have been plowing his fist into their belly about now. But all he could imagine was pressing his dick against Nikki's backside and sandwiching her between them.

"Nothing happened between us, I swear." Nikki's eyes were wide, her fingers twisted together.

Shit, she thought he was mad at her? Had that bastard Wade thought she'd cheated on him? Had he been the jealous sort? What was it Brett had told him about Wade? He kept his voice gentle. "I know."

If he was honest with himself, he could think of a reason why Brett might think he'd be jealous. One he himself had given his friend ten years before. But hell, he wasn't a raw kid anymore. If Nikki preferred Brett to him, then he was man enough to stand back. It would be like slicing his wrists open to let her go, but he wasn't about to destroy their friendship, especially if she didn't want him. Which made his fantasy that much more bizarre.

"So you're not angry with me? With us?"

"Nope." He toed off his boots before opening the screen door. Moving slowly, he approached her. Once he was close enough, he stroked her arms until her shoulders dropped and her death grip on herself eased. God, she was amazing. Her family had walked away from her—actually blamed her because Phil was an asshole, she'd lost everything she owned, and here she was pulling herself together. Talk about a steel backbone.

"You know, seeing you with Brett made me kind of hot. If he hadn't peeled out of here so fast, I might have suggested—"

Shoot, boy, you can't tell her you were considering a threesome. What type of pervert would she think you are?

The type of pervert you are, dumbass. Sheesh. "I heard what he told you about your stuff. Are you okay?"

Unfortunately Nikki didn't let it drop. "What would you have suggested?"

He recognized the way her eyes zeroed in and focused solely on him. He'd seen her use that dominant look on one of her more stubborn colts. Man, that was hot. Sweet and innocent one moment, all business and power the next. He shook off the lingering fantasy of the three of them getting hot and sweaty between the sheets. That was never going to happen. "Nah, never mind. Just an idea—" *fantasy* "—I've had."

But he couldn't stop thinking about how fantastic it would be to have his cock buried in Nikki's sweet pussy while she sucked Brett off. He adjusted his jeans covering his hard-on. Like she'd go for that little scenario. If he even suggested it, he'd be the one with Brett's fist in his gut.

"An idea? Involving Brett?" She must have been having a few fantasies of her own from the blush that crept up her neck and filled her cheeks. Damned, if she didn't look even more innocent. And as sexy as all get out.

He pulled down the neck of her shirt and peered beneath the fabric.

"What are you doing?"

"Seeing if that blush you've got going extends all the way down. Hey, look at that, it does."

She slapped at his hand until his finger popped from the fabric. "Do you ever think of anything but sex?"

"Sure. I think of food sometimes too." He couldn't resist teasing her, especially when she rolled her eyes. At least she wasn't looking like a puppy someone had kicked, like she had when he'd arrived. "Nothing like a nice grilled steak. Baked sweet potato with some marshmallows roasted on top. S'all good."

She opened the oven and gave him a delicious view of her ass. "It's not a steak, and there's no sweet potato, but I did make you this."

Whatever it was, it smelled delicious. Of course, so did the woman who'd made it. He peered over her shoulder and inhaled. She'd never know it wasn't her dinner he was sniffing. "What is it?"

"It's a tortilla casserole."

As she set the dish on a trivet, it struck Dillon how he looked forward to meal time since she'd moved in. How many hot meals he'd eaten with her sitting across the table from him instead of him standing, alone, at the counter eating cold Sunday leftovers his mother had packed? Why had he not realized before the simple pleasure of curling up on the couch with her instead of staring at the television, the canned laughter and commercials his only company. Even the thrill he got in racing home to find her waiting for him.

Home. That's what it was. This wasn't just a house anymore, a place he came to sleep. This was his home, the way he'd dreamed it would become. Having Nikki here made the difference.

"So I've been thinking." She turned to face him, resting one hip against the table. "Since Brett doesn't figure they'll ever recover any of my stuff, I should probably start shopping for a new bed, that type of thing. Start replacing everything I've lost."

The image of her greeting him every day shattered into a thousand shards as if she'd taken a sledgehammer to it.

"What?" He swallowed, hoping she hadn't noticed how his voice had gone up a full octave until he sounded like his youngest brother Matt before his voice broke last summer. "What's wrong with our bed?"

"There's nothing wrong with *your* bed, Dillon. But it's time for me to move back to my place. To have my own bed again."

No fucking way was she moving out now. Didn't she realize how right they were together? He stared at her as she placed the plate she'd heated on the table. "You can stay here. As long as you want."

"What are you asking me, Dillon? What are you saying?"

"I'm saying I want you to stay here. With me. Forever. Marry me, Nikki." *What the fuck?* Where the fucking hell had that come from? Yet as a part of his brain sat back and examined the idea, marriage to Nikki felt right. Yeah.

Marriage. The two of them together. Waking up to her beside him. Going to bed with her too. Talking in the evenings. Doing things together. How come he hadn't seen it before?

Not meeting his gaze, she toyed with the fork she'd used to stir the casserole. "I've been married once, Dillon. It didn't work out, remember? I'm not sure I want to get married again. Not yet."

Not an outright no. All right, there was still hope, especially since she'd said not yet, not *not ever.* "Maybe sometime in the future?"

She nodded. "Perhaps. There's still a lot we don't know about each other, Dillon. I don't want to rush into a decision I'll regret. I've been down that road before."

"So we'll live together for a while. I'll give you as long as you need." He crossed the distance between them, took the fork from her hand and turned her to face him. "Ask me whatever you want to know about me. I'll tell you anything you want to know."

CHAPTER 11

What did she want to know about him? What had she wished she'd known about Wade before they'd gotten married?

Start with the big one. See if her question, and her response, would scare him off. "Do you want children?"

He didn't go running. Instead he skimmed his hand through his hair, then nodded slowly. "Yeah. Not immediately. I'd like some time with you first. But yeah, I'd like kids."

"I'm not sure I can give you babies, Dillon."

There it was. That look people gave her when she told them. That goddamned "Aww, I'm so sorry" look she despised.

"Don't give up hope, Nik. Mom had a miscarriage between Griffin and Ethan. She went on to have three more healthy babies."

He'd even softened his voice. Damn it. What was it about people? "You don't understand. I don't know if I could get pregnant again, let alone carry a baby full term."

He cupped her face with one hand, running one calloused thumb along her jaw. "Oh, baby, I'm not looking for a broodmare. Besides, there's always adoption."

That's what her doctor had said too. Wade had dismissed the

idea out of hand, saying he wasn't taking in someone else's bastard. "It's not the same as having your own flesh and blood."

Dillon frowned. "I don't know if I agree. Brett's as close to me as my other brothers, even if we don't have the same genes—closer, even. I know my mom and dad love him as much as the rest of us."

Right, how had she forgotten they'd taken Brett in and treated him as if he was a Barnett born and bred?

Even knowing she might not be able to give him children, he still wanted to marry her. A sense of hope for the future, a future with Dillon, soared, making her giddy. Maybe…no, this was going too fast. She forced her dreams to stop spinning through her head and attempted to dim the smile that wanted to burst from her heart.

"What if…what if I want to go back to school? Would you be okay with me having to study all night instead of…" She shrugged. "I don't know, sitting with you watching a movie?"

He grabbed a chair and shoved it toward her, then flopped into the bench opposite once she sat down. "You'd like to go back to school?"

"I'd planned on it back in high school." Before she'd found out she was pregnant. "I'd like to take a course in genetics, maybe go for a degree in stable management."

Dillon's face lit up. "I think that would be great. Texas A&M's got an equine management degree, and there are some great courses you can take online these days too, if you want."

He jumped up and ran into his office, talking the whole time. "You could take genetics and reproductive physiology. I'm pretty sure they have a course on forage and pasture crops if you wanted to go in that direction. Maybe we could plant some of our own feed for the horses, make use of some of my land."

He carried his laptop back and powered it on, then grabbed the chair beside her while he waited for it to boot up.

Whenever she'd talked about going to school to Wade, he'd

snarl and sulk. Yet Dillon—she'd never seen him so animated. Being around such confidence was infectious, and she wanted more. Resting one hip against the table, she threaded her fingers through his hair, as if she could capture the energy he radiated.

What would it be like to live in a household with someone so enthusiastic and upbeat all the time?

It had been heaven, her conscience answered, reminding her she'd been here over a month. A month without fighting or yelling, a month where they'd shared the chores as well as laughs. She felt more at home here than she did in her own house. The warmth of happiness bubbled up inside her.

"You wouldn't mind if I went back to school?"

His jaw dropped as if she'd asked a foolish question. "Why would I mind? You've got a passion for those horses of yours, Nik. You should feed it."

She launched herself into his arms. "Oh, Dillon. Thank you! You're the first person who's listened to me and taken me seriously in I don't know how long."

"You want to really thank me?" Dillon nuzzled her neck, driving all other thoughts from her head.

She tilted her head to give him better access. "Let me guess, get up to the bedroom?"

"Why waste the energy when we've got a perfectly good table right here?" Reaching over to his laptop, he snapped the lid shut with one hand and placed it on the bench. "Stand up."

Thirty seconds later, she shivered when her naked back contacted the cool wood of the table top. "Dillon, this can't be hygienic."

"Oh, we'll wash the table down later, don't you worry about it." He leaned over her to press a kiss to first one tightly furled nipple then the other. "Stay there for a minute. I'll be right back."

She lifted herself up on one elbow as he rummaged around in the cupboard. "What are you looking for?"

He paused long enough to cast a glance over his shoulder. "Uh uh. Lie back. The master's at work."

Rolling her eyes, she obeyed him. Moments later, something cold and hard landed on her belly making her jump. "Sheesh, Dillon!"

"Ooops, sorry." He scooped up the can of whipped cream he'd dropped and placed it beside the bottle of caramel sauce.

"Dillon, you aren't..."

He winked as he grinned down at her. "Sure am. Now lie back."

Without giving her a chance to object, he spread her thighs wide and settled at the end of the table between them. "Dessert before dinner. Yum."

His boyish grin disarmed her enough to follow his instructions and not think about what he was going to do. Fingers gently parted her folds, and seconds later a hot tongue swiped between them, driving her breath from her. Dillon Barnett knew exactly what to do to excite her, inflame her.

She couldn't stop her giggles, however, when he sprayed a ring of whipped cream around then over each beaded nipple. The giggles changed to soft pants as he licked the white crown from each point. He drizzled the caramel in her cleavage and over her belly, swirling it in random designs with his tongue.

The heat of his breath, combined with the warmth of his tongue on her belly, had her muscles tightening. Her blood pulsed just beneath the surface of her skin that was quickly become overly sensitive, her body anticipating the path. Her hips lifted off the table when his teeth nipped the tender skin just above her hipbone.

"Dillon."

He leaned over her to kiss her nose. "Sssh. Just feel, baby."

Her pulse spiked when he resumed lapping the caramel from her body. She shivered when he skimmed a line of cream around her belly button, followed by a swirl that ended just above the neat triangle of hair covering her mound. He drizzled the caramel over the swirl then capped the bottle. "Ooops, dripped some."

Instead of the grin he'd given her earlier, his look was pure hunger. She couldn't stop the tremble that swept through her. He lowered his mouth, lapping and nipping her clean, then moved lower until his tongue touched her clit. He licked it lightly, then sucked until she pressed into him, grabbing the edge of the table for support.

The *hsss* of the spray can gave her barely a moment's notice before the cool cream coated her breasts once again. While his tongue returned its attentions to cleaning her, his fingers broached her pussy, teasing the sensitive tissue inside.

Her mind stopped working, swamped with the sensations he was creating. Her body shuddered, her leg muscles tensed, her need for release greater than she'd ever felt before. And still he drove her higher, harder, until she fought to breathe against the overwhelming urges. His thumb swiped over her clit one last time. She cried out, her body jerking against him, her climax slamming through her in a tidal wave.

Before she could finish, he straightened, overturning his chair in his haste. He hooked her ankles over his shoulders, unbuttoned his jeans, freeing his heavy erection. She couldn't take her eyes off the turgid head as he palmed it. He drove the breath from her when he thrust balls-deep into her still-pulsing channel, then slowly withdrew, his shaft glistening with her juices.

"Please, Dillon, I need you inside me."

"Hang on a sec. You got me so hot and bothered, I got ahead of myself. I need to make sure you're protected." He fumbled with his jeans for a condom and, once properly sheathed, surged back inside her again. Her sensitive tissues could feel every millimeter as he pounded into her in hard, fast thrusts, his fingers digging into her hips, holding her in place.

With each forward thrust, the table beneath Nikki moved until it hit the chair rail on the side wall. Dillon held nothing back. The kitchen reverberated with the sound of their flesh slapping together, the table pounding the wall in the same rhythm. She'd never felt so desirable, so wanton.

Another orgasm ripped through her, her body clenching him, milking him. His head rolled back as his cock swelled within her. One thrust, two and, with a shout, he stilled, spilling everything he had into her.

Nikki's eyes fluttered closed as he slumped over her, resting his head on her breast. It took all her energy to lift her hand and stroke his hair.

"Say you'll stay with me, Nik. Don't leave."

He sounded like a little boy entreating his mother not to leave him on his first day of school. She'd not had a choice with Wade, her hand forced by her pregnancy. Was she jumping into this relationship without thinking things through? She'd only dated one guy before, and she'd ended up marrying him. Which made Dillon only her second boyfriend. Maybe she should take some time, date someone else, so no one could say she'd rushed into another relationship.

Except she couldn't imagine life without Dillon. He'd climbed into her heart when she wasn't looking.

She loved him, plain and simple. With a depth she didn't think possible a month ago.

"What'll I do with my place?"

"You could rent it out for now." Dillon had obviously been thinking about this, or at least was able to see further ahead than her. "Griffin's looking for somewhere to live; he's finding it tough staying at home after living on campus."

"What if…what if things don't work out between us? Then I'd have to kick him out."

"Griff'll understand. Besides, Mom would welcome him back with open arms."

He lifted his head up, or at least he tried to—some of his hair stuck to her skin. "Come on, we both need a shower."

CHAPTER 12

LESS THAN FOUR HOURS AFTER HE'D LEFT, BRETT PARKED HIS CAR beside Dillon's truck. He switched off the engine and sat there.

You don't have to do this in person. You could drive a mile down the road and phone Nikki, ask her if she's all right. You'll be able to tell if she's telling the truth or not.

So why had he driven out here again? *Because your gut's been twisted in a knot for leaving Nikki to face Dillon alone. You know you have to face Dillon in person.*

He rested his head on the steering wheel. He could do this. He had to. Nikki deserved the happiness Dillon could give her.

Coward! Steal her away from the Barnett bastard. Or don't you have the balls, you whiny brat?

"Shut up, pop."

He didn't remember taking the keys out of the ignition or opening the car door. He didn't remember walking up the path to the kitchen door. All he could focus on was the pounding of his heart like a big kettle drum, drowning out all other sounds. The knob turned under his hand and the door swung open, a cool blast of air-conditioned air rushing over him.

He found Dillon wiping down the kitchen table, his hair clinging to his neck in damp curls and his shirtless chest glistening. He'd either just had a shower, or he'd just had a long hot sweaty bout of sex. *Please let it be a shower he'd just taken.*

"Hey, Brett what you doin' back so soon?"

That was it? Dillon wasn't going to go ape-shit about finding Nikki in his arms? Just "what you doin' back so soon?" Was he totally oblivious?

Brett couldn't stop himself from blurting out, "How's Nik? Where is she?"

Dillon's grin widened until all Brett could see were those fucking white teeth. He looked so fucking smug. The look of a man who was sexually satisfied. He sat down at the table and stretched his feet out in front of him, crossing them at the ankles. "She's upstairs. Having a nap."

Shit, it wasn't a shower that had made Dillon's hair wet. At least it wasn't *only* a shower. If it wasn't for his latest news on Phil—and the ten-ton invisible weights someone had permanently attached to his balls—he'd turn around, walk away and never come back.

"I asked her to marry me."

If Dillon had grabbed his gun from his holster and shot him point blank, it couldn't have hurt more. "She say yes?" *Please say no.*

Dillon's confident grin faded. "Sorta. She agreed to live with me for a while, give us a shot."

Should he be happy she hadn't said yes outright? He stomped on the ember of hope that flared up. *Nik's better off with Dillon, and you know it. He's got the Barnett name behind him. He owns his own company. You're a hanger-on. A Barnett wannabe-but-never-will-be.*

"I'm happy for you, man." He buried his head in the fridge, pulling out a beer.

"You wanna grab me one while you're in there?"

Brett grabbed a second bottle and handed it to Dillon. His foot stuck to something on the floor. He stalked to the cabinet beneath the sink and grabbed a sponge. "You spill something earlier?"

Dillon's lips quirked up, as if he had some private joke. "Nik and I, uh, had some dessert earlier on. Some of it must have dripped without us noticing."

What had Dillon done? Stripped her naked and then laid her on the kitchen table and… Oh, shit, yeah, Dillon had been cleaning off the table top. That's probably exactly what he'd done.

Was there no place in the fuckin' house he could be without visualizing the two of them going at it?

Dillon took a long swig from his beer then wiped his arm across his lips. "So there's no chance of getting any of Nik's stuff back, huh?"

"No." Brett swiped at the floor and tossed the sponge in the sink. He settled opposite Dillon and drank from the long neck before forcing himself to focus on his report. "The department got authorization to follow the activity on the credit cards Phil obtained under Nik's name. It looks like Phil thought he'd get clever and tried to squirrel some money away for a rainy day. We found accounts in Waco, Fort Worth, Arlington, Waxahachie and Cleburne. There's not much money left but—"

"—But that means he's still in the area."

The speed with which Dillon picked up on it surprised him. It shouldn't have, but it did. Focusing on work helped ease the pain of having to walk away from Nik. No. That was bullshit. It still hurt as if someone had rammed an icepick into his chest and twisted the damned thing. "Yeah."

"How much is left?"

"A couple hundred maybe? From what we could see, he's

running through it pretty fast. The only thing we can figure is he's gambling or back to buying drugs."

"Fuck. She's not ever gonna get anything back, is she?"

"No." He rubbed the back of his neck, a useless attempt to eliminate the knot that formed there long ago. "We've frozen the accounts but it won't help Nikki much at this point."

"Phil's not the sharpest crayon in the box," Dillon said. "It won't take him long to fuck something up or piss someone off enough to call the cops on him." He slammed his bottle down on the table. "Goddamn, that fucker pisses *me* off. Why would he treat Nikki like his own personal bank? Why would he steal from his own sister? The one person who gave him a hand up? It doesn't make any sense."

"Since when did life make sense? I gave up trying to figure that out by the time I was eight." When he'd realized other kids' fathers didn't beat on them just for walking into the room.

"Yeah." Dillon dropped one leg from the chair and straightened, knocking the neck of his beer bottle against Brett's. "You were better off once you got away from that sack o' shit who called himself your father."

Better off? Hell, yeah. He hadn't realized what a real man was until he'd gone to live with the Barnetts and saw how Mr. Barnett could command respect without using his fists. He doubted to this day Dillon realized how lucky he was.

Uncomfortable with the memories, he got up to grab another beer. He was just opening the fridge when Nikki appeared in the doorway. Instead of the braid she'd had her hair in at noon, it now cascaded down her back like a thick ginger waterfall. His fingers twitched, remembering threading them through the silky mass, wanting to bury themselves in it, to have it brush over his belly, his cock.

She was still wearing his shirt, but the cutoffs were missing. There was something incredibly erotic about how she'd had to roll up the sleeves so they didn't flop over her hands. His gaze skimmed down her long legs, trim from riding her horses, to her bare feet, her toes curling away from the cool tile. Damned if she didn't look sexier than any Victoria's Secret model.

"Hey Brett." A blush filled her cheeks, and her gaze burnt him to the core.

He chanced a glance at Dillon, who met his gaze and gave a smug yeah-she's-got-that-well-fucked-look-and-I-put-it-there grin before turning back to her and patted the back of the bench beside him. "Come sit down over here, darlin'."

She padded over to the bench and settled on it, tucking her legs up under her. Dillon wrapped his arm around her waist and slid her closer beside him. A blind man couldn't have missed the connection crackling between them. Right now Brett felt like he had x-ray vision. Maybe he could retrieve the icepick from his chest and use it on his eyes.

Unable to watch the two nuzzling each other, Brett turned back to the fridge. "Hey, Nik? You want a beer? Or would you rather have some iced tea?"

"Any root beer in there?"

After retrieving a bottle and opening it, he handed it to her. When her hand brushed his as she took it, he had to fight the groan that rose in his throat.

He watched her lift it to her mouth and tip the bottle, spellbound by how her lips fit around the top, how the long column of her throat moved as she swallowed. Is that what she'd look like with his dick in her mouth, swallowing his come?

Not going to happen, buddy, so you can just forget that fantasy.

Aware of the contemplative look Dillon gave him, he dragged his gaze from Nikki and focused on his own bottle. This had to stop, this longing for her. The fantasy of holding her in his arms as they fell asleep together, of waking up beside her, would never happen. So why did he keep torturing himself?

Dillon broke into his thoughts by asking if they were hungry.

"Starving." She graced Dillon with a beatific smile, one Brett would have given anything to have directed his way. "Brett? What about you? You hungry?"

Yeah, but not for food. What I want to taste is Nikki's...*give it up. You'll never taste her again.* Talk about forbidden fruit.

He should walk out. Leave.

Coward. If he left now, he'd never be able to face them across the dinner table. Here or at the Barnetts'. Which meant he'd have to cut himself off from the only family he'd known. Again.

Dillon took his choice from him when he shoulder-checked him. "Park your keister, buddy, you're in my way. Dinner's coming right up."

Knowing he had to either suck it up or lose his best friend, he claimed the chair opposite her.

True to his word, Dillon slid the plates in front of them ten uncomfortable minutes later.

Because Nikki and Dillon spent more time discussing her horses and keeping the Arabian lines pure than eating, Brett finished his meal before them. While they talked, he leaned against the wall, watching her, soaking in her enthusiasm. She had such a joy about her, a passion about her precious Arabians' bloodlines. Her face came alive, and her hands punctuated her points in graceful arcs. At one point she put down her fork and picked up her root beer. Instead of her fingers curling around the bottle, he pictured them curling around his dick.

He was just settling into the fantasy when the phone rang. Dillon checked the caller ID then picked it up. "Hey, Ma, what's up?"

Two minutes later he hung up and frowned at Brett, then glanced between him and Nikki. "Gram's in a tizzy. Something's disturbing her chickens, and she wants me to go check it out."

Seeing his chance to escape, Brett pushed his chair back. "I'll go."

Dillon waved him off. "Nah, don't worry, I've got it."

He patted his jeans pocket to ensure he had his keys, then grabbed his hat. After brushing a quick kiss over Nikki's lips, he headed to his truck.

With a sigh, Brett stood up and held out his hand to help Nikki out from behind the table. "Guess we'd better clean up."

It took them less than two minutes to stack the dishes in the dishwasher. Two long, awkward minutes where Brett was hard-pressed keeping his eyes off the way his shirt hugged the curves of Nikki's breasts. The way the hem rode up when she reached up to close a cupboard door, promising a peek at her taut little ass. How pathetic was it that he was jealous of his own damned shirt?

Nikki leaned against the counter as he filled the soap dispenser in the dishwasher door. "Dillon asked me to marry him."

"I heard." It came out as a whisper. He cleared his throat. "He also said you didn't say yes."

"Once bitten, twice shy, you know?"

He closed the dishwasher, then fiddled with the buttons, trying to buy time. "There's also the saying if you fall off a horse, it's best to get right back up again. Dillon's a good guy. He'd be there for you whenever you need him. Him and his family. You won't go wrong marrying him."

"Yes, he is a good man." A sympathetic look flickered across her face then disappeared, as if she knew that wasn't what he wanted from her. "But you're a good man, too."

A good man wouldn't be fantasizing about fucking his best friend's girl, his conscience mocked. He shrugged her off, turning away, only to have her follow until she was directly in front of him.

She caught his face between her palms and forced him to look at her. "You are! You put your life on the line for strangers every day. And I know the Barnetts love you as much as if you were born to them. That says a lot about your character."

If she only knew where he wanted her to put her hands. Then she'd see his real character, discover the dark needs he kept carefully hidden, not only from her but also from Dillon. "I'd do anything for them."

She searched his eyes for a moment. "Do you ever wonder where we'd be if it had been you who had stopped for me that night?"

Too many times to count, but it always came back to "But it wasn't me, was it?"

"What if it was?"

He opened his eyes. She was looking at him with such compassion, even love. The knots in his stomach twisted even tighter. "We can't play that game, Nik. You're with Dillon. You've made your choice."

"Have I?"

"You're here, aren't you? Just leave it at that. Please?" He stepped back, leaving her hand hanging in mid-air for a second before she dropped it. "You're better off with Dillon. He's good for you. He's got a family who will love you. He's got this farm where you can keep your horses." *He's better than me; he's not* damaged.

"Love isn't about money. It's not about how much land a man has. It's about how much he loves me. How much I love him."

"Dillon loves you." *You may not have admitted it to yourself yet, Nik, but you love him, too.* The words might have been broken glass, the way they tore at his throat.

"I know he does."

Something in her tone made Brett wonder if Dillon actually said those three important words?

"Do you love him?" *Even though you haven't accepted his proposal?*

She frowned a little and stared at the door where Dillon had last been. The hesitation gave Brett hope. Then she nodded. "Yes."

He sat down on the chair with a thud. See? She'd made her choice.

Except it wasn't him. She'd chosen Dillon.

CHAPTER 13

Whatever was going on with Brett, Nikki couldn't figure it out. He'd always been calm, always stoic. Sometimes his control was downright scary. But right now she was afraid he was on the brink of losing it.

She wanted to put her arms about him, hold him tight and not let go. She wanted to tell him she loved him too. Which confused her. So it would definitely confuse him.

She considered his last statement. *Had* she made a choice between him and Dillon? Was she rushing into a relationship with Dillon too fast? It's not like she'd put a lot of thought into it. She'd been having fun—holy hell, she'd loved spending time with Dillon, in his bed, on his kitchen table. A blush crept up her face at the thought of all the places in his house they'd made love. Yet here was Brett, and she didn't want to close off that choice either.

Damn it, why did she have to choose between them? Stupid societal rules.

Though, she had to admit, she wasn't sure she'd be very accepting if Dillon brought some other woman home and expected her to share their bed with someone else. Right. She had a choice, and she'd made it. At least that's what everyone kept telling her. Neither of them was a bad choice but a choice had to be made. She just wasn't sure she'd made it for herself yet.

"I love you too, you know. I always have."

He lifted her hand and pressed a kiss against her knuckles. "Thank you."

Thank you. Wow, that's all she got? No 'I love you too?' So there wasn't a choice to be made. She pulled her hand away from him and leaned back, studied him for a moment. How had she read him so wrong? "I hope you'll always be my friend."

"Of course we'll always be friends," he assured her though his voice sounded hollow, like something inside him had broken.

"One day you'll find someone you love. You deserve someone who loves you. Someone better than me."

His knuckles clenched until the skin stretched taut, the veins on his forearms bulging. "I'm not good for anyone."

Where was this coming from? "Why do you think you aren't good enough You're as good a man as Dillon." Not better. Different. But definitely just as good.

"No. I'm not." His eyes opened, pain filling his eyes. And his voice was rough, betraying the struggle he was having with himself. "I've got a drunk for a father. My mom ran off when I was little. I've got nothing to offer anyone. Dillon's got the whole Barnett family behind him. He owns a ranch, while I live in a rented apartment. He's got his own business, with employees. Responsibilities. Connections all around us. Don't you see? That's why I had to back off. He can offer you so much more than me."

Her breath stuttered in her throat. She barely made it to the chair before her legs folded under her. "Back off? What do you mean you backed off? Are you telling me you lied to me when you said you didn't want to date me?"

"Yes." The word was little more than a breath, barely making it past his lips.

All his hesitations, the number of times she'd caught him looking at her, the way he'd held her out on the lawn the night she'd been robbed, and again on the couch when she'd sworn he'd been about to kiss her. Despite his denials, he had been attracted to her. It all made sense.

"Oh, Brett." She covered his hands with hers. "Why didn't you tell me right from the start that you were interested?"

Had she done something—said something—that made him back off?

"I couldn't. I owed it to Dillon to give him his chance with you."

"You *owed* it to Dillon?" What type of debt meant he had to stand back from someone he was interested in? She chewed on her lip as she wondered if perhaps Dillon had done something to warn Brett off. Called in some boyhood pledge or…no, Dillon had invited him to come stay with them. He wouldn't have threatened Brett. She squeezed his hand. "What do you owe him for?"

Brett lifted his head, allowing her to spy the bleak expression on his face. His eyes searched hers, the blue piercing deep into her soul. "My life."

"I don't understand." A movement on the porch had her looking past Brett. Dillon had returned and was standing on the other side of the screen door, listening. When he saw she'd noticed him, he shook his head and put a finger to his lips, signaling for her not to give him away. What the hell was going on? She forced her eyes back on Brett. "What are you talking about? How do you owe Dillon your life?'

"I used to live a couple farms down from his parents' place. My mom took off when I was three, so it was just me and my father. He…" He swallowed and pulled away from her, lifting one hand to run his fingers through his hair. "He was okay some days, but other days he drank. He was a mean drunk."

She waited as he took a deep breath, not wanting to interrupt him, afraid he'd stop talking, knowing that he was probably telling her something he hadn't spoken of for years. "The night before Dillon's tenth birthday party, Pop got to whaling on me for something or other. I don't even remember what it was for now. It didn't matter to him. He didn't need an excuse; I just had to be in the same house with him. Anyway, he beat me up pretty good that night."

Nikki exhaled as quietly as she could, tears prickling beneath her lids. She forced herself to stay quiet, to not interrupt him.

He rubbed the bump on his nose. "He broke my nose. I think that was the second time he broke it. He lost it after that, worse than he normally did." He rubbed his left arm, but from his expression she could tell he was so lost in his memory he was unaware he was doing it. "All I could do was curl up in a ball on the floor. So he started kicking me." His hand covered his right side. "He said I was a sniveling coward who was damned well going to take his punishment."

Her hand trembling, she touched his wrist, stroking it gently. She ached for the little boy he'd been, wishing she could wipe such horrid memories from him.

His eyes closed, and he took a couple deep breaths before opening them again. "Back then, I used to be scared of the dark. To teach me not to be a coward, he used to lock me in a work shed and leave me there overnight. He dragged me out there again that night. I begged him not to leave me, but he just kicked me again and told me to stop my whining. Then he shut the door on me. I hurt so much, Nik, and it was so cold, I thought I was going to die."

"Oh, Brett," she whispered, her voice strained from trying

not to weep for him. He needed her strength, not her tears. "You were just a little kid. You must have been so terrified."

"Dillon noticed I didn't show up for his party the next day, so he came looking for me afterward. Pop came out back later. Told me the *Barnett bastard* had been by. Said he'd told him that I was *out somewhere*. He laughed about it, said he hadn't even had to lie. He thought he was so fucking clever."

No words—of comfort or of any other kind—sprang to mind. She covered his hand with hers. He flipped his over and clasped hers like it was a lifeline and he was about to drown.

"I begged him to let me out, Nik. I begged him for water because I was so fucking thirsty. But he just walked away and left me there. "

Nikki covered her mouth with her free hand. The tears she'd been fighting burnt a trail down her cheeks. Her throat constricted against the grief radiating from Brett, and the ache in her chest spread until each breath was a struggle.

She glanced over at Dillon, who was leaning against the doorframe, out of Brett's sight, the same look of despair on his face she felt on hers.

"When I didn't show up for school on Monday, Dillon came looking for me again."

Dear God, he'd been locked up for three days? Thank God Dillon's birthday was in April, not mid-summer, or Brett might not have been alive three days later. As it was, it was a wonder he'd survived at all.

"This time Pop was gone. He was at a bar, I found out later. Anyway, I guess Dillon knocked on the front door but when no one answered, he came around back, where he knew I kept the spare key." His voice died off as if he were trying to gather himself. It took a couple minutes before he picked up the story again. "I heard him calling, so I yelled for him to let me out. That's when he broke the lock and found me."

"Thank God," Nikki breathed.

He went on as if he hadn't heard her. "He ran off for a while. I thought he'd left me like Pop had, but then he came back with some water. I guess he must have phoned his folks too because a couple minutes later, Mr. Barnett showed up with the cops. He took me to the hospital and told the doctors to send him the bill. He and Mrs. Barnett visited me every day. Once I was released, they took me home with them and told me I was going to live with them from then on."

He raised his head; his eyes were dry, but filled with raw pain. "Don't you see? If Dillon hadn't come looking for me? I don't know how much longer I would have lasted. I owe him my life, Nik. If it means I have to give up a shot at being with you, that's a small price to pay compared to what I owe him. To what I owe all the Barnetts."

He let go of her hand and pushed himself to a stand, then hesitated as if undecided what to do, a state she'd rarely seen him in. "I gotta go."

Nikki reached out to touch his arm, but he walked toward the front of the house without looking back. A minute later, the front door slammed and his car roared away.

Dillon let the screen door bang in the frame behind him. He'd taken his hat off and was running his hands through his hair. "I had no idea he felt he owed me like that."

He swore and buried his fist in the wall beside the door, drywall dust floating down over his boots. "Goddamn. The fucking idiot, he never once told me he was still interested in you. He's been my best friend. How come I didn't see it sooner?" His voice broke. "Oh God, why didn't I see it?"

"Because he made sure you didn't." That she hadn't.

"But I should have. Goddamn it, Nik, he's more than my best friend. He's even more than a brother to me than Matt or Griff." His eyes scrunched shut, as if blocking back tears.

His other fist curled at his side. "Shit, Nik, if you knew what I did to him that night after Tater's party. If you knew how I acted. I was such a first-class prick and all that time, he…"

For years she'd tried to scrub away the memories of those last few months of high school. To forget the hasty marriage to Wade that for the first few months had seemed so wonderful then turned ugly so quickly. She dragged up the past and tried to focus on what else had happened, but failed. "What happened, Dillon? What did you do?"

"Right before Tater's party, there was this Garth Brooks concert I wanted to go to." He prowled the kitchen in a random pattern. "My cousin Jimmy had a couple extra tickets and offered to take me and Brett if we wanted to go with him and his girlfriend."

"Wait a minute, it's coming back to me. Brett told me why you didn't come to the party. Your parents found you'd snuck out when you weren't supposed to and grounded you."

"Yeah. I'd let my grades slide, and it was a school night so Mom and Dad said we couldn't go. We'd decided to go anyway, except Brett got sick. I didn't want to miss it. I swore him to secrecy, then I snuck out the window and hoofed it over to Jimmy's place. But I hadn't counted on Mom checking in on Brett before she went to bed. She found my bed empty. When I got back she and Dad were waiting. They busted my ass big time and grounded me for two weeks. I was so pissed off because I wasn't allowed to go to the party, but Brett was."

He rested his head against the wall. "He was so happy when he came home from the party. Shit, Nik, he couldn't stop smiling. I hadn't seen him like that since my parents told him he'd be staying with us, that he wouldn't have to go back to that scumbag of a father. Then he told me about how he'd kissed you, how you'd two had necked all evening." He thumped his forehead against the wall. "I was so fucking jealous—of him getting to kiss you, of him getting to go to the party when I couldn't. I hit him. He didn't even defend himself. He just let me whale away on him. Dad had to haul me off of him." His fist hit the wall again, making a hole beside the first one. "Oh Christ, I nailed him so hard I just about bust his nose. The same way his father had. Why had I never put it together before?"

She covered her mouth with her hand. Dillon had beaten up Brett? He'd never said a mean thing against anyone in his life that she'd ever seen. He treated everyone like his best bud; he'd never let anything get him down. "How could you have hurt him like that? Brett was your best friend. What were you thinking?"

This was the reason she hadn't seen Brett for so long after that night. Was this was he didn't want to admit he still wanted to date her?

"I was nearly eighteen, damn it. I thought I…ah, hell, I was stupid and confused, and I didn't think about what I was doing."

She folded her arms across her chest. "I hope you apologized to him."

"I did. Later. When he finally came back."

"When he finally came back," she repeated. He hadn't been sick the way Dillon had said? Nikki took a step back. "What do you mean, 'when he came back'?"

He rested his forehead against the wall. "A couple days after I pounded on him, Brett and I got into another fight because I'd believed a lie someone else had told me about him."

"What was the lie?"

"I found a condom in the back of my car. Someone told it was Brett's. That you and he had made out that night."

What the fuck? "We didn't. Yeah, we kissed, but nothing more."

"I know. Now."

"Who was it that lied to you?" And why did you believe them?

A despair-filled gaze flicked over her and away in an instant. "It was Wade."

Had Wade had his eye on her even back then? Was the condom tale his way of clearing out any competition?

"I wouldn't listen to anything Brett said so he took off," Dillon continued. "The next day he wasn't in the house or anywhere and we realized he was missing. My parents called the police, but they were told that he was eighteen so he could legally leave if he wanted. The only person who looked for him was Tiny.

"I didn't mean to drive him away, Nik. Honest, I didn't. I felt so bad afterwards, but I couldn't find him to apologize. He was gone almost a week before Tiny found him living on the streets in Dallas. It took another week for Mom and Dad to convince him to come live with us again."

He inhaled deeply again. "But when he came back, he moved out of our room and moved in with Griff. He froze me out, Nik. Even after I'd apologized to him."

"Sometimes saying you're sorry isn't enough."

A strange look flickered across his face. "That's what Dad said."

"But you're friends now. So he must have accepted your apology eventually."

"Not at first. He started hanging out with Tiny whenever Tiny was off duty instead of hanging out with me the rest of that semester." Dillon finally opened his eyes, his expression as bleak as Brett's had been earlier. "Then instead of applying to Aggie the way we'd planned, he applied to Boston College, got accepted and moved away."

Would Brett think everyone he loved had deliberately hurt him again? "We have to find him, Dillon. We have to show him we care about him. That we worry about him."

"Yeah. You're right." He scrubbed his hands over his face, then bent down to pick up his hat. When he straightened, he looked at her for the first time since he'd walked in. "Are you coming back here after this, Nik?"

"Let's find Brett before we start worrying about where I'm going to live."

Would she come back here? Or would she go back to her own place, date Brett perhaps? Or at least learn exactly who Dillon was before she got in any deeper. God, what a tangle it had all become.

CHAPTER 14

Dillon eased his truck off the road and parked it behind Brett's car. "He used to come here when we were kids. Before he came to live with us. He called it his thinking spot."

He switched off the ignition but stayed in place, his hands clenching the steering wheel. "You know the weekend his dad beat the crap out of him? Before I checked his house, I'd come out here on my bike. I knew things were tough at home, so I figured maybe he'd run away." He rubbed his thumbs into his eyes. "After he moved in with us, we used to come here all the time to fool around once our chores were done. We had us some good times here."

"Let's go find him." Nikki opened her door and hopped down to survey the area. It was typical Texas brush, buffalo grass and bluestem fighting for space with prickly pear and yucca. Perfect rattlesnake country. While she'd never been bitten, Rascal had tangled with one the previous summer. After seeing what he'd gone through, she'd been cautious ever since and was glad she'd taken the time to put on her boots instead of her sandals.

Dillon grabbed what he called his whacking stick from the

back of the truck and swung through the grasses to scare any snakes into retreat.

He skirted a section of Bull Nettle, making sure she didn't come in contact with any of the stinging hairs. A few steps later, he reached down and plucked a yellow flower, sticking it behind her ear with a half-hearted smile. "Tickweed. Just to make sure you don't pick up any fleas."

"Gee, thanks." What a romantic story to tell her friends—the first flower he'd given her was a flea repellent. Chuckling, she touched the blossom, knowing she'd treasure it anyway. If they ended up staying together. Her smile faded.

"This place is beautiful in the spring." Dillon tapped the ground as he approached a fallen branch to scare any rattlers. "The whole field is covered in Indian Blankets."

His love of the land must have sprung from the days he'd spent right here, she realized. She tried to picture him and Brett as youngsters running through the fields, playing tag or, more likely, cops and robbers.

They reached the crest of the hill. A creek, its waters higher than normal from the storm they'd had the day before, wound its way through the harsh terrain, widening out at the far end to a pond that probably dried up in the summer heat. But today, it glimmered bright blue, reflecting the sky above.

"Takes your breath away, doesn't it?" Dillon wrapped his arm around her waist. A part of her land—and his— looked exactly the same. To her it was harsh land, rock and dirt and weeds. But now, standing here, she tried to see it through his eyes. Not scrub, but mesquite trees laden with grape vines marking the river's path, lush greenery combined with the water-worn rocks lining the creek's banks. Thick marsh grasses lined the edges of the pond, the occasional bird swooping down in sudden arcs, catching bugs skimming along the surface. At the far end, a stand of sweetgums and loblolly pines stood as silent sentinels, guarding the pond.

"Come on, Brett's probably up ahead. There's this one spot he used to like to sit."

They scrambled down the bank, following the creek along its meandering path until it widened and became the pond. While Dillon continued, Nikki paused and shielded her eyes from the sun as she scanned the area. It took a few moments, but she finally spied Brett sitting beneath the overhanging branches of a massive old beech tree halfway down, tossing pebbles into the water. As they approached, he stiffened and turned his head away from them.

Dillon hesitated, the first time she'd ever seen him unsure. "Maybe we should just leave him alone for a while."

"No, he needs to know we're here for him. Both of us."

Yet he still hesitated. "I don't know, Nik. Brett's a private person. Even when he was in the shed, his arm and ribs all busted up, he didn't want me to see how much he was hurting."

"Then you can stay here. But I'm going to him." Not taking her eyes off the hunched figure beneath the beech tree, she skirted Dillon and continued along the side of the pond.

As she got closer, she could see Brett's jaw tighten, the tension in his shoulders and arms, how he looked like he was prepared to jump up and run.

"Brett?" she said softly, slowly her pace. "Are you all right?"

"You here to tell me how you feel sorry for me? Poor little abused kid and all that crap?"

The bitterness, the sarcasm in his voice sliced through her. She did feel sorry for him, but she knew he didn't want to hear any form of pity. Any more than she'd wanted to hear "you can always try again" or "it wasn't meant to be" about her miscarriage.

She ducked under the branches and sat beside Brett. Dillon moved behind both of them to hunker down on Brett's other side.

"We're here because we were worried about you." She

chanced having him bolt by placing her hand on his upper arm. "You're my friend, Brett, and friends are there for each other."

He stared at her for a second, then nodded and stared at the pond again.

No one said anything for another few minutes until Brett swore and threw a handful of pebbles into the water at once. He stood up. "I can't do this, Nik. I can't pretend anymore."

Before he could take a step away, Nikki reached out and caught his hand. "Brett, wait. Please."

"What do you want of me?" His voice was husky, as if he'd been screaming for hours. Maybe inwardly he had been.

"I want you to talk to me. And to listen. Please."

Though it took him a moment, Brett finally settled into place beside her.

"At the very beginning of this, I asked you if it was all right to go out with Dillon, and you said you were fine with it."

If Brett saw Dillon straighten and stare at her, he didn't give any indication. She shoved away the thread of guilt that arose. They hadn't been dating then, and she'd been perfectly within her rights to check to see if Brett was interested, she told herself. She turned her attention back to Brett, reaching out to touch his arm with her fingertips, to re-establish the contact she'd had with him.

His eyes closed at her touch. "You deserve to be happy, Nik. You're happy with Dillon, and he's happy with you. He loves you."

"But you love her too, don't you?" Dillon said quietly.

It took a long moment before Brett nodded.

"Except you decided to be noble and not interfere, didn't you?" Dillon's voice was still quiet though she heard the anguish in it.

"Because you didn't want to lose your best friend, your family, the way you had before, didn't you?" Nikki continued when Dillon couldn't.

"They're all I've got, Nik. I don't have anyone else." He took a deep breath and looked at Dillon. "When I went to Boston? I was miserable. Your mom phoned regularly, and Griffin emailed me every once in a while, but it wasn't the same. I couldn't stand being alone like I'd been before. I love your family, Dill. I'm not about to let them be ripped away from me. Not again."

Dillon tossed the husk of a beechnut into the pond. "You could have come home more often, you know. They're your family too. Matthew, Lilly, especially Griffin. They missed you. They used to rag on me about you all the time. Shit, Brett, all you had to do was say something, and I would have backed off and let you date her too."

"This time," Brett snapped.

Dillon winced and nodded.

"You may not see it but I do. They're caught in between, and if they talked to me, I'd know they'd feel like they were being disloyal to you. I couldn't do that to them. I was used to being alone, to not having anyone when it was just my pop and me. But once I'd been part of your family, gotten used to having people care for me, talk to me like I was worth talking to, I couldn't live without them. I can't live without them." His voice was rough, as if he'd swallowed glass and each word tore his throat apart. He turned back to face Nikki. "I'm sorry. Maybe I should have told you, I don't know. You've always been special to me. You always will be, but I couldn't lose Dillon or the Barnetts. I can't." The bleak look Brett gave her was one filled with need, with love, but no hope. "You deserve better than me, Nik."

Tears prickled in her eyes, and her heart ached for the boy he'd been. "You shouldn't think about yourself that way, Brett. You're a good man. Any woman would be lucky to have you. I would have gone out with you if you'd asked me back in high school. Maybe I would have ended up married to you instead of Wade."

Dillon's eyes widened for just a second before they closed. He exhaled and swallowed. When he opened his eyes again, his eyes were dark with misery. "I can't tell you how hard this is for me to do, but I love you both enough that I'm prepared to step back. Nik, if you want to date Brett instead of me, I won't hold you back."

"Oh, for Christ's sake." Brett jumped to his feet again. "Do you think that's why I told her about how you saved me? Do you think I haven't seen the connection between you? Shit, Dillon, the electricity between you two would fucking electrocute me if I tried to get between it."

Nikki stood up, irritated to be spoken about as if she weren't there. Before she could say anything, Dillon rose to his feet. "Do you think I'm gonna feel good about being with Nikki, knowing I stole her away from you? Do you think I wanna look at her from here on in wondering if maybe she stayed with me out of some sort of misplaced loyalty instead of love? That I'm some sort of rebound from Wade that maybe she regrets?"

Nikki's jaw dropped. If he'd punched her in the gut, it couldn't have hurt more. At the same time, she felt guilty she'd been flattered that Brett had wanted to date her, as well as resentful that he hadn't asked. But did Dillon really think she was with him as some sort of rebound affair? Or was he using it as an excuse to back out of his proposal? "So you're going to walk away from me? Just like that? What about your proposal?"

He took off his hat and ran his hands over his head. "It meant what I said, Nik. These past few weeks haven't just been about getting into your pants. I want to marry you. I love you. I just..." He stared at his feet, his voice dropping to a mumble. "I'm not good at saying it, that's all. It makes me feel like a wuss."

His admission softened her anger. "It wasn't *just* about getting into my pants? Sheesh, Dillon, how romantic can you be?" The urge to smile faded when she realized they hadn't resolved a thing. "So now what do we do?"

"You're going to have to decide between us," Brett said softly. "And whatever you decide, Dillon and I'll have to find a way to live with your decision so it doesn't split us apart again."

You're going to have to decide between us. The words she'd been dreading hung over her like Damocles' sword.

Nikki sprang to her feet, pacing along the side of the pond. She loved them both, and now they'd expect her to choose between them? No matter who she chose, she'd end up hurting the other. She'd end up hurting part of herself. "I can't decide between you right here and now."

Two days ago, she would have chosen Dillon with no hesitation. Now? There was no way she could choose between them. Not without seeing if maybe there was some spark still between her and Brett. She had to know that she hadn't jumped into the arms of the first man who'd come along, so she'd never have any regrets when she and Dillon had a fight. And she knew they would have fights; it was part of living with someone else.

Brett walked over to her and stroked her arms. "No one's asking you to make a decision right now."

Dillon took a breath and joined them. "Look, Nik, I'm not saying this is easy for me to do. It's ripping my guts out, but I don't want you to choose me out of a sense of obligation. I know you've been there before. I don't want to be who you 'settled' for. If you choose me, I need to know it's because you want me. Because you *love* me. I won't settle for anything less."

"Don't you understand? I can't choose one of you over the other. Not now. Now that I know I've come between you before." She looked between them. "How am I supposed to choose and not be terrified you'll end up hating each other?"

"Get to know us," Dillon suggested. "Stay at my place, the way you have been. I'll move into the spare bedroom with Brett. We'll take it a day at a time."

A blush creeping up her neck, Nikki shook her head. "That's going to be awkward for everyone, isn't it? It would be better if I move back to my place."

"If you're going to learn about us, to decide between us, you need to see us at our worst as well as our best. Both of us. You've been living with me for over a month. Brett moves back in and you get to know him better." He hesitated a second before exhaling. "You should let Brett take you out for dinner or whatever you two want to do and see where it goes from there."

"And you'd stand back if I decided to sleep with her?" Suspicion laced Brett's tone.

"If *we* decided to sleep together," she corrected.

Dillon looked ill, but he nodded. "Yeah. I would."

Brett swore. "Bullshit. You beat the crap out of me when I told you I'd kissed her back in high school. And now you're all noble about letting me sleep with the woman you asked to marry? Tell me another one, Barnett."

"I'm not eighteen anymore. And I can't begin to tell you how sorry I am I reacted the way I did. I've already apologized. I don't know what more you expect of me. But I'm not prepared to jeopardize my relationship with either of you. Please, Brett, it's killing me to do this; I need you to trust me. If Nik says she prefers you, I'll step aside. Hell, I'll be your best man at your wedding." He stuck out his hand and waited for Brett to shake it.

His hand hung there for almost a minute as Brett eyed him. "Don't you think it should be Nik you're asking, not me?

They both faced her, Dillon asking, "What do you say, Nik?"

"What do I say? I say you're both nuts." Nikki paced along the edge of the pond, putting distance between them before she turned to face them again. "From where I'm standing, I've got a couple of choices here. My favorite right now is to move back to my place and not date either of you. I'll raise goats and morph into an eccentric old lady everyone laughs at."

"I'm not liking that option," Dillon muttered.

Brett rolled his eyes at Dillon. "What's your other choice, Nik?"

"I can move back to my place and date you both, take my time before making my decision." That was the logical choice. So why didn't she like it?

"You don't have any furniture at your place, remember? It would take a helluva lot of money to replace it all." Dillon seemed determined to keep her at his place.

While she loved staying at his house, Nikki knew it wasn't the best idea. And yet, she didn't want to leave. What happened if she left Dillon and he realized he didn't want her, and she'd lost the best man she'd ever known? What if Brett didn't... Arrrgh. Damn, she was getting so tangled up by guilt and desire.

"Stay at my place, Nik. Give it a shot." The anguish on Dillon's face, straining his voice, tore at her conscience.

"Please?"

CHAPTER 15

On the way home, Nikki debated staying at Dillon's or moving back to her place a dozen times. While she'd decided it was best if she left, the words never made it past her lips. Maybe she had latched onto the first man who came along, and her feelings for him weren't love so much as a way to combat her loneliness. Maybe he was a rebound affair, and she'd regret hooking up with him later, though she thought that possibility slim.

But how would she know? Before this month, she'd only been with one man.

For the rest of the afternoon, she was aware of how quiet they were, aware of how Brett angled his body away from Dillon, aware of how Dillon's eyes followed her every movement with a hunger—and anguish.

She should have ended the charade before they had dinner. But she couldn't. Damning herself, she toyed with her food, aware of the long silences and the strained air that now filled Dillon's home. Lying in Dillon's bed alone that night only heightened her confusion. She loved Dillon. She was sure of it.

So why couldn't she just say it out loud and tell Brett he'd blown his chance, tell him she'd made her choice?

Over the next couple of days, their conversations were stilted, but gradually they relaxed when there were only two of them together. The strain reappeared when all three shared the house.

Most nights, she'd go to bed at the same time as Dillon, then get up when Brett got home. They'd curl up on the couch together, her giving him a backrub when his shift—or their circumstances—left him particularly tense. Other times he'd lift her feet on his lap and massage them. They discovered they liked the same shows, though their taste in music differed. She liked classic rock, he liked country music.

Instead of making her decision easier, she enjoyed both men's company. The longer she delayed, the more she realized it would be impossible to choose one over the other.

A week into their agreement, Brett disappeared for a while as soon as Dillon's truck pulled into the driveway. He returned home a couple hours later, a garment bag hooked over his shoulder.

"I want to take you out on a real date this evening, just you and I." He looked at Dillon, his expression set in what she now thought of as his cop-neutral expression. "Do you have a problem with that?"

Dillon looked up from his sketchpad. "Nope, no problem. I gotta work up this proposal for the Snider place."

The bag proved to contain one of the most beautiful black cocktail dresses she'd ever seen, and a pair of fuck-me stilettos that fit her like a dream. "It's beautiful."

He shrugged, but she could tell he was pleased. "If you don't want to wear it, it's okay. The clerk said I could take it back if it didn't fit or you didn't like it."

"No, I love it." She'd never have bought something like this for herself. That he went through the trouble of going to the mall—something she'd discovered both he and Dillon considered the equivalent of bamboo under the fingernails— told her how important the evening was to him.

Frowning at the mixture of excitement and trepidation warring within her, she took the bag and headed up to her bedroom. When she turned to close the door she found Dillon standing in the doorway. She tried to read the expression on his face, in his eyes, but he'd closed himself off.

Frightened that she may already have lost him, she wrapped her arms around his waist. "I don't have to do this. I won't go out with Brett if you don't want me to."

He cupped her face between his calloused palms. "I told you before, I don't want to be someone you settled for. So if you have to go out on a date to prove to yourself or anyone else that it's me you want, I guess Brett's the only guy I'd trust you with."

She buried her face in his chest, taking a deep breath and holding it. Although he'd taken a shower when he'd come home from work, there was a spicy scent she couldn't attribute to his usual brand of soap, a scent uniquely Dillon's. "I don't know if I can do this."

He kissed the top of her head. "No regrets, Nik. About anything. Now you'd better get ready. Brett's waiting."

He lifted the bag she'd draped on the bed and handed it to her. He started to leave, but stopped in the doorway and spoke over his shoulder. "Nik? If you guys want to…you know, explore things between you? Don't feel guilty about it, all right? I'll understand."

He was seriously giving her permission to sleep with someone else? A crack appeared in her heart, threatening to widen with the slightest movement. "How can you not be jealous?"

There was a long pause before he answered. "You need to find out if Brett can make you happier than I can…" His voice fractured, and he cleared this throat. "I love you both too much to get in your way. I don't want you—either of you—putting aside your own happiness because you're worried about me or how I'll react. I've interfered once already. So you do what you have to do to be happy."

"You make me happy, Dillon," she whispered.

"I need you to do this for me, Nik. I need you to do this for Brett. Promise me you won't back out. Promise me that you'll give Brett the chance I took away from him back in high school."

"I—"

"Promise me, Nik. Please."

"I promise I'll give Brett a chance."

Dillon left her alone without looking back. She stared at the dress Brett had brought home for her. She should just hand it back to him, tell him she'd made up her mind. So why was she unzipping the bag? Maybe that alone told her she needed to find out for herself if she was ready to commit to Dillon. To anyone.

Almost an hour later, she came out of the bedroom to find Brett waiting outside, wearing a somber black suit and striped tie. He drove her to a Dallas restaurant, complete with waiters in tuxes. The menu the maitre d' handed her didn't have prices on it, but she suspected the bill could have paid the month's mortgage.

"You keep staring at me." She touched her hand to her hair. "Is there something wrong? Tell me I don't have something stuck between my teeth."

He shook his head. "I just can't believe we're here. Together." He reached across the table and twined their fingers together. "You have no idea how long I've wanted to take you to dinner. Out on a date."

His intensity flowed across the table, winding along her arm and around her body. How had she lived with him, sat across from him at breakfast and lunch each day for the past weeks and not noticed the raw sexuality surrounding him? How had she not noticed the small scar above his left eyebrow, or how his eyes with the darker blue ring around a sky blue center dominated his rugged features? Had he always looked at her with such longing? No, not longing, it was more than that. His look promised long nights of mind-numbing kisses followed by slow tender sessions where he explored every inch of her body.

The need for him had her drawing a shaky breath and pressing her thighs together in an effort to ease the growing ache. *Why didn't it feel wrong to be attracted to two men at the same time?*

"Nik? Are you all right?"

All she could do was nod.

On the drive back, silence hung between them like a dark curtain. Every now and then, Brett took his hand off the steering wheel to touch her knee or caress her hand. Before she knew it they were out of the city and heading down the interstate toward Dillon's. "Thank you for not suggesting we stay at a hotel tonight."

He glanced over at her. "I have to admit I seriously considered it. But I figured if I made reservations, you'd feel obligated to have sex with me. I don't want you to feel obligated to me for anything, Nik. Especially not for sex."

"I don't feel obligated." Horny as hell, yes. Needy, achy, those too. Obligated? Not a chance.

"I don't want to pressure you, Nik. If we're going to take things to the next level, I want it to happen in its own time and for the right reasons."

"What if now's the right time?" she whispered.

He brought her hand to his mouth. The gentle way he pressed his lips to her knuckles scorched her. "I'd love to, but I want you to be sure about this. About us. It could ruin all our friendships—you, me, Dillon. It could change things between us completely."

"I know." She rubbed her thumb over his. It would change

things. But she'd promised Dillon to give Brett a chance. "Does it bother you that I've made love to Dillon?"

Another mile passed before he answered. "Does it bother you that I've made love to other women?"

"No. You weren't going with me, so why would I hold your past against you? But you know what I mean. I don't want to come between you two. Not again."

"What happened in the past wasn't your fault. What happened this time isn't your fault either. Way back when this all started, you asked me if I was interested in you and I wasn't honest with you. I'm the one at fault. Not you." Even in the dim lighting of the dashboard, she could see his fingers tighten around the steering wheel. "I shouldn't have even suggested this date. I should have just walked away."

Yet he hadn't.

"Maybe we need to look at tonight the same as ripping off a bandage."

"What do you mean?" He glanced sideways at her.

"Maybe we should get the sex out of the way right at the start. Make sure we click together in bed. That we don't bore each other or do something that turns the other off. Why waste time?"

Holy shit, was she really suggesting this? But at least they wouldn't waste months dithering. That way if they didn't click, she'd walk away without a second thought. Not that sex was the most important part in a relationship but for all she knew, Brett could turn out a dud in the sack. As shallow as it made her feel, she wasn't prepared to put up with another long stretch of boredom in bed. And maybe, ten, twenty years down the road, she'd at least be able to say she hadn't jumped into the bed of the first man who invited her. That she'd…well, shopped around didn't exactly sit right with her, but it was the closest comparison she could come up with.

Brett must have felt the same way. "That makes it sound like you're taking me out for a test drive."

She forced a smile, although she knew it lacked conviction, and shook her head. "You know what I mean. I want to know how we are together in bed. Dillon won't be home for a while yet so we won't have to worry about him listening."

"It didn't bother you that I was in the next room listening to you and Dillon the past couple of weeks." His tone was flat, a muscle in his jaw twitching betraying his struggle at control. He shook his head. "Sorry, that didn't come out the way I wanted it to. It's just…listening to Dillon, knowing…"

"Hey, I didn't know how you felt," she reminded him gently. "Neither did Dillon. We weren't trying to show off or make you jealous or anything."

"I know." He pulled the car off on the side of the road. After he'd put it in park, he half turned in his seat. "I'm not saying you were trying to rub my face in anything. It just damned near killed me listening to what was going on." He exhaled noisily. "Dillon's so fuckin' loud, it was hard to ignore."

She couldn't stop the giggle that bubbled up. "Yeah, he is." Her smile faded as she imagined how she would have felt if she'd had to listen to Wade fucking one of his girlfriends while she was in the next room. God, that must have been hell for Brett to lie in the next room and have to listen to their lovemaking.

"Look, I know Dillon's said it's okay for me to date you, but I don't want to get in his face about it. I feel like I'm poaching on his territory. And frankly, I'm still worried he'll get pissed off, not only with me but with you too."

"Dillon's the one who suggested that we should go out on a date. He made me promise to give you a chance. I'm not one to break a promise, Brett. Besides, we both know there's something between us, some spark we need to work out before I can make a decision."

She lifted his hand to rub his knuckles over her cheeks. The heat in his eyes told her he wasn't as unaffected as he tried to pretend. "Let's just go home and see what happens from there. All right?"

Nodding, Brett eased the car back onto the road. Less than ten minutes later, he parked in front of Dillon's house. "Maybe we should go to my place instead."

"No, we're here now. And Dillon's isn't here. So it's not like we'll be rubbing it in his face, right?"

"Right." Though he didn't sound convinced.

She held her breath when he leaned over and kissed her. Instead of a careful kiss on her cheek, he pressed his lips against hers. She stiffened for a second, then parted her lips slightly, accepting his advance.

He tasted of a lingering essence of the wine they'd shared earlier and a crisp, unique flavor that set her head spiraling into a vortex of need.

He buried his fingers in her hair, pulling her hard against him, taking control of the kiss, thrusting his tongue into her mouth. Warmth flooded her belly, and she moaned.

"God, how many times did I hear you do that through the bedroom wall and wish it was me?" he muttered around the kiss.

The ten years since they'd last kissed compressed as if it had been a day, then floated away. She forgot they were in the front seat of his car, forgot they were parked in front of Dillon's house. Only the two of them existed in the world.

Outside a nighthawk screeched as it chased bugs flying around a lamp Dillon had installed by the barn. Inside, soft moans filled the car as they explored each other.

She curled her fingers through his hair, enjoying the way it rasped in the back. Where Dillon's shoulders were wider from doing heavy work, Brett was more streamlined, but she had no doubt he was equally as strong. He was harder than he'd been back in high school, stronger. Yet she knew he'd never hurt her.

He skimmed his hand down her side to her hip, his fingers digging in for a moment as he shifted her angle. On the trip back to her shoulder, he brushed the sides of her breasts that grew heavier with each minute they kissed. "Do you know how many nights I lay awake back in high school, remembering how you tasted? How you felt in my arms? The feel of your lips against mine?"

"I wish I'd known." *I wish it had been you who had been my first lover.*

As if he could read her mind, he pressed one finger over her lips and shook his head. "Don't. That's history. We're two different people now."

He may have been different, but she still felt the awkward teenager she'd been the first night he'd kissed her. But she wasn't that girl anymore. She didn't want to be that girl ever again.

"Let's go inside," Nikki whispered. "I want to kiss you without a console between us."

He stroked his thumb down her jaw, his eyes unreadable in the shadows. "I don't feel right about doin' it in Dillon's house. I can drive us to my place."

"He's not here, remember? And he gave us his blessing." She caught his hand and slipped it beneath the hem of her dress. "Touch me again."

Every part of him stilled while his eyes searched hers.

"Touch me," she repeated. "Everywhere."

Moving ever so slowly, his hand crept higher on her thigh, until he reached the silk of her thong. "Are you sure?"

She'd never been so sure of anything in her life. She shifted, giving him better access.

Brett's fingers slipped past the silken barrier, parting her folds, slick with her arousal. She closed her eyes, concentrating on the sensations enveloping her. The warmth of his breath on her cheek, the rasp of his beard, the lingering scents of his aftershave. The strength of his shoulder cushioning her head.

She gave in to the pleasure he kindled as his fingers teased her clit. Sometimes hard, sometimes feather-light, each movement drove her higher and higher. He dipped his fingers into her core, touching a spot that had her tilting her hips until they barely rested on the seat. He fondled her, petting and stroking until she was trembling, unable to draw a breath. And still he drove her higher, capturing her gasps with another kiss.

His fingers touched places she hadn't known existed until this past month. His thumb brushed over her clit at the same time his fingers plunged into her inner muscles, until she could no longer contain the heat blossoming inside her.

"Let go, baby."

Her body out of control, she clutched his forearm as her release exploded like a Fourth of July rocket, spreading through her whole body, setting her on fire. Brett murmured something to her, his voice rough and dark. She was beyond understanding anything but sensation, the vibrations of his words rippling through her chest, working their way down to his fingers deep inside her, setting off fireballs at their tips.

As the fireworks faded, her body melted against him.

"Thank you," he whispered, pressing a kiss to the side of her forehead. He withdrew his fingers and straightened the fabric that had bunched at her waist.

Before he could pull away from her, she caught his hand and lifted it to her lips, kissing the fingers that had brought her such pleasure. She touched the tip of her tongue to his index finger. Hearing his breath hitch, she curled her lips and sucked the full length of his finger into her mouth, tasting the musk of her own juices. His heart raced beneath the hand she'd flattened over his chest as she stroked her tongue over the fleshy pad. She slid her hand down his chest, over his abdomen until her palm reached the hard length of his cock. After unzipping his fly, she slipped her hand beneath the fabric and freed him from the confines of his trousers.

He was different than Dillon, different than Wade. Longer than one, thicker than the other.

"God, Nik, I love feeling your hands on me."

He wrapped her fingers around his shaft and pumped their joined hands a half dozen times, harder than she would have dared. He'd closed his eyes and rested his head against the seat, the expression on his face no longer the blank mask but a mixture of pain and pleasure.

"I've got a better idea." She untangled her hand from his and lowered her head.

Ignoring the console jabbing into her ribs, she stretched her lips around the smooth head of his cock. Her eyes fluttered closed as his fingers tunneled into her hair, his thumb stroking lazily over her neck just below her ear. Holding the base of his cock with one hand, she took him deep into her mouth until her lips touched her fingers then slowly withdrew. He was everything she'd imagined, his potency pulsing against her tongue. Power contained in a velvet sheath, yet lurking beneath the tender way he held her, a sense of barely contained danger.

CHAPTER 16

THE WARM, WET DEPTHS OF HER MOUTH, THE STRENGTH OF HER tongue and the mind-blowing suction she used on his cock had Brett closing his eyes in a desperate attempt not to lose complete control. Christ, she was a goddess made for sucking his dick.

He'd planned to seduce her slowly, to start off with opening a bottle of her favorite wine he'd stashed away a couple nights before. Then he'd kiss her. Touch her. Get her worked up. Together they could work their way to her bedroom. Slowly. Gently. Tenderly.

At least he'd made her come first. But in the front seat of his fuckin' sedan like a horny teenager? Why hadn't he taken her up on her invitation when she'd suggested they go inside?

He groaned as she sucked him so deeply, the head of his cock bumped her throat. Instead of gagging the way he'd expected her to, he could feel her lips curling up, and she started humming. *Oh, shit, yeah!* When she slowly withdrew until only the head stayed between her lips, it was everything he could do not to push her head down and fuck her talented mouth like the barbarian he was.

As she pumped her mouth, her hips rose and fell to the same rhythm. He lifted her behind off the seat, encouraging her to kneel so he could slide his hand between her legs and cup her mound. With a moan she ground her clit against the heel of his hand while his fingers plunged into her pussy. Her juices covered his palm as her humming grew louder, more frantic, the vibrations sending an electrical jolt through his shaft and straight to the base of his spine.

Desperate, he pulled her off of him. Her eyes were glazed, her lips red and swollen as she looked at him in confusion. The scent of her arousal—musky and sweet at the same time—filled the car, inflaming his senses.

"Not here. Not like this. I want to be buried inside you when I come." He removed the keys from the ignition and opened his door even as he was stuffing his dick back into his pants. Anxious to get her inside, he nearly jumped over the hood of the car to open her door before she could.

As soon as she'd cleared the car door, he slammed it shut, grabbed her hand and half dragged her to the house. She giggled that it took him three tries to stab the key into the lock, only to discover the door had been unlocked the entire time. What would it feel like to make her giggle while she had his dick in her mouth?

Heaven. *Sheer* fucking *heaven.*

Once they were inside, he threw the deadbolt and plastered her back against the front door. Without a care for her dress, he pulled the neckline down over her breasts, catching her bra with it. The fabric pulled taut, holding her breasts up like a trophy. Holy crap, her breasts were so pretty, the plump nipples jutting out, begging to be suckled. He captured one taut bud with his mouth, lashing it with his tongue, scraping both top and bottom with his teeth.

She pressed her breast deeper in his mouth as she sought his erection again. He captured her by the wrists and braceleted them with one hand above their heads, stopping her from touching him. If she did, he'd shoot off in his pants.

With his other hand, he freed himself, then trading her breast for her mouth, he hitched her skirt out of the way and positioned himself at her entrance. With a curse, he realized he'd forgotten one important step and had to release her hands while he fumbled in his back pocket for a condom. Once properly protected, he repositioned himself, driving her breath from her when he buried himself to the hilt with one thrust.

So fucking fantastic.

Her body was firm against his, speaking to the hard work she did in the stables and the hours of riding her horses. He rotated his hips, her channel so hot and tight, it about drove him insane.

A dark primitive side of him tried to claw its way out, wanting to pound into her, to spill his come deep inside her, to leave his scent all over her so any other man around would know she was his. He nipped at her shoulder, rasping his teeth over her smooth skin, half worrying he'd leave a mark, the other half hoping he would.

He tortured himself by pulling out of her in a long, slow glide, which proved to be an agonizing pleasure as her body enveloped him. Just as slowly he rocked back into her until the head of his cock nudged the hard flesh of her cervix. His body trembled, especially when he noted she took every inch of him deep within her without complaint.

He buried his head in the crook of her neck, inhaling the perfume she'd dabbed behind her ears, tasting the salt of her sweat. At some point he didn't remember, she'd undone the buttons of his shirt, and her breasts rubbed against his chest, driving him crazy with lust.

"It's gonna have to be fast, baby. I can't do this slow."

"So what are you waiting for?" She hooked one ankle around his waist and tilted her hips as he pounded into her. Her fingers dug into his shoulders as though she'd be launched through the door if she didn't hold on to him. She made the softest little mewling sounds while her internal muscles clenched his dick.

The door banged against the frame each time he slammed into her, and her cries changed to gasps. The sounds combined with the wet sucking sounds of their flesh slapping together, filling the hallway and echoing up the stairs. His lips curled into a smile at how they were making as much noise as when she and Dillon…

He drew back when he realized what they were doing in Dillon's front hall. He glanced around, noticing for the first time that except for the hall light, the house was dark. Then he remembered Dillon's truck hadn't been out front. He released his breath in relief.

"Brett?" Nikki half wailed. She grabbed his ass, attempting to start the motion he'd stopped. "Don't stop now. I'm so close."

She was so fucking gorgeous with those heavy-lidded eyes and sweat-glistened breasts. His cock jerked inside her tight little pussy that clutched him even tighter than her mouth had in the car. He cupped her face, brushing his thumb over her plump lower lip. "Do you know how beautiful you are?"

"Brett," she cried in a desperate voice. "Please."

Her pussy clenched him, her rippling muscles milking him in a desperate attempt to coax him to continue. Even as he hesitated, she bucked, once, twice. With a fierce growl, he withdrew then thrust into her, burying himself to his balls. She gasped then moaned louder and louder with each surging thrust, her back slapping against the wood of the door.

Her muscles clamped around him as she surrendered to her release. He lasted two more thrusts before he joined her, his body shaking as his balls drew up, his come pulsing in hot spurts deep within her.

DILLON HELD HIS BREATH, hoping they wouldn't notice him lying on the couch, his softening dick in his come-splattered hand.

Brett eased out of Nikki, who lowered her feet to the floor. They sagged against each other for a moment, then Brett murmured something in Nik's ear and the two disappeared from view. The creak of the stairs told him they'd headed to bed.

He blew out a long breath, his body shuddering. Damn, it had been hot waking up to see Brett pulling Nikki's dress down over her breasts. He'd briefly considered letting them know he was home, but then they'd started fucking right there in the hall, and he didn't want to interrupt them. He'd gotten so turned on by their display, he'd had to undo his zipper to relieve the pressure. Before he knew it, he'd been stroking himself in time to Brett's thrusts.

Thank God Brett hadn't turned around and spotted him. Although he wondered why Brett had paused the way he had. Had he heard him perhaps? Sensed he was there?

Dillon shook his head. Maybe pausing was part of Brett's technique, some sort of delayed gratification?

It should bother him more than it did that Brett had just thoroughly fucked Nikki. Instead he'd found it so fucking erotic. It had made him so hard he'd wanted to join them, to watch Nikki's eyes unfocus again, to hear that deep-chested groan Brett made when he came.

Christ, he was so fucked. There was no way he could suggest that Nikki not make a choice between them, or suggest that she choose them both. If he did, she'd race back to her place while Brett planted his fist in his face before he'd finished his sentence. They'd never understand what he was suggesting.

Hell, he didn't understand it.

CHAPTER 17

Dillon eased himself into the hot tub with a groan. He'd come home from work aching and sore. Nikki had pushed him down on the couch and given him a backrub that had him soft everywhere but the groin.

Damned if Nikki hadn't suggested this dip and then dropped every stitch she had on to entice him. If he hadn't been so tired, he'd have bent her over the arm of the couch and taken her from behind.

When he pulled her to sit on his lap, he noticed she was having trouble meeting his eye. And that her thumbnail had been chewed down–a habit he'd noticed she only did if she were worried about something. He also couldn't miss the tension in her shoulders. Hellfire, she'd needed a massage as much as he had.

"You're feeling guilty about going out on that date with Brett last night, aren't you?" Guilt gnawed at his conscience that he'd not admitted he'd watched them.

Nikki buried her face against his neck and nodded.

"Brett and I had sex last night." She'd said it so quietly he barely heard her confession over the hot tub's motor. If her jaw hadn't been touching his neck, he may not have even realized she'd spoken.

He cupped the back of her head with one hand while he drew lazy circles along her spine with the other. "I told you, no regrets, okay? I want you to make sure you're making the right decision, no matter who you choose."

But damn it, he'd hoped they wouldn't be as great together as they had been last night. The hallway practically glowed from the heat the two of them had thrown off.

"When did you get home? I didn't hear you come in."

Ah. Guess this was where he should come clean about his little act of voyeurism.

"It wasn't too late. After I'd dropped off my estimate with the Sniders, I stopped off at TJ's Grill and watched the Rangers game." Here was the opening where he should tell her how Ethan had ended up dropping him off because he'd had that third beer and didn't think he should get behind the wheel. Which might explain why he'd ended up sacked out on the couch instead of in bed.

He leaned back against the jets, wondering why the hell he'd prevaricated. This was the perfect opportunity for him to admit he'd watched the two of them. It was not the time to admit that not only had it not bothered him but he'd fucking well jacked off to watching them fucking, because that was just too perverted to admit.

Luckily, Nikki had been asleep when he'd had one of his guys pick him up and take him over to the bar to retrieve his truck that morning.

They were still soaking when Brett came home from his shift, calling, "Anyone home?"

"Hey, buddy, we're out here."

A few minutes later, Brett wandered out onto the deck, carrying a beer. He must have gone upstairs to change because instead of wearing his uniform, he was wearing a Barnett

Landscaping tee and a well worn pair of blue jeans, with bare feet. When he noticed Nikki sitting beside Dillon, he slowed, a frown creasing his forehead. "Am I interrupting anything?"

"Nope, not at all." Dillon leaned back, stretching his arms along the edges of the tub. His cock hardened as he remembered the night before. His imagination expanded the possibilities, picturing the three of them in bed together. God, that would be so fuckin' hot. He'd love to have a ménage, love to watch Nikki go down on Brett while he fucked her from behind. Did he dare risk it? Why not? The worst they could do is say no. "Why don't you ditch the clothes and jump in with us?"

"I don't have any trunks."

"I'm not wearing any." Dillon held his breath when Brett eyed the hot tub with a wistful look. "Nik, would it bother you if Brett drops trou?"

"What sane woman would object to having two hot guys buck-ass nekkid on each side of her?" A flush filled her cheeks, though whether from the heat of the tub or her anticipation of being naked between them, Dillon couldn't tell.

With a shrug, Brett turned away and peeled off his shirt. His jeans and jockeys hit the deck moments later.

Dillon straightened. A large purple bruise covered the spot where Brett's ribs had been broken when he'd first come to live with them. That sucker probably hurt like a sonuvabitch when he breathed. Damn it, so much for Brett taking part in any bedroom calisthenics tonight. "Those are some pretty bad bruises, bud. You okay?"

Covering the area with his arm, Brett lowered himself into the water. He hissed when the heat reached his chest. "Fine. It probably looks worse than it feels."

Nikki gasped and scooted closer to Brett. After a brief struggle, Brett dropped his arm and allowed her to examine the knuckle-shaped bruises.

"What happened?" Nikki asked.

Brett's eyes closed, though Dillon couldn't tell whether he battled pain or struggled to contain his burgeoning erection. "Just a little scuffle during a bust. Nothing to worry about."

"You get it looked at?"

"Yes, *mom*. Nothing's broken."

Nikki hmmed, and rose up on her knees, commanding,

"Turn around."

"Why?"

"Because you look like you need a massage." She swatted him on his shoulder. "Trust me. Turn around."

"Better do what she says, bud." Dillon sank his shoulders beneath the water, his eyelids half lowered as he watched Brett attempting to cover his hard-on. "Besides, she gives a wicked back rub. You'd be a fool to turn her down."

With a sigh, Brett shifted so she'd have access to his back. She moved closer, nestling her knees on either side of his hips, then dug her thumbs into his shoulders.

Brett groaned and leaned into her touch, allowing her to concentrate on a particularly stubborn knot. His head rolled to the side, resting against her breast. Each time she dug her fingers into Brett's shoulders, her breast slid up the side of his head, the stubble of his hair grazing her nipple until it was a stiff peak.

Holy hell, he'd never realized how hot voyeurism could be. He shifted as his own erection throbbed in the pulse of the jets. If they kept this up, there'd soon be more than just water frothing.

Unlike Brett, he didn't try to hide his groin from her gaze; there was no way he could disguise the heavy erection bobbing in the jetting water.

Aw, hell. He was probably digging up snakes, but damned if he could pass up the opportunity now it had plonked itself down in front of him.

He palmed his cock, stroking its length, making sure Nikki could see what he was doing. "Watching both of you, being here, all three of us…I was thinking that maybe…" His voice dropped so low it sounded like he was growling, but he couldn't control the lust rampaging through him.

Brett understood him at once. He gave his head a small shake, a warning dark in his eyes. "Don't go there, Dill. Once you've crossed that line you can't erase it."

Nikki settled back on her heels. "What are you two talking about?"

Neither man answered her, though their unspoken communication crackled through the air between them. *Come on, bud, we can do this. Trust me.*

"Dillon? What do you mean? What line are we crossing?" she repeated.

Brett finally broke off the starefest. "Dillon's suggesting we have a threesome."

Nikki wanted to blame the jetting water for the way her clit tingled, or for the full heavy feeling of her breasts. She wanted to blame the steam rising around her for the way her body tightened, squeezing the air from her lungs. But she knew it had nothing to do with the hot tub. The heat spearing through her came from thinking about being sandwiched between the two men. Her breasts ached from her fantasy of seeing Dillon's dark head bent over one breast with Brett's golden head over the other, of them touching every part of her body. Of Dillon in her pussy, and Brett…oh, Brett filling her mouth as she kneeled in front of him, or stretching her ass as he reamed her from behind.

"What do you say, Nik?" Dillon asked.

She jumped, realizing she'd been so lost in her fantasy that he'd closed the distance between them.

What did she say? *Yes. Hell, yes!*

"Brett—" She broke off her question. How lame would it be to ask if he'd still respect her in the morning?

When he turned to look at her, the emotion in his eyes, the longing, shocked her. His gaze dropped, lingering on her throat, her breasts, lower. Each spot his eyes stopped at burned like he'd branded her. He took equally long on his path back up her body, but instead of meeting her gaze, he looked past her. To Dillon.

She cleared her throat, her voice barely a whisper, but her plea came through as loud as if she'd shouted. "It couldn't hurt just once. Could it?"

Water cascaded off him as he surged to stand in front of her. With another glance at Dillon, he cupped her face and brushed his lips across hers, his thumb caressing her jaw.

Her eyes fluttered closed as his lips sealed around hers, his tongue tickling the seam of her lips. So gentle, yet the hand holding her in place was so strong. Calloused in places Dillon's weren't. She relaxed her jaw and let him deepen the kiss. The hard length of his erection pressed into the soft flesh of her belly. All too soon he broke the kiss, though he didn't release her.

He gaze moved from her to Dillon. "Does this bother you? Watching me kissing Nikki?"

"Nope. It makes me as horny as hell watching you two. Whodathunkit?" Dillon pressed his body against her, his hand sliding around her side to cup her breast, his erection nudging the small of her back. The crisp mat of his chest hair tickling her shoulders, he was a pillar, supporting her as her legs trembled beneath their onslaught. Her hips rotated, grinding against Brett's erection in front and Dillon's behind. Both men groaned in succession.

"Inside." Dillon pulled away first. "Upstairs. Now."

Nikki sucked in a breath at his command. Fantasies were one thing, reality totally different. She couldn't even picture the mechanics of making love to two men at the same time. She gave up and decided they'd figure it out upstairs. With a shrug, she relaxed and let herself ogle Dillon's tight behind when he climbed out of the hot tub. The man had the best frickin' ass of anyone she'd ever seen. She loved clutching it as he pumped into her, feeling the play of muscles beneath her fingers.

Dillon grabbed the towels they'd placed there earlier, handing one to Nikki. Before she could take it, Brett reached around and snagged it, snapping it open and wrapping it around her. Her body heated, turned to liquid when he tucked the end into her cleavage, his palm grazing her breast, drawing her nipple into a tight bead. She pressed her thighs together against the ache starting deep inside as she imagined what she was about to do.

Dillon toweled himself off then tossed his to Brett. As Brett dried himself, Dillon opened the door and led Nikki into the house. The air conditioned air had goosebumps forming on her skin. He smiled and flicked one of her nipples poking against the terrycloth. After Brett's earlier contact, that simple touch had her shaking.

He must have seen it as his eyes burned into her, and his voice grated in need. "Let's get you upstairs and dried off."

Completely unselfconscious of his nudity, he strolled ahead of them and bounded up the stairs. As Dillon disappeared down the upstairs hall, Nikki realized Brett was hanging back. Her tongue hit the floor when she saw him standing there, his towel slung low over his hips. *He has no idea how hot he looks, does he?*

He held out his hand, waiting for Nikki to place her palm in his. "Nik? Are you okay with this? Just because Dillon suggested it doesn't mean you have to..." He tilted his head to one side in question. "It's not too late to back out, you know."

"I want to try this, for all of us to be together like this, even if it's just for tonight. But I need to know if *you're* okay with this. If it'll make things difficult, more awkward being around us—me—tomorrow." She felt the blush rising up her neck. "I guess what I'm saying is, will you still respect me in the morning?"

"Baby, I'll always respect you." Her bones melted when he cupped her behind, pressing his erection into her belly. Snuggling closer, she kissed him until he broke off with a groan. "If we keep this up, I'm going to come before we begin."

As they reached the top of the stairs, she hesitated. "Brett? What about you? Do you want to do this? I mean, isn't it sort of weird for you to be naked around Dillon? Two guys in the same bed at the same time?"

There was such a long pause, she wondered if he might change his mind and walk away. "I don't think I can back out now, Nik."

ADMITTING that beneath all her nerves, she was turned on by the prospect of being with them both at the same time, Nikki followed Brett into the bedroom. They found Dillon already busy stripping the top covers off his bed. Brett released her hand and headed into the bathroom. He returned moments later with two more towels. He tugged the one she'd wrapped around herself from her, then snapped out a fresh one. "This is all about you tonight, Nik. If there's anything you don't want to do, just say so, and we'll stop it, okay?"

The rough texture of the towel brought her skin alive as he patted her dry. Coupled with the gentleness of his ministrations, it completely undid Nikki. Especially when he stepped behind her and wrapped one arm around her waist, pulling her so she rested against his broad chest, his erection warming the small of her back like a fiery brand. With his free hand, he cupped her breast, rolling the nipple between his thumb and index finger until her pussy spasmed.

Her imagination had nothing on the reality of Brett's hardness behind combined with Dillon's strength in front, or the passion radiating from both men. She'd never felt so beautiful, so worshipped, as she did right now.

Closing her eyes, Nikki nestled her head in the crook of Brett's shoulder, inhaling his clean, masculine scent. A whimper of pleasure escaped her when someone—she could only guess it was Dillon—cupped her other breast, and a pair of firm, warm lips closed over the nipple. At first he was gentle, lapping with his tongue, but then his lips tightened around her, and he suckled her with hard tugs. Her pussy throbbed with each pull of his mouth until her whole body ached with the need to be filled, to be sated.

Dillon released her breast and pressed soft kisses over her belly. Wrapping his hands around her ankles, he urged her to part her legs wider. Her eyes fluttered open. Dillon knelt between her feet, his cock jutting hard and thick from its nest of dark hair as he glided his thumbs up the inside of her thighs and between her folds. He lowered his head onto her thigh, his beard scraping the tender inner flesh. His eyes flashed dark as he traced one finger, coated with her cream, over her lips. "Turn your head, Nik. Let Brett taste you."

As soon as she did, Brett kissed her, nibbling and licking her essence coating her lips. He groaned into her mouth, his hot cock twitching against the crack of her ass.

"She tastes so sweet, doesn't she?" Dillon's breath blew hot across her center and had her body shuddering in response. She hauled in a shaky breath to see her fantasy half realized— Dillon's dark head between her thighs, compared with the golden hairs dusting Brett's arm as it banded her waist.

Behind her, Brett's breath was harsh in her ear. "Do you like that, baby? Do you like feeling me playing with your breasts while he's eating your pussy?"

"Yes." God, yes, it was heaven.

Still Dillon teased and taunted her, driving her to the brink then easing back. His tongue stabbed at her clit, his fingers broached her, curling, teasing as Brett plucked at her nipples. Her world condensed to the sensations of these two men pleasuring her, her bones liquefied and her head spun with the bursts of light and heat exploding within.

Just as her knees gave out entirely, Brett picked her up and laid her on the bed then lay beside her. Her eyes opened, her lids heavy, as Dillon crawled beside them.

She jumped when Dillon lifted her foot, but relaxed as he massaged it. He caressed her ankle, then her calf, his calluses adding an additional thrill to the sensation of him touching her so gently. Brett mirrored his attentions on her other leg, laying a soft kiss on her knee. They moved up her body, bypassing her mound, until they reached her breasts. Her breath hitched to see Dillon's dark hair mingling with Brett's gold as they suckled and lapped her nipples.

Though her fantasies had been pretty wild on occasion, she'd never imagined they'd come true. She wouldn't have dared imagine that she'd ever have the two men she cared for—loved —making love to her. That Dillon, and Brett too, would put aside their own egos, their own needs to see to her pleasure. To fulfill her fantasies.

Oh sure, she was pretty sure they'd probably fantasized about having threesomes too, but she doubted their scenarios would include the two of them with one woman. More likely they'd fantasized having multiple female partners. Wasn't that every guy's dream? Yet here they were, with her.

Brett pulled away from her breast and caught a length of her hair, wrapping it around his hand. He leaned down to whisper, "So beautiful. You are so beautiful, Nik."

Before she could reply, he caught her lips with his, brushing a soothing kiss over them at first. Tasting, testing, just like he had before. She threaded her fingers through his hair and held him, allowing him to explore her mouth, granting him anything he wanted. Because she wanted him just as much.

The sensation of kissing Brett while Dillon continued to tease her breasts had her sighing and giving into the sheer pleasure of the moment.

With a groan, Dillon pumped his hips so his cock rubbed along her thigh. His breath harsh as he panted, he pulled away and sat back on his heels. "Hey, Brett, why don't you scoot on up to the headboard there?"

Once Brett was in place, Dillon flipped her over, positioned her between Brett's outstretched legs and lifted her behind so she was on her hands and knees.

Brett's thick cock bobbed less than a foot away from her face, the head bulbous and heavy, the shaft jutting proudly from his nest of dark golden curls. Shifting her weight onto one hand, she curled her fingers around it and stroked the smooth length of his shaft. His breath hissed as he inhaled. A flicker of pain crossed his face, reminding her of his injured ribs. She let go of his shaft and moved until she was over him. His cock stroking the soft skin of her belly, she pressed a kiss to his bruises. "Are you sure you're up to this?"

He chuckled as he stroked a knuckle down her cheek, then lifted her head so she was forced to look at his face. The blue of his eyes darkened and flashed. "I'm sure, baby. I'd be an idiot to turn down an opportunity to make love with you."

Not fuck you. Make love with you. She understood the difference. If there had been any last lingering doubts about the threesome, his statement would have squashed them completely.

Without breaking eye contact, he murmured, "Dillon, are *you* sure about this?"

"*I'm* sure about it," she murmured. Making sure he still watched her, she bent down and licked up his shaft, swirling her tongue around the swollen head.

His touch gentle, Dillon stroked her behind. "Suck him down, baby. Show him how good you are with your tongue."

Lowering herself to her elbows, she slid the head between her lips and gently sucked. Brett groaned, his fingers tangled in her hair, pressing her down. She increased the pressure and took him deep into her mouth. Dillon played with her clit at the same time. Giving head had always turned her on, but to be played with by someone else at the same time she had a cock filling her mouth doubled the intensity of her own needs.

As if he knew what she needed, Dillon settled himself between her legs. Instead of the cock she'd expected to part her pussy, his beard rasped the tender inner skin of her thighs. Seconds later, his tongue lapped at her labia. She parted her legs, giving Dillon better access. He held her hips steady as he made a meal of her.

She hummed in approval around Brett's shaft and stuck her hips back toward Dillon, rotating them as much as she could. At first she felt awkward, afraid she'd bite down on Brett's shaft as Dillon teased her clit.

"It's all right, baby, I've got you." Brett held her head in his hands and assumed control, thrusting his cock in time with Dillon's licking.

Chuckling, she swallowed him deep again, using her tongue to tease the sensitive head as it slid past. The first cracks in Brett's control appeared; he started panting, his hips lifting from the mattress, jamming his shaft against the back of her throat. If she could do nothing else for him, she'd give him everything she had tonight.

Dillon's noisy slurping soon became all she heard as his tongue hit all the right spots. Brett pulled her off of him, letting her concentrate on her own pleasure. Panting, her body tightened as she ground against his face, her orgasm rocketing through her until her head spun and left her dizzy.

Opening her eyes, she discovered Brett staring at her as if she were a chocolate cheesecake he wanted to devour. "She's beautiful when she comes, isn't she?" Dillon scooched up the bed until he was lying beside her, a smug look on his face.

"Damned straight she's beautiful." Brett tightened his grip on her head, lifting it until her mouth hovered over his cock. "My turn."

Her body still trembling from her own orgasm, she cupped his balls and rolled them. Stroked the spot right behind them. A bead of pre-come welled at the tip of his cock. Her tongue curled over the engorged head, lapping him clean as delicately as a cat. Sweat beaded on his upper lip when she sucked the entire head between her lips, using her tongue to stroke around the edges, needing him to lose all control, wanting him to know that his pleasure was just as important as hers.

"Ah, fuck! Yeah!" Brett's hips surged up until the head of his cock hit the back of her mouth, his come jettisoning down her throat. Glorying that she'd made him lose control, she swallowed the pulsing releases. Though his come was thicker, it tasted sweeter than Dillon's salty essence. She swallowed it down, licking the last traces off with gentle swipes.

Once his cock softened, he stroked her hair. There was a softness in his expression that spoke of love and passion.

Nikki stroked the bruises on Brett's ribs. "Are you all right?"

He cupped her jaw and pulled her down to him. "I'll be fine."

She nuzzled his face, his beard scraping her cheek. "Liar."

His lips were still tilted into a smile when he captured her mouth with his. He worshipped her with his mouth and his tongue, needing no words to tell her how he felt.

When Dillon caressed her back, she broke off the kiss and turned to him. His eyes were as dark as Brett's were light, filled with an intensity that took her breath from her. He lowered his head, his lips grazing hers, his taste mingling with Brett's.

"I love you, Nik." The warmth of his breath as it wafted over her cheek wound around her heart, binding him to her. She slipped to the side until she was lying between them. Dillon caught her mouth with his again. By the time they parted, they were both panting, Dillon's erection pressing hard against her mound.

"Turn over, babe."

Dillon lifted her on her hands and knees, then slid behind her until the front of his thighs slid slick against the backs of hers. Grasping her hips hard, he rode her hard, the only sound in the room the wet sound of his balls slapping her clit, his harsh breath and her moans.

Nikki lost her breath when his cock jerked inside her channel, her muscles clamping around him, holding him, forcing him to work to withdraw each time. The friction created an agonizing pleasure that had her sobbing in need.

"Look at Brett, Nik. Let him see what you look like when you come."

Not knowing where she got the strength to obey him, she forced her eyes open.

"Oh, baby, you're so beautiful," Brett whispered. His cock jerked against his belly, as if confirming his statement.

She gave up trying to think when Brett reached beneath her and rolled her clit. The pressure sent her over the edge, her pussy milking Dillon's cock as her muscles contracted around him.

Her orgasm triggered Dillon's and he thrust once more, shouting as his cock pulsed deep inside her.

CHAPTER 18

As Dillon pumped into her, Brett supported Nikki, holding her shaking body as she rode out her orgasm. How he wished he'd been the one to make her come, to make her eyes glaze over the way they were right now.

He wanted to go down on her pretty pussy and taste her—he'd been in too much of a hurry to take the time the other night. He wanted to stab his tongue into her, to have her legs wrapped him again, her fingernails scoring his back as he buried his cock deep inside her. He wanted to feel her spasm around him as she came, to empty himself into her until his balls were bone dry. Then he wanted to mount her and do it all over again.

Though Nikki might not have realized it, he'd noticed just who had been the one to make love to her. Oh, sure Dillon had let her give Brett a blow job, but he'd kept the prize for himself. He wanted more than Dillon had granted him. He wanted all of Nikki. To himself.

The blow job she'd given him had been fantastic. What else would she want to try, let him do? What had she done with Dillon already?

Dillon pulled out of her with a wet sucking sound and staggered into the bathroom muttering, "Be right back. Gotta get rid of this raincoat."

Two seconds later, Nikki pulled away too, telling him she had to clean up as well. Left alone in Dillon's bedroom, Brett stared at the ceiling.

In the other room he could hear Dillon say something that had Nikki giggling. They were his two best friends, yet he'd never felt so alone.

Why the hell had Dillon suggested this? And what the hell would happen tomorrow when they had to face each other in the light of day? Despite Dillon's earlier assertion about not having any regrets, he wondered if he would find himself kicked to the curb again the next morning?

Would Nikki have second thoughts about two guys who would willingly share her?

By agreeing to Dillon's goddamned impulsive suggestion, would he lose any hope of a future with Nikki? With either of them?

"What's the matter, buddy?" Dillon crawled up to his side of the bed and flopped down on his pillow. "You look like you lost your best friend."

Gee, why would I think that? He couldn't tamp down the sarcasm boiling inside. "Ten years ago, you beat the tar out of me for kissing her, Dill. What the fuck are you going to do when you decide you regret tonight?"

"I was eighteen and stupid. I promise you, buddy, I'm not gonna regret tonight. Ever." Dillon lifted himself up on one elbow and watched as Nikki returned from the bathroom. "Nik? I think Brett's worried we're gonna kick him out. You got any regrets?"

Nikki snuggled up to Brett, smiling that same beautiful smile she'd given Dillon in the kitchen a few days before.

His heart lodged in his throat, realizing it was all for him.

Maybe he'd still be around tomorrow. Maybe he still had a chance with her.

She shook her head, causing her hair to brush over his chest in an erotic caress that had his cock hardening again. "Why would I regret showing you just how much I love you both?"

Emotions swamping him at her pronouncement, Brett swallowed hard. He threw one arm over his eyes, unwilling to let either of them see the emotion he couldn't keep from his expression. It was either that or let the tears that prickled beneath his lids spill down his cheeks for everyone to see. He hadn't let himself cry since he was a kid. He'd learned early not to show any type of emotion, and he couldn't let her—anyone, even Dillon—know how she affected him. He couldn't give anyone that type of power ever again. Yet here she was, bit by bit, pulling down the barriers he'd built.

If Nikki chose Dillon instead of him, it was going to hurt worse than any beating his father had given him. Even if she did choose him, he doubted Dillon would be as magnanimous in defeat as he'd promised. Either way he'd lose—in winning Nikki's love, he'd lose Dillon's friendship. If she chose Dillon over him, he couldn't be able to bear watching the two of them together knowing she'd loved him, just not loved him enough.

She shifted until she was draped over top of him again, her body a comforting blanket. Something brushed his cheek. "Hey, are you okay?"

Her simple touch shattered the remaining walls. He wrapped his arms around her, holding her tightly as if she would float away if he didn't.

"I love you," he whispered, the words tumbling out before he could stop them. He held his breath once he realized what he'd done, the power over him he'd handed her.

"I love you too." There was no hesitation to her words, no equivocation that left room for doubt.

He opened his eyes and found her watching him, her eyes

still heavy from her arousal, her cheeks flushed and lips swollen from taking his cock between them. She was the most beautiful woman he'd ever seen.

Then he realized what she'd said—and who else had heard. Dillon met his gaze evenly. He swallowed against the joy and relief filling him. No matter what came out of tonight, he wasn't going to lose Dillon's friendship. Maybe, just for tonight, he could share his love with them both.

Holding Nikki's head between his hands, he captured her lips with his, thrusting his tongue in her mouth with a hunger he'd never known before. His hands roamed over her body, memorizing the spots that drew a reaction. He savored the soft gasps and moans when he found a particularly erogenous zone. He growled with delight when she rubbed her mound against his erection.

Flipping her onto her back, he worked his way down her body, letting his lips and tongue hit the spots he'd identified earlier as turning her on. The smooth skin of her belly, a half inch below her navel, the sensitive dent just above her hips on either side of her soft curls. He grazed his beard over the tender skin of her thighs until her legs splayed open, allowing him access to her swollen pussy. The musky fragrance of her arousal rose up and filled his senses until his head spun.

Dillon rolled on his side and began to play with Nikki's breasts. "You mind if I join in?"

Nikki answered the question by pulling Dillon's head to her breast. Brett closed his eyes, concentrating on teasing Nik's engorged clit, licking her essence. He shoved his hands beneath her hips and lifted her to his mouth. Her body trembled each time he flicked his tongue over her folds, teasing her.

Sweat dripped down his forehead and onto her mound, mixing with her dew. He groaned when her hips arched, pressing her into his face, coating his cheeks and jaw in her juices. She tasted so fucking good—no peach at the height of ripeness tasted as sweet. A man would never go hungry with access to such sweetness.

When her hands started fisting the covers, he stiffened his tongue and stabbed it into her, then withdrew it and sucked her clit. Over and over he repeated the action, driving her until she writhed beneath him. Sure she was approaching her orgasm, he looked up, needing to see her lose herself in pleasure again.

"Brett, please. I want you in me. Brett, please." Her breathy plea, using *his* name, not Dillon's, had him closing his eyes. There was no way he could let them see how much it meant to him that she'd beg him with such need. Such love.

Dillon rolled across the bed, grabbed a condom from the night table and tossed it to him. His hands trembling, Brett ripped the package and rolled it on. He poised himself above her, but hesitated, watching to see if Dillon would stop them.

Dillon didn't. Realizing Brett had stopped, he frowned.

"What are you waiting for? She needs you."

Not needing any further encouragement, Brett returned his attentions to Nikki. He lowered himself over her. Heat rose from her skin, calling to him, soothing him. The scent of her arousal clung to his chin, his cheeks, enveloping him. With one hand he guided the head of his cock to her opening, then pressed in inch by inch.

Though going slow damned near made him whimper, he forced himself not to rush. Last time he'd taken her against the door in a frenzy. This time he wanted to show he could be gentle. She deserved to be worshipped. Loved. Tonight he would give her anything she desired. No matter what his body wanted, all he cared about was her pleasure.

The pair were locked in each other's gazes, unaware of anything else, any*one* else, as Brett parted Nikki's swollen folds.

When Nikki grabbed Brett's biceps, begging him to take her harder, Dillon bit back the urge to groan and urge his friend to do what she asked. He understood Brett's need to go slow, while cursing his own lack of control. Even though they'd promised the night would be for Nikki, she'd ended up sucking down Brett's dick then later he'd pounded into her from behind, hard and fast. Oh, she'd come when he'd gone down on her earlier, and again while he was inside her, but she deserved to be pampered, to be cherished.

Brett knew that, and could control himself to put Nikki ahead of his own desires, to give Nikki what she needed, what she deserved.

They both deserved better than he could give them. He'd never shared a lover before, and he'd half expected to be jealous, but watching the love on their faces, seeing the care Brett took with Nikki, the total look of adoration on his face, hearing Nikki begging for Brett—not Dillon—to fill her had convinced him he'd been right in suggesting the threesome. He'd heard Brett's whispered declaration of love, but now he was seeing their mutual love firsthand. How could he be jealous in the face of such complete devotion? Of such selfless love?

This night wouldn't just be for Nikki. It would be for Brett too. To make up for that time ten years ago when he'd driven his best friend away.

Sometimes saying sorry isn't enough. Isn't that what Nikki had said? Would this be enough to convince Brett how sorry he'd been for hurting him?

What a shit he had been to let a fit of jealousy separate Brett from the only people he'd ever been able to trust. Yeah, tonight would be for both of them. Tomorrow they'd probably be wondering if things had changed, especially since Brett tended to overthink things. So tomorrow he'd make sure they didn't have any regrets over anything they'd done tonight.

Brett groaned when the full length of his cock nestled between Nikki's glistening labia. The deep-throated sound thrummed through Dillon's chest and into his balls.

Nikki's breath hitched and the look of sheer pleasure as her eyes fluttered closed had come leaking out of Dillon's dick, his balls drawing tight to his body.

Brett's languid movements as he withdrew from Nikki then slowly slid his cock in again, combined with Nikki's soft mewling, became an erotic dance, with Dillon an entranced spectator. Watching them make love so tenderly, compared to the frantic coupling they'd done against the front door and their obliviousness to his presence, made his voyeurism that much more erotic.

When Brett bent down and kissed Nikki, Dillon had to squeeze the base of his cock to stop himself from coming too soon. His balls ached when Nikki dig her fingers into Brett's ass, smelling the heady musk of their mutual arousal. His hips jerked in time to Brett's thrusts as they gradually increased their tempo.

Nikki's arms and legs wrapped around Brett while he held onto her as if she anchored him to the world, the two of them still joined in the most intimate way a man and a woman could be. Afraid of breaking the spell of their shared release, Dillon soaked in the love enveloping them, filling the room until nothing else existed.

Seeing his friends in the throes of passion drove Dillon over the edge. Not wanting to sully the gift they'd granted him, he grabbed the towel he'd discarded earlier, covering his cock as his release splattered over his hand.

After a long moment of the two of them clutching together, Brett rolled off of Nikki and, after disposing of his condom, settled on the other side of the bed beside her. Nikki reached out, tugging Dillon until he rested beside her.

"I'm sorry," she said softly. "I'm not sure how things work having to please two guys at the same time. Would you like me to—" A blush staining her cheeks, she withdrew her hand from his and reached for the towel covering his groin.

"Don't. You don't have to apologize." Before she could

remove the towel, he caught her hand, lifting it to his mouth and kissed it. "It was beautiful to watch."

"Don't you need—"

"No, Nik. Sssh. I'm fine." He stroked her face, caressing the tender skin just above her eyes until they fluttered closed. "Go to sleep, baby. I'll be right here."

He reached down and snagged the sheet. Brett grabbed the other side, his look cautious as together they draped it over Nikki. That his friend still didn't trust him not to betray his word cut as deep as any knife. "You should get some sleep too, buddy."

After a short hesitation, Brett nodded, then he stretched out beside Nikki.

Once Dillon turned off the remaining light, he lay back on the pillows, aware Brett was staring at the ceiling the same as he, both listening to Nikki's soft breathing. If only there was some way the three of them could stay like this forever. Because if there wasn't, he had to make sure Nikki chose Brett. There was no way he could in good conscience come between two people who shared such love, such devotion. But the thought of making good on his promise, of standing as Brett's best man, was going to hurt more than having his balls ripped out through his throat.

CHAPTER 19

Nikki awoke to a hand stroking the arm she'd thrown over Dillon's warm hard body. Giving a groan of contentment, she snuggled closer and buried her face in his chest. "I could stay here all day."

"As much as I'd love that, we're gonna have to get up soon or we're gonna be late."

"Late? For what?" She cracked open one eye and found Dillon watching her. Though his lips were quirked up in a smile, there was a strange expression in his eyes as they looked past her. Her eyes opened wide, finally realizing there was another warm hard body—with an impressive erection—cuddling her back.

"It's Sunday, remember?" Brett murmured against her shoulder.

"Which means we have dinner at my parents' place." Dillon brushed a kiss over her hair and patted her hip. "Hit the shower, sweet cheeks. I promised Mom we'd be there in a half hour."

"A half hour? I can't get ready in a half hour." She dashed to the bathroom and screeched when she got a look at her hair. "Oh my God, I can't go to your mother looking like this."

"What's the matter? You look fine."

She tugged at the tangles and the bump of hair on one side. "Fine? This is not fine, Dillon."

"It's only a family dinner. You've been there a half-dozen times now. Well, maybe four because we missed last week."

She turned on the shower and stepped into it, ducking her head under the water. "Exactly. It's your *family* dinner." Shampoo. Where the hell was her shampoo? "That means your mom. And your dad."

There it was. Water running into her eyes, she grabbed the bottle and squirted it on her hand, then slapped it onto her head. "Your brothers. Your sister."

She scrubbed, trying to work up a lather. "It's your whole freaking *family*."

Not to mention that I've just slept not only with you but your foster brother too! Yet he expected her to waltz in between the two of them as if nothing had happened?

Why wasn't the damned stuff lathering? She stared at the bottle. Shit! It was the conditioner!

Brett rolled from the bed and joined them in the bathroom. He shot Dillon a glance Though he was wearing his cop face, which meant she couldn't tell if he was amused or concerned. "I think Nik's concerned about facing them after what we did last night, Dill."

"Uh, gee, d'you think?" She ducked her head under the spray again and washed as much of the conditioner out as she could, then squirted the shampoo directly onto her hair.

Dillon frowned as he peered over Brett's shoulder. "They won't know. I'm not about to tell them. Brett won't either."

Fuck, sometimes guys could be so clueless. It didn't matter who else knew. She knew. How the hell was she going to look at Mrs. Barnett in the eye again?

She slammed the shampoo bottle onto the shelf but only got

half of it on the ledge and it fell off onto her toe. Her shriek echoed off the bathroom tile. "Goddamn it!"

"Go call your mom, Dill. Tell her we'll be late and to hold dinner until we get there." Before Dillon could argue, Brett shut the bathroom door and locked it, leaving Dillon on the other side. He stepped into the shower and wrapped his arms about her. "Breathe."

She tried to push him away, frustrated that she was losing control while he was so calm. "But—"

"Ssshh. Just relax. Take a deep breath." Once she had, he told her to take another, and another, rocking her until she was limp against him. "Don't worry about the Barnetts. They won't judge you."

"But—"

"No. No buts." He tightened his arms around her and tucked her soapy hair under his chin. "They are the nicest people I've ever met. Dillon's right. They don't know you slept with both of us, and we're not about to say anything. Even if they did know, they'll be nothing but polite to you."

"Until I leave."

"No, even then they won't say a word against you." His hand rubbed up and down her spine. How did he know how to say just the right thing? "They're good people, Nik. You can trust them to treat you right."

"That's why you're so afraid of losing them, isn't it?"

"Yes."

She pulled away and looked up at him. "I'm glad they took you away from your father so you could live with them."

"So am I." He tucked her back against him. "So am I."

On the way to the Barnetts' house, Nikki sat between them. The fifth time she reached for the radio, Dillon grabbed her hand and held it flat against his thigh. "Stop worrying."

"I was just going to turn it up."

"You turned it down less than thirty seconds ago. You've

been playing with it all the way here." He shared a glance with Brett. "Do you want me to turn around? Call

Mom and tell her we're not coming?"

"Would you?"

"I could."

She eyed him suspiciously. "Why did you say it like that?"

"Like what?"

"The way you dragged it out like that. What are you implying, Dillon?"

"We cancelled out last week, and I missed that week you first moved in too, remember? Mom said if I cancelled out this week, she'd round everyone up and bring them all over to my place."

"She would, too," Brett agreed.

"Then she'd make us do the dishes afterward." Dillon frowned and turned onto the county road leading to his parents' place. "There are a lot of dishes to do on Sundays. Like quadruple the amount we normally have."

"Dillon, doing dishes is not a chore when you've got a dishwasher." They both looked outraged at her statement. It wasn't until she settled back, thinking she'd won her argument, that she realized Dillon was pulling into his parents' driveway. Shoot. They'd tagteamed her into not watching where they were. Now it was too late to back out.

Dillon parked his truck beside a beat-up old Chevy half ton. "Hey, Griff's home."

He hopped out of the truck and swung Nikki down. She noticed that Brett kept a decent distance away from them. While she knew it was necessary to maintain the illusion, she wanted to hold his hand.

She was chewing on her thumbnail when the front door swung open. Mrs. Barnett swooped onto the porch with a smug look on her face. She hugged Dillon first, then Brett, and turned to Nikki. "I'm so glad y'all could come today. With Griff working all over the state these days and Ethan at college, it's the first time the whole family's been together in ages."

She led them into the house, talking over her shoulder as she went. "When Dillon phoned, I thought he was going to try to cancel again. But I told him that if he did, I'd just pack everything up and bring everyone over to his place."

As they passed the living room with its faded couch and upright piano, Brett leaned over and whispered, "You didn't believe us, did you?"

She shook her head as they entered the dining room. While she already knew Dillon's family, her nerves jumped to see Dillon's brothers, Griffin and Matt, grinning a smile identical to Dillon's as if they knew full well what had happened the night before. Middle brother Ethan and Dillon's sister Lilly sat on the opposite side of the table. While they were nodding and smiling, they didn't make her stomach flip-flop. She took a deep breath and took her seat, telling herself she could get through this meal.

At least until she glanced to the head of the table where Dillon's father sat, a frown on his face, his dark eyes, normally sparkling like Dillon's, solemn and penetrating. She wiped her hands on her skirt. Did he suspect what had happened?

From the chair to his left, another pair of sharp chocolate eyes scanned her.

Mrs. Barnett placed her hands on the shoulders of Dillon's grandmother. "Nicole, you remember Jackson's mother, Ruth, don't you?"

"Yes, ma'am. How are you, Mrs. Barnett?"

Gramma Barnett flicked her gaze from Nikki to Dillon for a moment then turned to Brett and pursed her lips. From the few times she'd met Dillon's grandmother before, she got the feeling that little escaped the woman's attention. With a curt nod of her head, Gramma tapped on the table.

"Glad to see y'all made it this week. Now where's dinner? I'm hungry."

Feeling as if she'd just been judged, and passed inspection, Nikki exhaled a slow breath.

As plates were passed around the table, and the family settled into a half-dozen different topics in which everyone voiced an opinion, Nikki gradually relaxed. She'd half expected that Dillon might try something inappropriate considering he was sitting right beside her, but he kept his hands to himself the entire time.

The main course finished, they'd moved on to Mrs. Barnett's famous apple crumble pie when the discussion drifted to the headlines. Dillon reached over and grabbed the last slice, bobbling his plate when his grandmother changed the direction of the conversation.

"Did you see that story on the news the other night about a woman over in Cleburne who was arrested for marrying two men without them knowin' about the other?"

Trying not to draw too much attention to herself, Nikki leaned close to Dillon and whispered, "Please tell me you didn't say anything to her about me dating both of you."

"I swear I never said a word," he whispered back.

Gramma Barnett frowned at them and pointedly raised her voice. "Apparently, she travelled a lot for her job, and neither suspected the other existed. From what I saw of the report, she'd been married twenty years to one, then married another half her age over in Austin a couple years back. Both men said they were both as happy as a pig in shit." An earthy chuckle erupted, starting deep in her belly. "At least until they found out the other existed."

Nikki chanced a glance sideways at Brett and met his puzzled gaze. He lifted one shoulder a half inch and shook his head. Was it merely a coincidence that Gramma Barnett had mentioned the subject? Or had she picked up on something they'd done—some way they'd looked at each other?

Faith joined her mother-in-law's laughter. "As long as she didn't have to do their laundry, good for her."

Mr. Barnett wasn't as forgiving. "Mother, Faith! What type of example does that set for Lilly?"

The conversation hitting a little too close to home, Nikki sipped her iced tea in hopes it might cool the blush creeping into her cheeks.

Gramma Barnett stabbed the last bit of pastry on her plate and waved it toward Nikki. "Nothin' wrong with a woman living with two men, Junior, s'long as everyone's amenable to the arrangement. Look at this little filly and how she's keeping your boys so happy."

A chorus of "Gramma!"s echoed around the table while Nikki choked on her drink.

"What? It's an honest opinion." Gramma Barnett thumped on the table. "What woman wouldn't be tempted by two fellas as good lookin' as my boys? If she's not, there's somethin' wrong with her."

Dillon's father fixed his mother with a glare. "I hardly think this is the appropriate venue for this discussion, Momma."

"Bah." She leaned toward Nikki as if she was going to whisper a secret, but didn't lower her voice. "My grandparents had a permanent threesome all their adult lives. Betcha Dillon never told you that before."

"No way! Really?" Lilly piped up, though instead of shock, her eyes were wide with interest.

"I could hardly tell her something I didn't know myself, Gram." Despite his tan, Dillon's cheeks bore an unmistakeable hint of a blush.

"Yup." She dabbed her mouth as delicately as if she were presiding over a state dinner, then realizing she had the attention of the whole table, placed the napkin on her lap. "And

I'll tell you somethin' else—they weren't the only ones in the county with more than two to their bed."

She glared around the table as if warning anyone who dared challenge her. "Times were hard back then, and there weren't as many women around as there are now. According to my daddy, his daddies decided instead of fighting for the hand of the woman they loved, they'd all live together. Musta worked out because they're even buried side by side by side out in the churchyard." She pointed at Nikki then waved her bony finger between Brett and Dillon. "You should do the same thing. You'd be a fool to pass up the opportunity to bed down with such fine-looking specimens. And it'll keep these boys on their toes—make 'em keep you happy both in the bedroom and outta it, in case you decide to kick one o' 'em out. The good Lord knows young Dillon here needs something to keep him out of his mischief."

All the eyes that had been staring at Mrs. Barnett trained on Nikki, waiting to see her response. Feeling like a bug under the microscope, Nikki looked to Dillon for help. That was a futile hope, as he was dissecting the remains of his apple crumble. For his part, Brett stared at his plate, his brows drawn together. No help there either. The pie that had been so delicious moments before now lay as heavy as a rock in her stomach. "Um, th-thank you for the advice, Mrs. Barnett. I'll certainly keep it in mind."

"You do that." Mrs. Barnett put down her fork and pushed her plate to the center of the table. "Close your mouth, dear. You'll attract flies." She stood with a groan then shuffled to the door. Halfway down the hall, she called, "Jackson, get off that keister of yours and drive me home. Or are you gonna make your poor old momma walk all the way?"

Mr. Barnett's chair scraped across the floor as he pushed it back. "Coming, Momma."

No one else moved or said a word until they heard the front

door close. Then everyone erupted in laughter at exactly the same moment.

"Oh, my lord, that woman." Mrs. Barnett placed a hand on either side of her face in mock dismay.

"Well, I think she's great," Lilly declared. "I hope I'm as sharp as her when I'm that old."

"Lord help us," Dillon muttered.

"Boys, you're doing the dishes today." A chorus of masculine groans greeted Mrs. Barnett's directive, but every one of the men stood up and started gathering dishes.

Facing Nikki, Faith gestured to the other room. "Why don't you come into the front room with me, hon? Lilly, I believe you had homework this afternoon? Don't you have that book report?"

"Which means she wants me to get lost while she grills you, Nik," Lilly said in a stage whisper. But she left the room.

Feeling like a horse smelling the nearby glue factory, Nikki followed Mrs. Barnett to the living room.

"Normally I'd ask you to forgive Lilly, but I'm afraid she's right today. I have been dying to talk to you." Faith sank onto the couch and patted the back of it in invitation. "I've been wondering if Brett's gotten any leads on your brother's whereabouts?"

"Oh." The dread that had been attached to Nikki's heels like a deadweight dropped away. She sank onto the couch in relief. "Last I heard, the police found Phil's car. He'd sold it to someone in Temple." And she'd overheard Brett telling Dillon that the money Phil had transferred from her accounts to his had run out. "Brett doesn't think they'll ever be able to get any of my things back."

"I'm sorry to say that if Brett says they won't, they probably won't." Faith smoothed her skirt and frowned. "I was so worried about him when he said he was going to join the police force. This isn't Dallas or some of those other nasty places, but still, folks around here can get into trouble. Don't get me wrong, I'm proud as punch of him. But I worry about him as if he were my own flesh-and-blood."

"I can tell. And he loves you like you were his mother."

Mrs. Barnett's cheeks turned red, but Nikki could tell she was pleased to hear it. "You didn't know Brett when he was a boy, did you?"

"No, I was a sophomore when my family moved here."

Faith grabbed a photo album from a shelf filled with albums and flipped open a page, as if she knew exactly what picture she wanted. "This is what he looked like shortly after they moved here."

Nikki ran her finger over the picture of a solemn-faced, twig-thin Brett staring at the camera, a taller and sturdier Dillon grinning broadly, his arm slung around Brett's shoulders. "He's so skinny."

"I don't think his father worried overmuch about feeding anyone but himself. Do you know when Children's Services came in to inspect the place, he had over two dozen empty cases of beer in the kitchen? They found dozens more piled up on the back porch. The man must have drunk beer like it was soda pop."

Faith reached over and flipped the page. "This is a year later, once he'd come to live with us. As you can see, he's got a bit more flesh on his bones."

He'd also grown taller and was now the same height as Dillon. What she noticed most was the smile on his face. Not as confident as Dillon's, but a definite improvement over the previous picture. The haunted look in his eyes had disappeared, the stern lips were now pulled into a mischievous grin. He was happy. Because of the Barnetts.

Her heart ached at seeing the change in him after knowing what he'd survived. He deserved to be happy. If she chose Dillon over him, would she end up driving Brett away from the only real family he'd known? She blinked rapidly, trying to stave off the tears that threatened to fall.

She hadn't asked to end up torn between the two of them, and yet here she was, faced with an impossible decision between two men she respected, cared for...loved.

"He was always a scrapper, though. Course, it got him through a lot. Some of the other boys used to think because he was skinny, that meant he was frail, and others hassled him about his father being an ex-con, but he sure set them straight right quick."

Nikki flipped through the pages, examining photos of Dillon and Brett as they matured through middle school and into high school, recognizing them as they'd been when she'd moved to town. She stopped at their graduation photos. Brett's smile that had been present in the previous pictures was once again absent. Even more telling was the absence of Dillon's usually ever-present grin.

Faith frowned when she saw what page Nikki had stopped on. "That was such a horrible time. Dillon attacked Brett, not just once but twice.." She sniffed. "When Brett ran away, I was terrified. I was sure we'd lost him forever. I was terrified what he'd do, where he'd go. That maybe he'd get hurt, or hurt himself. I was so angry at Dillon because he wouldn't tell me what had happened." Another sniff. "They still haven't."

Wishing she could disappear into the floor, Nikki closed the book and flattened her hand over the cover. "They were fighting because Brett kissed me, and Dillon was jealous."

"Is that the way of it, then?" Faith said just as quietly as Nikki had admitted it. "I'd often wondered if there was a girl involved, but they're both so pigheaded neither would tell me. Even after Brett came back, the two of them didn't talk. Next thing we knew Brett was going to school in Boston, and we barely saw him at all."

"I didn't know they fought until a couple of weeks ago.

Please understand, Mrs. Barnett. I wasn't trying to make trouble between them. Dillon had never showed any interest in me before Brett kissed me."

Neither had said anything other than a polite hello or howdy in the halls for the rest of the semester. By the time Brett had come back from his first year at college, she was married.

"And now here you are, all together again."

Did Faith know that she was sleeping with both of them? She chanced a look up, if only to try to figure out just how much Dillon's mom knew.

Instead of condemnation, she saw sympathy on Faith's face, heard understanding in her voice. "You care for both my boys, don't you?"

Miserable, she nodded and stared at her hands still flattened over the album. "They want me to decide between them."

Would her choice split them apart again? Would Faith blame her if her choice caused another schism between the two men, within the Barnett family? She looked up at the old woman, expecting to see ... what? Condemnation? Anger? Would she be warned off, told to leave both Brett and Dillon?

Instead Faith sighed. "Oh, honey, you're the baby in Solomon's Wisdom, aren't you? Only it's the two men you love splitting you apart."

CHAPTER 20

"ALL RIGHT, LET'S GET THIS DONE." BRETT GRABBED HIS PLATE and stacked it with Nikki's. "Matt, you're washing. Griffin, Ethan, you're on rinse detail. Dillon and I will dry."

Solutions often came to him when he was working at mindless tasks. Maybe the dishes would help him sort through the myriad of questions assailing him. Like what the hell had tipped Gramma Barnett to what had happened last night? As much as he'd wanted to blame someone else, he knew neither Dillon nor Nikki had said anything. Which meant that canny old woman picked up on some vibe resonating from them. How soon before the others clued in?

"Aw, man, why do I have to be the one handling the dirty dishes every Sunday? Why can't Ethan or Griff do the washing this week?" Matt complained. But he plodded over to the sink and turned on the water, squirting the dishwasher detergent into the stream. "We could at least buy a dishwasher. You've got one, Dill. And you live alone."

"There's three of them now," Ethan reminded his youngest brother. He leaned a hip against the counter while they waited for the sink to fill. "Hey, Dill? Did you know about Gramma's grandparents? Was she telling the truth, or was she yanking our chains?"

Good question. If Gram had said something, maybe that's where Dillon had gotten his idea for the night before. He studied Dillon as he opened the pantry.

Dillon's face showed only puzzlement when he handed another towel to Brett. "I don't know. I can't say I've heard those stories before."

Maybe Dillon's subconscious had remembered them? Nah. Brett had been a cop too long and saw conspiracies where there were none.

After scraping off a plate, Matt plunged it into the water. "So is she right? Are you two doin' Nikki at the same time?"

Before Brett could react, Griffin popped Matt on the back of his head. "Moron, you don't ask a question like that. Shee-it."

"Hey! I was only askin'. 'Sides, Gramma's the one who brought it up. I didn't see you objecting to her talkin' about it."

Griffin snorted. "Yeah, like that would go down well."

"Didn't you see how red Dillon turned?"

Couldn't have been much redder than he was right now. Only then it had been from embarrassment. Right now, Dill looked like he was ready to take the boy down and pound the words back down his throat. Pretty much the same feelings he himself was fighting.

Not realizing the jeopardy he was in, Matt continued, "I think they are both doing Nikki—"

That did it. Brett lunged. Just as his fingertips grazed Matt's shirt, Dillon and Ethan grabbed him.

At the same time, Griffin hooked his elbow around Matthew's head and put him in a headlock. "You wanna get your face smashed in, fuckhead? You better apologize and fast."

"For what?" Matt grunted as he struggled to free himself.

Griffin rolled his eyes toward the ceiling. "For disrespecting

Nikki, you frickin' dipshit. Jesus, Matt, I can't believe we share the same DNA. You're such a jerkwad sometimes."

"All right already. I apologize." Once released, he brushed a hand through his hair. "I just think it's cool that they're both doin'—"

With a groan, Griffin hauled Matt out of the kitchen and onto the porch, cursing him all the way. "Don't worry, I'll take care of him."

"Let me go, asshat." Matt's whining died off as Ethan joined Griffin in hauling their youngest brother away.

The pounding in Brett's ears subsided. With Griffin, Dillon and Faith by his side, and from the sounds of it Gramma Barnett's approval, it didn't matter what anyone said about what had happened the night before if it ever got out. The Barnetts would be there for him, as well as Dillon. Supporting them no matter what.

Maybe Dillon realized it too, from the stupid grin spreading across his face.

"I'm betting Matt staged that specifically to get out of doin' those." Dillon waved toward the counter full of dirty dishes.

Brett shook his head and cracked a smile. "I bet you're right. The little shit. And it worked too. Come on, I'll wash, you dry."

His good mood dissipated as the sink filled with water. It was the first time he'd been alone with Dillon since the night before, and the doubts about the evening, about whether Dillon had heard him whisper that he loved her, about why Dillon had suggested the threesome in the first place, flooded back.

Wondering how to broach the subject, he washed the dishes with such a vigor he wondered how he hadn't broken everything he touched.

Were his questions best left unasked? Unanswered? Leaving his hands immersed in the water, Brett stopped scrubbing, trying to read Dillon's body language.

Dillon closed the cupboard door and broke the silence. "Go on, say it. I know you've been wanting to."

"Did you convince your grandmother to make that shit up about her grandparents?"

Dillon's mouth flapped open. "No! Hell, no."

"Then why the hell did she bring it up out of the blue like that? Something had to have put it in her head. And since you're the one who's always over there, I'm figuring maybe you said something to her."

"How should I know what goes through that woman's mind? Besides, you've been with me the whole day. When would I have had a chance to say jack shit to her without you knowing?"

Dillon was right; he'd not been out of Brett's sight since they'd gotten up. "What were you expecting me to ask then?"

"Nothing. Never mind."

Dillon leaned a hip against the counter and glanced around before lowering his voice. "While we're on the subject. About what Gram said, about the three of us living together? Maybe we should think on it some."

What the fuck? Fulfilling a fantasy for one night was not the same as a permanent threesome. Did Dillon not have a clue what a can of worms he could create? "No. We shouldn't."

"Why not? It would solve a buttload of problems."

"Because it's not done, Dill." Damn it, what the hell was Dillon thinking? There was no way in hell's half acre they could pull off such a ludicrous idea.

Besides, if he agreed to Dillon's scheme, he'd find himself shut out more and more as time went by. Being reminded how it was Dillon's house they lived in, how Dillon made more money with his business than he did as a cop. And given enough time, Nikki would grow tired of his shiftwork and turn to Dillon, and he'd find himself shut out completely. Although maybe it would be fairer to Nikki. Being a cop's wife wasn't a picnic.

Dillon kept his voice low, but his passion came through like a class-five tornado. "Why should Nikki have to choose one of us over the other? Why can't we just keep on the way we have been? I'm happy, you seem to be, and so does Nikki."

The good feelings that had filled him drained as surely as if someone had pulled a plug. "You fucking selfish bastard. You think you're going to lose her to me, don't you? Because she made love to me the night before last. So you figure you'll cut your losses and offer to share her like she's some goddamned horse?"

Dillon cursed. "Come on, Brett. Think about it. Could you be happy knowing you'd never feel her sweet little pussy around your dick again?"

Brett stared at him. How fucking shallow could Dillon get? "Is that all Nikki is to you? A good fuck?"

"No, of course not."

He crossed the distance between them until he could feel Dillon's breath on his face. And Dillon could feel his. He used their difference in height to his advantage and for good measure gave him his best cop stare. "If sex is all you have going with Nik, I will take her from you and not lose a lick of sleep about it."

To his credit, Dillon didn't back down, didn't even flinch. "I love Nikki. It's not about how good she is in bed. I love everything about her. I want to protect her and help her. I love coming home and knowing she's there waiting for me. I love getting her to laugh. I want to comfort her when she's sad and care for her when she's sick. I want her to know that I love her."

And there it was. It wasn't about sharing Nikki. It was about Dillon getting his way. Dillon didn't need to resort to fists. Not this time. No, he'd discovered a more subtle way to win Nikki's love.

Grinding his jaw, Brett stepped back. "That's it, isn't it? It's chafing your ass that you might lose her to me."

"All I know is it'll kill *either* of us, no matter which of us she chooses. I heard you tell her you love her last night. She's told me she loves me too, you know. I may not have said the words, but I love her too. So yeah, it's tearing me apart to think she could go home with you, and I'd never get to be with her again."

Though he kept them at his sides, Dillon's hands had clenched into fists, and his feet were planted shoulder-width apart. Brett recognized that stance; Dillon was gearing up for a knock-down-drag-out.

Dillon's eyes narrowed. "You know, it just occurred to me. I gave you my word that if she chose you, I'd stand aside, that I'd support you both. But I didn't hear you say anything back. What are you plannin' on doing if she chooses me over you, Brett? What would you do if you discovered last night was her way of sayin' goodbye to you? Would you step aside? Or would I have to keep my double ought with me, just in case?"

Brett's breath froze in his lungs. Was their lovemaking last night her way of saying goodbye? Is that why Dillon had proposed the threesome? Had the two of them planned it? Was it some sort of perverted way for Dillon—or Nik— to control their break-up? To give *poor Brett* one final fuck before he was sent on his way?

When they'd woken up Nikki hadn't been cuddling him. She'd been all over Dillon, with him spooning her from behind. Maybe the evidence had been right in front of him, and he'd missed it. "Has Nik decided?" he asked, the words strangling him.

The stiffness to Dillon's stance relaxed, his shoulders slumping, his hands relaxing. "No. Not that she's said to me."

He forced himself to ask the one question he hadn't been able to ask since that day back by the pond. "I know you said you'd come to our wedding, but if Nik did choose me, could we still be friends, Dill? Or would we back to where we were in high school?"

Without any sort of hesitation, Dillon met Brett's gaze. "I won't pretend it wouldn't hurt like hell but yeah, we'd still be friends. I don't want to lose either of you. Not again."

He meant it, Brett could tell, but saying it was one thing; doing it was a horse of a totally different color.

Dillon shuffled closer, dropping his voice. "But listen to me for a sec. No matter who Nik chooses, one of us is going to get hurt. I don't want to get hurt, but you know what? I don't want to see you hurting again either. Does that make me selfish? Damned straight it does. But what if Gram's got the right idea? What if none of us have to get hurt? What if we just let things continue the way they were last night, this morning? The three of us. Together. Every day. Every night. From here on in. A 'til-death-do-we-part type of commitment."

Brett exhaled. As seriously fucked-up as it sounded, he could picture it. Besides, it would be nice to know that Nikki would have someone to lean on if he bought the farm one night. He rubbed the bruises on his ribs. What if that bastard last night had pulled out a knife or a gun instead of using his fists? If he and Nikki had been married, she'd have been visited by the sheriff and would be planning his funeral right about now. This way, she'd have Dillon to take care of her.

"Maybe if we were living in California or, I don't know, some big city where no one knows their neighbors, we could get away with it. But here? Where everyone and their brother knows when you scratch your fuckin' butt? Can you imagine the talk about Nik—and us? You saw what Matt was like just now. You heard what he was saying about her. Imagine that type of trash talk from strangers on the street, or in a store when Nikki's all alone without us to defend her. Do you want to subject her to that?"

"Okay, so people might talk for a while, but then it'll die down. Some other scandal will replace us as the topic of choice. You've seen it a thousand times before. Look at when it came out that old lady Jenkins was havin' that affair with Joe Miller. Sure, everyone talked about it, called her a cougar 'cause she was boinking a man almost thirty years younger. But now they've been living together for close to five years. No one bats an eye anymore. And look at Sheriff Crawford—he's lived with the two Cade brothers with not a woman in sight for close to fifteen years, yet he's still getting voted into office every term." Dillon was right.

Shit, were they seriously considering this? Could they make it work? "I can stand what people say about me, but do you think Nikki would go for it? Could we protect her from the gossip?"

There was a moment as Dillon hesitated before he nodded slowly. "I think so. If my family can accept it, I think we'll be fine."

Since Dillon's family was related to most everyone in the county, Brett had no doubt Dillon was convinced of his confidence in the Barnett name being enough to sway public opinion. But Brett wasn't so sure. After all, neither he nor Nikki was a Barnett.

They worked in silence until he plunged another dirty saucepan into the water. "If Nikki says no, we don't pressure her, right? We respect her decision, no matter what it is."

Dillon had the good grace to look offended. "Of course. You think I'm that much of a dickhead?"

"Hey, you said it, not me."

"Thanks a lot for the vote of confidence." Dillon took the pot Brett handed him and dried it. Once he'd balanced it on top of the others underneath the cabinet and closed the door, he wadded up the towel and stared at it for a moment. "I love Nikki. I'd love nothing better than to have her live with me for the rest of my life. But I don't want anything to..." He cleared his throat. "You're like a brother to me, Brett. You're...what I'm trying to say is...you and me..."

"Yeah, I get it. You love me." Though he tried to keep the remark off-hand, Brett felt the heat rising into his face even as his throat closed in again.

"Yeah." Dillon exhaled. "Yeah, I do. I just…I'm not good at saying it. Especially to guys, you know?" He took another deep breath. "Look, last night, when you and Nikki were making love…well, that's just it. You two were making love. I don't want to come between that. If it comes down to it, if she can't make a decision, then I'll step back."

While part of Brett whooped in relief, another part of him wanted to sink onto a chair and bury his face in his hands. "Why would you do that, Dill? Why would you walk away from a woman you say you love?"

"Because she's happy with you. And you're happy with her. And you both deserve to be happy. And…" Dillon ran his hands through his hair until he resembled a porcupine with his quills ready to shoot. "You lost your chance with her before because of me. Think of it as me doing the right thing finally, setting the record straight."

Torn between wanting to say "too little, too late" and "about fuckin' time," he realized Dillon had missed the point. "I appreciate the gesture, but I don't think that's your decision to make, Dill. It's Nik's."

Still, the broken part of him inside, the part Dillon had fractured years ago, the part he'd hidden away and tried to pretend didn't still hurt, eased. No matter who Nikki chose, they'd still be friends.

Dillon shrugged one shoulder. "Yeah, I know. Look, while I've got you alone, I've been wanting to talk to you about that."

Brett's hold on the pot he'd been washing tightened, every muscle tense. "About what?"

"About what happened senior year."

Using all his concentration, he placed the pot back in the

water and released it before turning to face Dillon. He opened his mouth to say something but no words came out.

Dillon stared at his boots and took a deep breath before looking him straight in the eye. "I'm sorry for being such a prick. I shouldn't have beat on you when I'd not told you I liked Nikki. Looking back on it, I'm surprised you ever came back to Texas, and even more surprised that you still talk to me."

Had Dillon forgotten the countless times he'd stepped in and stopped him from getting beat up when he and his dad had first arrived in Barnett county? Or how many times he'd awoken from one of the endless nightmares he'd had the months, years, after he'd come to live with the Barnetts and found Dillon crouched beside him, willing to talk late in the night until the demons receded? No matter how many times he swallowed, he couldn't clear the lump that formed in his throat. He waved to the other room where voices of the various Barnetts floated to them. "You guys are my family, Dill. I couldn't walk away from you all like that."

Dillon broke eye contact and started examining his boots again. "So you came back because of them? That's it?"

"No. I had other reasons too." Reasons he didn't want to get into here. Then he realized what Dillon needed. "Yes, I missed you. I missed our friendship. I didn't know if we'd ever be friends again when I came back but I thought it was worth a shot."

After another deep breath, Dillon raised his head again, misery clouding his eyes. "I'm real sorry. For everything I did back then." He stuck out his hand. "You're a better man than me, Brett. Will you accept my apology?"

Brett eyed Dillon's outstretched hand. "You're not gonna wanna hug me or some touchy-feely shit like that, are you?"

Dillon's grin lit up his face. "Nah, this is Texas after all. I'll settle for a good old-fashioned handshake."

Brett grabbed the towel Dillon had left wadded up on the

counter and dried his hands with jerky movements. Despite the assurance, when he clasped Dillon's hand, he found himself dragged into a hug, Dillon slapping his back.

"Geez, Dill." He extracted himself and turned back to the sink, not wanting Dillon to see how much that hug had affected him. "Shit, if Nikki had walked in right then, she'd have thought we're going all *Brokeback Mountain* and would hightail it out of Texas, let alone your place."

After popping Dillon one in the shoulder, Brett walked out of the house. He jumped off the porch and wandered over to the pasture, resting one foot on the fence as he stared at the grazing horses. If he was lucky, Dillon wouldn't follow him and expect him to talk because, goddamn it, his fucking throat had closed up again.

There had to be another way than having a permanent polyamorous relationship. Hell, he couldn't even get his tongue around the words, let alone the idea. Yet no matter how many times he turned the solution around and examined it from every angle, the only way everyone could win was if Nikki never made a decision, if they continued living together, the three of them.

What would the Barnetts think in reality? Let alone everyone else in Barnett county? And yet...and yet it might be the perfect solution.

What the hell was he thinking?

CHAPTER 21

Nikki climbed into Dillon's truck and sat quietly as Dillon and Brett said their good-byes to the Barnett family. To her relief, neither man said much on the way home; everyone seemed lost in their own thoughts. The only sign Dillon gave that he knew they were in the truck with him was when he took his hand from the steering wheel to squeeze her thigh. Brett held her hand the whole way home, his thumb brushing over hers, though she wondered if he was even aware he was doing it as he stared out the window.

Without speaking they headed to the living room where they all sat on the couch, once again Brett and Dillon sitting on either side of her. Dillon wrapped an arm around her waist and pulled her to rest against him, while Brett lifted her feet onto his lap and gave her a foot massage. The shadows grew long, leaving them in the dark as they watched television, though for the life of her, Nikki couldn't say what they were watching.

His daddies decided instead of fighting for the hand of the woman they loved, they'd all live together kept repeating in her head. Was a permanent threesome feasible? Could it work? Or was she just grasping it as a solution because she didn't want to lose either man?

What about Brett and Dillon? Did they both really want her? Or were they locked into some private battle they'd never resolved ten years before? Would they come to their senses one day and realize they were settling for sloppy seconds by sharing her? Would she have to watch one or the other—or both—leave in a few months' time, when the excitement of the forbidden wore off?

There'd be no escaping any public censure, no matter how accepting Dillon's grandmother might be of their arrangement. She doubted Dillon's father would approve of the example they'd be setting for the rest of their children, especially Lilly. Dillon wouldn't be willing to risk his father's approval. Brett wouldn't either.

Brett also had to deal with the public on a daily basis. What might happen if he had to testify at court? Couldn't a defense attorney use their relationship as a weapon to destroy his credibility?

She rested her head on Dillon's shoulder. She'd said she loved them both, and Brett had returned the words. Oh, boy, he'd returned them with feeling so deeply she felt it down to her toes. Dillon loved her too. He'd even asked her to marry him. And he'd shown it in so many ways. He loved Brett too, or else he never would have stepped aside the way he had by the pond. That selfless act had done more to cement her respect, her love for him than anything else.

If she chose one of them, she had no doubt she'd see little of the other again. Oh, they'd wish her and whoever she chose well, but it would hurt too much to stay around. But if she didn't choose, if she chose Gramma Barnett's solution, society could crush them all.

She held two good men's fates in the palm of her hand, fates that with one word could be destroyed.

Dillon finally picked up the remote and switched off the television. "We need to talk, Nik."

The seriousness of his tone had her tensing. Dillon was rarely this serious. Her brain ran through the various scenarios. He wanted her to decide between them now. She clutched the hand Dillon had snaked around her waist.

Maybe Dillon regretted last night and wanted to ensure it never happened again. Or maybe he'd decided that a woman who would agree to that fantasy wasn't the type he wanted to settle down with after all.

Maybe he was going to tell her to move back to her place?

It might make things easier, give her some breathing space. But she liked having them around, having someone to talk to in the evenings, to cuddle with in the mornings. Her place would be so empty. She'd never been alone. She'd moved from living at home with her parents to being married to Wade. And within a couple of weeks of him moving out, Phil had moved in.

Maybe that's why she'd agreed to let Phil stay with her. Maybe she'd never grown up. Maybe she'd never been responsible for herself. Never proven herself.

Dillon caught her hand and stroked the fleshy part at the base of her thumb. "This afternoon, while you were talking with Mom, Brett and I were talking about what Gramma Barnett suggested. About the three of us living together."

They were considering it too? She glanced between them, waiting for Dillon to crack a smile or Brett to frown and tell Dillon off. Instead they watched her intently.

"Wait a minute. You're serious about this? About us..." she twirled a finger between the three of them. "About the three of us living together. Permanently?"

"Yeah, we're serious, Nik." Brett rested a hand on her thigh. "Neither of us can picture life without you. We think we could make it work."

It took all her concentration to breathe, to force air past her narrowing throat. Was she really considering this as a viable alternative? How insane was that?

"We both love you, Nik." Dillon sought out her hand again. "We both want to be part of your life. What do you say?"

"How about you're both nuts?" And so am I for even considering it. Even though it would be fantastic to have you both in my life.

"Come on." Dillon was like a pit bull with a bone. "Have the last few weeks been that horrible? Didn't you enjoy last night? Having two hot men at your beck and call?"

Realizing her mouth had fallen open, she snapped her jaws together. "You mean, you expect that the three of us would sleep together like that all the time?"

Brett cleared his throat. When she glanced at him, she caught the last of some look he'd given Dillon, but couldn't decipher what it meant before he replaced it with his cop face. "We wouldn't expect you to have sex with us both at the same time—"

"Unless you want to," Dillon interrupted.

"—but we could work out some sort of sleeping arrangement."

"You mean, like you get every other day with me?" Unable to sit still any longer, she pushed herself off the couch and walked to the window. Nope, that wasn't working. She needed to move while she thought about this. She paced in front of them, unable to wrap her head around their proposal. "Or Dillon gets three days a week, you get the other three, and I get a day off? What day would I get? Wednesdays? Or is that negotiable?"

Dillon snagged her hand as she passed him. "You're overthinking this. It's not that hard. I go to bed early most nights, and Brett comes home late. You go to bed with me in the evening and wake up with him."

She couldn't miss Brett rolling his eyes. "We haven't exactly worked out all the details, I admit, but we'll find a way to make it work."

"How did you let him talk you into this scheme? You're normally the less impulsive one."

"Because the alternative," Dillon tugged her onto his lap, "is that you choose one of us, which means the other has to walk away."

Brett shifted until he was beside Dillon. "We both love you, Nik. Neither of us can stand the idea of walking away from you. Of never being with you again."

Shoot, two men professing to be in love with her, willing to share her for a chance that she'd love them? How could she not find that romantic? She buried her face against Dillon's chest. "I love you both, but I don't see how this could work."

Brett reached over and stroked her hair. "You don't have to make a decision about it right now. We're putting it out there as an alternative. So you don't feel pressured to choose between us."

When she'd been considering it herself, she'd thought the whole idea outlandish, but with them both onboard, both sitting there so reasonable, so serious, maybe it deserved some thought. If nothing else, it gave her an alternative, or even a chance to buy some more time to make a decision about which man she preferred.

"How long have you two been considering this?" She pulled away from Dillon. "Is that why you suggested last night?"

Dillon cleared his throat. "To be honest, last night has always been a fantasy of mine. That you both agreed to it was gravy on the biscuits."

Brett snorted. "Bet your fantasy never included me before."

"Yeah, you're right. Normally it's me with a little girl-on-girl action and not another dick in sight." Hangdog didn't begin to describe Dillon's expression, but the color creeping into his cheeks had Nikki rolling her eyes. "But you have to admit, last night worked out pretty good. Neither of us has any complaints, and you both seemed to enjoy yourselves. So why not make it permanent?"

Shooting Dillon a bemused look, Brett answered, "Dillon's telling the truth. We only started discussing keeping it permanent after Gram suggested it this afternoon. So what do you think?"

Her amusement died. "I don't know." She chewed her thumbnail as she met Brett's even gaze. "Won't you lose your job? Polygamy's illegal, after all."

"There's nothing illegal because we're not getting married, we're all of age and no one's being unduly influenced."

Dillon's sense of humor hadn't fled. He chuckled. "Besides, I can't see Sheriff Crawford ordering a raid on the Double Bar because we're havin' a permanent threesome. Not after some of the stuff you've told me about him."

"Dillon," Brett growled. "That wasn't supposed to go any further than us." He cupped her cheek. "You'll always have the choice to stay or to go. You'll be free to leave at any point. I promise."

She huffed in exasperation. Leaving wasn't as easy as he implied. Not for her. Besides, it wasn't just about them. "It may not be against the law, but it's not exactly accepted by today's society, despite what your grandmother says. I can't see your parents accepting the three of us living together in sin. Well, maybe your mom, but your father didn't seem too thrilled with the idea of a woman living with two guys at the same time. Did you see the look on his face when his mother was talking about her grandparents? He definitely wasn't happy."

Nikki shook her head. "I don't want you—either of you—to have to cut off your family for me. Besides, a relationship isn't just about sex. It's about who does the laundry and the dishes and the cooking." All of which had fallen to her in her first marriage. "It's about respect and trust and honesty."

"We've all pitched in so far, haven't we? And believe me, I haven't lost any respect for you because of last night, if that's what you're worried about," Dillon insisted. "As for my folks, they'll come around."

Brett didn't look so sure.

"It's not just your family we have to be concerned about. What if Brett has to testify in court, and the attorneys decide to ruin his credibility in order to defend their client? I don't want to put him through that."

"So we deny it. They won't be able to prove anything. It could be that you're living here with Brett, or maybe you're living with me and Brett's using the room over the garage. No one's going to know exactly what goes on in our bedroom. For all you know, they might accuse you of living here to cover Brett and me planting a few post holes in each other."

Brett swore as he rolled his eyes. "Thanks, Dill. I needed that image burned into my brain."

She had to smile at Dillon's faith in people, faith she'd long since lost. "People will still talk, Dillon. I'm surprised they're not already." If they had, she'd have moved out faster than Rascal snapped at a fly. "I'm not sure I can handle it again."

"What do you mean *again?*" Brett asked.

"I went through the gossip mill the last couple years I was with Wade. I'd go into stores, and people would get real quiet when they saw me. Then as I was leaving, I'd hear them start up again. Others couldn't wait to tell me how Wade was cheating on me." She took a deep breath. The only other person she'd spoken to about this had been her lawyer. It wasn't any easier now. If anything it was harder because she cared about what they thought. But they had to know what she'd endured. They had to understand what she wouldn't accept ever again.

"One day this woman—I don't know her name, but I'd seen her around before. Anyway, she came up to me in the middle of the grocery store and told me about how she'd fucked Wade the night before. How she'd sucked him off for everyone to see at the Boot-T Bar. She even had a picture of them on her cell phone that a friend of hers had taken of them. That's when I decided to go for the divorce."

Dillon tightened his hold about her hips, pulling her snug against him. "First off, neither of us is going to cheat on you. I'd beat the shit out of Brett if he did, and I'm damned sure he'd do the same to me. We love you, Nikki. Both of us. Yeah, there's going to be some talk, but you know how the people around here are. We'll be old news soon enough. And if anyone gives you any problems, you just tell us and we'll look after it."

"What'll you do? Go beat the tar out of them?"

"No, but they might find themselves with an extra load of manure piled up against their front door. Maybe dumped in their pool." When she didn't smile, he sighed. "It was a joke, Nik. Brett and I will always be here for you. We'll find some way to help them realize how stupid it is to spread gossip. My mom can stop a body cold with her stare. And once she lights into you, you'd cuddle a hornet if she told you to."

While she knew they meant what they said, it didn't make accepting the solution any easier. "I need time to think about it, all right?"

"You've got your whole life." Brett stood and held out a hand. "Come on, it's time for bed. Dillon's gotta get up early tomorrow."

When all three of them ended up in Dillon's room, she couldn't help smiling and shaking her head. As bizarre as it seemed, crawling into the bed between the two of them felt more natural than being in the bed alone.

CHAPTER 22

A PART OF BRETT'S BRAIN REGISTERED THE SOUND OF COUNTRY music playing for just a second before it stopped. Confused, he opened his eyes and realized he was in Dillon's room, with Nikki plastered against him, her hand flat on his belly, her body snuggled up to him, her breath caressing his shoulder. He looked up and saw Dillon sitting on the side of the bed, fumbling on the floor for his pants.

Dillon looked over his shoulder with an abject look on his face. "Sorry, I couldn't find the shut off for the alarm quick enough. Go back to sleep. I'll be out of here in a sec."

Chancing waking her up, he stroked the length of Nikki's hair that draped over his chest like a silken ribbon. "Do you ever feel like someone's going to wake you up, and she'll disappear?"

Dillon smiled. "Nah, she's right where she's supposed to be. With both of us."

"Can we make this work, Dill? Can you watch me touching her and not be jealous? I don't want to end up fighting the way we did before."

"How can I get angry or jealous when I see how happy you make her? And she's happy with me too. That's all that matters."

Dillon reached over and stroked another section of her hair. "She needs us both. She already knows we love her and would do anything for her. She'll come around. In time."

"You have to admit, a permanent threesome is pretty out there. What if she wants to choose between us after all this? What if one of us—" *you* "—decides we don't want to share her anymore?"

"So we bust our asses to make sure she doesn't have any doubts. We do everything we can think of to prove how great the three of us together can be."

With a soft sound, Nikki shifted to lie on her back, though she didn't wake. The sheet covering her dropped away, exposing her breasts.

Dillon grinned when the sheet tented over Brett's groin. "Never figured you were a breast man. Always thought you were an ass man."

"I like every part of her." Her butt, her mouth, her eyes, and oh, those pretty plump lips surrounding her pussy. Who could resist the sight of her, her taste?

"Have you noticed how she likes it when her breasts are played with?" Dillon cupped one of Nikki's breasts and stroked his thumb over the nipple. It hardened immediately. Nikki sighed and rolled her hips into his hand. "It's like they have a direct connection to her pussy."

He had noticed, but watching Nikki's natural response had his cock so hard it ached. If he couldn't relieve the pressure building in his balls, it would mean a trip to the shower and a quick hand job. "Do you think she'd mind if we woke her up?"

"I'd say it all depends on how we wake her up." Dillon's grin widened. "Shall we?"

His breathing heavy, Brett lowered his head over one of Nikki's breasts. A second later, Dillon lowered his head to her other breast, using both teeth and tongue on the taut bud. Brett waited for the anger to kick in, expecting the inner caveman who'd wanted to mark Nikki only days before to swamp him, to shove Dillon away from her so he could claim her for himself. To his surprise, the caveman stayed quiet, assessing the devotion and passion Dillon had as he suckled Nikki's breast.

Nikki's throaty purr of contentment told him they'd woken her, especially when she stroked Brett's hair. Brett paused and watched Nikki's eyes flutter as Dillon played with her breast. The musk of her arousal—and Dillon's— filled the air. He'd never seen anything as beautiful as the love they obviously felt for each other; that they invited him to share it shoved any hint of jealousy away.

He slipped a hand between her thighs. Moisture coated his hand as he parted her folds and found the hard bud of her clit. Her spine bowed off the bed in response.

Abandoning her breasts to Dillon's attentions, he moved down the bed, flinging the sheet to the floor. Before he could ask, she parted her legs and allowed him to position himself between them.

The ache in his balls was unbearable seeing her spread wide, waiting for him to pleasure her. His nostrils flared when the scent of her arousal hit him full force. She may have been asleep, but she was awake enough to know she wanted this. Wanted them. He cradled her hips with his hands, lifting her to his mouth. Her taste exploded on his tongue, a heady nectar that had addicted him and held him in its thrall.

He stiffened his tongue and stabbed it at her clit, then returned to the areas on each side, teasing her. Licking and lashing with his tongue, he brought her to the brink and then eased off before she could come. Again and again he pushed her until finally he relentlessly sucked on her swollen nerve endings.

Her hips lifting off the mattress, pressing full strength against his hands, she writhed as her orgasm overtook her.

The mattress dipped when Dillon shifted his weight. She

murmured something about morning breath, and Dillon chuckled. "My dick doesn't give a damn about morning breath, darlin'. Open those pretty lips of yours, will you?"

Brett paused, watching as Nikki's lids opened slowly.

Her lips parted, and her tongue flickered over Dillon's dick.

Dillon's eyes closed. and his head rolled back. He knew just what Dillon was feeling. Nikki's tongue was sheer genius when it came to giving head.

After a few minutes, she pulled away. "I want you inside me," she whispered. "Both of you. At the same time. And not in my mouth. *In* me."

Dillon sat back on his heels. "Are you talking double penetration? One of us in your pussy and one in your ass?"

She nodded her head, her bottom lip caught between her lips as she glanced between them. "Please? Or would that freak you out?"

Brett rimmed her behind with his finger then broached it knuckle-deep. Her soft sigh and tightening muscles had him asking, "You been taken here before, haven't you, Nik?"

As he'd expected, she shook her head. "No, but I've read about it and know it can be done." When Dillon frowned, she reached over and stroked Dillon's dick. "I want to feel both of you come in me at the same time. Please?"

Without waiting for Dillon's approval, Brett rolled off the bed. If she wanted him up her ass, he'd gladly oblige. If Dillon wouldn't, he'd find some other way to satisfy her himself. "I'll get my lube. Nik, why don't you use Dillon's bathroom and get yourself ready?"

At her blank look, he explained what she needed to do to prepare for double penetration. Then he padded into the guest bathroom, where he took care of his bladder and washed up and brushed his teeth. Feeling ready to kiss Nikki, he dug through the drawer he'd claimed as his own for the lube, then headed back to the bedroom.

After tossing the lube on the bed, he opened the drawer in the bedside table to search for some condoms. He chuckled when he found an unopened package containing a vibrator, along with some fluffy fur-covered handcuffs, the tags still attached. He glanced at Dillon who shook his head and said, "Don't look at me. I would have bought leather cuffs."

Apparently the little minx had a kinky side he'd yet to discover, but he sure looked forward to fulfilling some of her fantasies.

Wondering if he should use one of her vibrators should Dillon back out, he turned around only to find Dillon staring at him, his eyes almost bugging out of his head.

"I've never taken a woman up the ass before," he whispered. "What do I need to know?"

Now this was a big what-the-fuck discovery he hadn't expected. Dillon had never tried anal? And here he'd thought Dillon had tried just about anything when it came to sex. "You're not doin' the anal part, Dill. I am. Once we're both inside her, it's mainly a matter of you coordinating your movements to mine. You'll figure it out pretty quick."

"What if..." He ran a hand through his hair, making it stick up in a thousand different directions. He'd never seen Dillon so unsure. "I don't know, what if she decides she doesn't like it?"

"Then we stop."

"What if I can't? She's blows my mind, Brett. I've never been so unhinged in bed with a woman like I am with Nik. What if I—we hurt her?"

"Nikki will tell us if it hurts. Relax, Dill. Nik's the one who suggested it, remember? If we focus on making her happy, it'll be fine." Wasn't it just a few moments ago that Dillon was telling him the same thing? "You may even enjoy it so much you'll want to be the one in her tight little ass next time."

Dillon eyed him. "You've done this before. I don't mean just the anal but the whole double penetration bit. You've had other threesomes, haven't you?"

"Yup." But Dillon would never weasel the details out of him. He'd given his word, and he'd keep it.

A quiet curse filled the bedroom. "Mom always tells Lilly it's the quiet ones she has to watch." Dillon's eyes narrowed. "You're not gonna want to cross swords, are you?"

"Don't knock it until you've tried it, Dill." Ignoring Dillon's mouth as it flapped open, Brett climbed onto the bed and waited for Nikki to return.

The look Nikki gave them when she opened the bathroom door knocked the breath from his lungs. Her lips tweaked at the ends in an innocent playfulness while her eyes promised a sensual experience he wouldn't soon forget. The hard-on that had softened returned with a vengeance. Once she lay between them again, they cuddled for a while, both men playing with her breasts, stroking every square inch of her. Despite his reservations, Dillon was soon panting, his hips grinding his hard-on into the mattress.

Lifting himself on one elbow, Brett covered her mouth with his, using his tongue as a promise of what he and Dillon would soon be doing within her. When she was squirming beneath him, her breathing heavy, he pulled away.

"Spread your legs for me, baby."

With that languid cat's movement, she obeyed him. Once again he dipped his head and played with her pussy, licking and lapping until her hips lifted off the mattress.

"Dillon, play with her breasts. Tweak her nipples the way she likes."

Moaning, Nikki writhed as he continued his onslaught on her pussy, thrusting two fingers deep in her, curling them to stroke her front wall. Moisture drenched his palm as she whimpered beneath their combined attentions. His mouth never leaving her labia, he slid his hand from her pussy and through her hot flesh to the tight bud of her ass. Using her dew as a lubricant, he inserted a finger to the first knuckle.

Her hips lifted, pressing into his invasion. Her legs wrapped around his shoulders, pulling him to her, not pushing him away. She was so responsive, so uninhibited when she dropped her defenses.

He pulled away long enough to apply lube to her entrance and his fingers, then broached her again, stretching her, preparing her for his invasion. Soon, her juices trickled out of her pussy, drizzling onto the fingers broaching her behind. She wouldn't get any more ready than she was.

"Okay, babe, how do you want to do this? Me from behind while we lie on our sides, or do you want to ride Dillon while I ride you?"

Her eyelids were heavy, her pupils large in the dim light.

"I want to be on Dillon, while you're behind."

His favorite position. On top and in control. Of both of them. "Suit up, Dill, then lie on your back."

Dillon grabbed a condom from the bedside table and tossed him one. "Anyone tell you, you'd make a good drill sergeant?"

"Some people like being ordered about in the bedroom." He raised a brow at Nikki's expression. Was she into submission? That would be interesting. From what he could tell, Dillon might be too. Shit, that was a turn-on he hadn't expected from either of them.

Working one-handed, he reached over to the condom he'd dropped beside him and rolled it over his cock. He spread the lube liberally over the sheath then waited for Nikki to position herself over Dillon. He just about groaned watching Dillon's dick disappear into her swollen labia. Fuck, that was so hot.

From the way she stiffened, she was having a hard time stopping herself from coming. "Not until I'm in there too, babe."

"Hurry. Please." Her breathless plea had him straddling Dillon's legs behind her in two seconds flat. He pressed her down over Dillon's chest and parted those beautiful taut cheeks of hers. The head of his cock nudged her rear entrance.

Holding her hips still, he let himself groan as he entered her snug channel. If he'd thought her tight before, with Dillon filling her pussy, her ass had less room to expand than it had for his fingers. He forced himself to pause even though his eyes wanted to roll to the back of his head at the warmth of her passage. Electrical shocks shot down his spine and tingled in his balls with the need to come.

Not yet. This was for her.

"Don't stop now." She pushed her hips back, taking his cock in another half inch in answer.

Pushing as slowly as he could, he pushed in until the full length of his cock was imbedded within her ass.

Then Dillon shifted, the swollen head of his cock rubbing along the thin membrane separating him from Brett's shaft. Their eyes met, Dillon's wide with surprise, darker than normal with desire.

Holding Dillon's gaze, Brett flexed his hips, stroking both Nikki and Dillon. If he could do nothing else this night, he'd find out just how much he could rely on Dillon's friendship. With that one small movement, he revealed a small part of himself he'd never dared reveal before. Allowed him a glimpse behind his façade.

In response, Dillon arched his hips, mimicking Brett's movement, returning the caress in kind. They both groaned when Nikki wiggled her behind against Brett's groin. He held her in place before he completely lost it.

Leaning over her, he buried his face into the crook of Nikki's shoulder, hiding the tears gathering in his eyes. Dillon was right. Making this a permanent arrangement could work; it had to work. Because the two people he cared about the most were sharing themselves with him in the most intimate way they could. He'd never felt so loved.

NIKKI SHUDDERED as Dillon slowly withdrew and Brett's cock jerked inside her behind, the delicious hot pain both torture and ecstasy. She'd never felt so full, so alive. And it wasn't just because she was filled both front and back, but everything about them being together. It was the heat surrounding her both back and front, the way Brett buried his face into her neck, his body shaking from need. The glazed look in Dillon's eyes as he stared at her—adoration, lust, love.

He'd been so sweet, the way he'd kept checking every two seconds as Brett had invaded her ass, so worried that they were hurting her. Didn't he realize the whole time every inch of her was ablaze? When Brett had stroked the front of her passage, she was sure she was about to explode.

Dillon caught her mouth with his and slowly buried himself inside her again in a long, slow glide. Sandwiched between the two of them, all she could do was feel. Feel Brett's warm breath as he kissed the side of her neck, feel his strength as he gripped her hips, the crisp hair of his legs rough against the back of her thighs. The softness of Dillon's lips compared to the harsh beard rasping her chin, his chest hair chafing her sensitive nipples while his belly rippled against hers.

Her hands clutched the bedding when Brett drew back while Dillon thrust in. Then they reversed, Dillon withdrawing while Brett buried his entire cock within her ass again. Both men groaned as her body tightened around him, trying to hold him inside.

As if they had coordinated their lovemaking, they alternated, one slipping in as the other slid out. Her body constantly clutching at them, attempting to adjust for being empty on one side and full on the other and then it all reversing again until her brain couldn't keep up. Her body reacted on instinct, accepting their dual invasion, reveling in being possessed by two men who cared so deeply for her, for each other, that they could put aside their egos and their needs to satisfy her.

Brett's hand left her hip and cupped her breast, squeezing her nipple until she hovered on the brink of her climax. Her whole body quivering, she pressed her breast into Brett's hand, angled her hips to accept them both deeper.

"Do you like this, baby?" Brett whispered in her ear, his breath sending a ribbon of need skittering down her neck, over her breasts. He surged deeper. Stars sparkled at the back of her eyes and her hips surged back to meet him.

"Yes, oh, God, yes. It feels so good. I want this every night."

Both men stilled, and she realized what she'd said. Every night. Had they taken that as her agreement to their suggestion? No, she couldn't let them think that. The whole proposal was so insane. "I mean, I'm…enjoying this."

Dillon's hand joined Brett's on her hips. The two of them quickened their pace; neither had the breath left to speak. The onslaught of their possession of her drove her over the edge.

She didn't have the air in her lungs to scream. She couldn't even gasp her release as her orgasm exploded in a violent wave. When she thought she couldn't come any harder, any longer, Dillon slid a hand between them. He didn't even have to press; just the simple touch of one finger as it slipped through her folds set her on fire. Her eyes could no longer see, but her pussy felt the thick length of his shaft pulse, felt the heat of Brett's come through the latex as he spilled his release at the same time.

Minutes later, they lay in a sweaty heap, arms and legs tangled together. Dillon stroked Nikki's shoulder and gave it a small squeeze. "You and Brett get some more sleep, Nik."

He kissed her cheek. "Love you."

She nestled into Brett's embrace, listening to the water running as Dillon showered, squinting against the dim light of the bathroom as he dressed. She could wake up like this every morning. Surrounded by the two men she loved and who loved her.

Dillon was almost to the door when she raised her head and looked over Brett's shoulder. "Dillon? Do you really think this would work? The three of us?"

"Yeah, I do."

"How can you be so sure? It would make things so complicated."

He shrugged. "There's nothing complicated about it. It'll work because we want it to work. We love you, Nik. You love us. That's all we need."

It couldn't be that simple. Nothing in life was that simple. Nothing in her life had been simple anyway.

As they listened to Dillon's truck start up outside, Brett pulled her head back to his chest. "He's right, Nik. We can make it work if you'd trust us."

CHAPTER 23

Day by day, another of Brett's belongings found its way from his place to Dillon's. First his shaving gear appeared beside Dillon's in the bathroom. A few days later, his shirts and jackets and uniforms filled a rod on the walk-in closet. Then his books, both fiction and procedural, crowded the shelves as if they'd stood there for years.

She had to admit she enjoyed lounging around in the evening with Dillon and waking up with Brett in the morning. She prized the time she spent with both of them, both in the bedroom and out of it. Never in her life had she felt so treasured, so loved.

We can make it work if you trust us, Brett had said.

She did trust them, but what they suggested was so...huge that saying yes, actually saying it out loud, was impossible.

Two weeks after they'd first proposed the arrangement, Dillon caught Nikki at the waist and swung her onto his lap at the kitchen table. "Hey, Brett? Are you hungry?"

Brett leaned against the counter and crossed his bare feet at the ankles. Even with the top button of his jeans undone and his chest bare, he had an air of danger about him. Or maybe she was confusing danger with the wolfish quality he brought to their bedroom some nights. "Yup, I could do with a bite."

"After that lunch your mom made?" Nikki poked Dillon in the belly. "Where do you keep all that food? How do you not weigh three hundred pounds?"

She paused when she caught the look between them. "You're not talking about meat and potatoes, are you?"

"Nope." Nuzzling her throat, Dillon slid his hands beneath her top. "I'm thinking I'm hungry for some dessert. Maybe a little Nikki à la mode."

Giggling, she jumped off his lap and raced for the back door, the wooden screen door slamming behind her. "You've got to catch me first."

She'd barely made it to the first step off the porch before Brett snatched her from her feet with a chuckle. "Looks like we've got some fast food here, Dill."

Her breath escaped softly when he caught her mouth with his. Dillon stepped behind her, his hands once again beneath her top, stroking her breasts. When her knees gave way, she sagged against him, giving in to the sensation of both men pleasuring her under the warmth of the October sun.

Her hands sought a path down Brett's chest to his unbuttoned fly. They'd just delved beneath the denim when a throat cleared from the path a half-dozen feet away.

It took a moment for her to recognize Tiny, considering he wasn't wearing his uniform. He took off his baseball cap and turned it in his hands, looking everywhere except at them.

"Didn't mean to interrupt." He frowned and hitched a thumb toward his battered pick-up. "I figured you'da heard me drive up."

Nikki jerked her hands away from Brett's fly and clutched them to her stomach only to realize Dillon's hands were still beneath her blouse. A whimper escaped her as she frantically searched for some way to explain that Tiny hadn't seen what he'd seen, but realized it was already too late. He'd seen them. All three of them.

Let the earth open up and swallow her now.

"Breathe," Dillon whispered. He slid his hands from underneath Nikki's top and put himself between her and their visitor, while Brett turned away and fumbled with the buttons of his fly. "What can we do for you, Tiny?"

"I just dropped in to see if Brett wanted to go to the shootin' range with me." Tiny cleared his throat twice while bright red flags of color appeared high in his cheeks. "I, uh, guess not. See you later, Brett."

Brett rubbed her shoulders as she stood on the porch watching Tiny drive away. "He won't say anything to anyone, Nik. Don't worry."

"But he saw us fooling around. All three of us." Reaching up to her shoulder, she clutched Brett's hand. "He knows. I know you believe he won't tell anyone, but suppose he does?" Thank God Tiny hadn't arrived five minutes later. She'd been that close to going down on Brett, and Dillon probably would have gone down on her at the same time. "Even if he doesn't, you still have to work with him. How will you be able to face him after this?"

How would *she* be able to face him again without turning beet red? Aw hell, he'd probably tell the guys in the police department, and she'd not be able to go into town again without everyone knowing.

Brett turned her to face him, then cupped her jaw and lifted it so she couldn't look away. "He won't say anything. And he won't judge either of us. There's no reason to panic. Trust me."

Dillon hitched a hip onto the railing. "This is your home, Nik. You can kiss who you want without having to explain yourself to anyone."

Brett leaned down to brush a kiss over her cheek. "As long as it's one of us you're kissing."

Shaking her head, she pulled away. "I don't think I can do this."

Without thinking about it, she headed to the barn.

"Nik—" Dillon started after her.

She faced him, holding up her hand to stop him. "No. Don't. Just...just give me some space, okay? I have to think about this."

Though they didn't say a word, they followed her to the barn and watched her saddle Bashir. She couldn't look at them as she swung onto his back and rode away from the barn, leaving them behind.

Bashir sensed her impatience and soon, they were galloping across Dillon's land. A check over her shoulder showed Dillon and Brett standing shoulder-to-shoulder at the barn door, watching but not following.

What was she doing? Had she just made her decision?

When she reached the section of fence they'd cut to let her animals through, she climbed down and unlatched the gate they'd put there in its place. She ran her hand along the steel. They'd worked so hard to help her. Both of them had helped her day and night, mucking out the stalls, feeding and exercising her horses.

More telling, they'd been concerned about *her*. Cared for her. Both of them had been more concerned than Phil or Wade had ever been. Or in all honesty, more concerned than her parents had been. Not only this past year, but when they found out Wade had been fooling around on her and her marriage was faltering. Or even when she'd lost the baby.

So why was she having such a hard time accepting their solution?

What was that saying about having her cake and eating it too? Damn it, that's what living with both of them was—an indulgence. They were a chocolate fudge brownie with whipped cream on top. She sure as hell loved the combination, even though she knew it would take one helluva lot of sweat in the barn to work off the calories.

She had no doubt they loved her, and she loved them equally in return. But was she being greedy holding them both to her, instead of letting them find someone they deserved? Someone who could give them kids of their own? Despite Dillon's protests that adoption would be fine with him, she longed to give him golden-skinned, dark-haired babies that looked just like him. Though Brett had worried about passing his father's genes on, with the right woman to encourage him, he'd be a great father.

The doctors had assured her that not only getting pregnant might be tough, but staying pregnant was a long shot. Neither of them should settle for damaged goods. They deserved better than her.

So why couldn't she give them an answer? The *yes* she longed to give them, or the flat-out *no* they needed to set them back on the right path.

With a sigh, she swung back into the saddle and urged the gelding through the thigh-high weeds. She pressed Bashir to jump the stream trickling through the middle of the property. His tongue hanging to one side, Rascal splashed through the water behind them.

Once they were in the main pasture she dismounted and headed to the front of the house. Her boots echoed on the worn planks as she approached the front door, Rascal's nails clicking on the wood behind her. Once she opened the door, he shoved past her. Nose to the carpet, he snuffled and snorted following unseen paths while she wandered through the deserted rooms.

In the few weeks she'd lived at Dillon's she had more happy memories than she did here. Wade had never lain beside her on the couch and cuddled late at night. Most nights he'd fallen asleep in the chair. The nights he *had* come home. How many times had she gone to bed alone, wondering where he was?

She wandered into the kitchen. She ran a finger along the counter, remembering the dinners she'd prepared, trying not to remember how many she'd eaten alone. Wade had never laid her flat on the kitchen table and made love to her the way Dillon had.

Had this house ever been more than a shell? A place to shelter her from the rain and the storms and the heat? Had it ever been a home?

Once. For a short time.

She walked to the picture window, remembering her excitement choosing the fabric for the curtains she'd made right after they'd been married.

She stopped at the door of her office, the room she'd originally chosen to be the baby's room. Those first few months of their marriage, she'd spent a lot of time in this room, painting it, picking out baby furniture, dreaming of holding a baby in her arms. A week after she'd discovered she may never have another child, she'd insisted Wade paint it from the soft pink it had been to a dark green, wiping any trace of her hopes for motherhood from her life.

"Are they good memories or bad?" Mrs. Barnett asked quietly from the far end of the hall.

"Both." She'd heard a car drive up and the front door open, but was surprised it wasn't Dillon or Brett. And relieved.

Using the boot of her toe, she nudged a box of papers she and Brett had packed. She'd already salvaged her notes on her horses, the vet bills, their blood lines. The rest of this was… trash. Like so many of her dreams from when she'd moved in. "How did you know to look for me here?"

Mrs. Barnett followed her into the office. "I stopped off at Dillon's. The boys told me you were upset and that you'd gone for a ride. When I drove by, I saw your horse outside, so I took a chance. I brought you a copy of that apple crumble pie recipe you said you wanted."

Nikki took the folded paper Faith held out and glanced at the neatly written recipe. "You could have left it with Dillon, but thank you for taking the trouble."

Faith tilted her head. "I've got some pretty strong shoulders, hon. Do you want to share whatever's weighin' you down?"

You mean tell you how I love both Dillon and Brett but am afraid I'll let them down? How I feel like I'm running from my problems to the security they offer? Like I'm selling out?

"I don't know where to start. It's hard to explain."

How could a woman with a husband who loved her and five beautiful children—six, if you included Brett— understand what even she didn't understand?

"Why don't you try me? No judgments, I promise."

She squared her shoulders and faced Dillon's mom. "Remember that conversation we had a couple weeks ago? About me having to choose between Dillon and Brett?"

Faith nodded. "I figured that was the trouble."

If she were seriously considering the permanent arrangement, she supposed this was the best person to start with. If Faith couldn't accept it, she'd have her answer. She'd walk away from them both before causing them problems with their family. "I'm sleeping with them both, Faith. Sometimes at the same time. Now they want me to stay with them. In a permanent threesome."

Faith pursed her lips and exhaled softly. "Oh. Y'all took Gramma B's suggestion to heart, didn't you?"

"It just sort of happened." She wouldn't dare blame Dillon. Or Brett. She'd been as much a part of the decision that first night they'd had the threesome. "I won't apologize for what we've done, Faith. I love them both."

"And yet you're here, while they're waiting for you back at the Double Bar."

"Can you imagine the talk when it gets out that the three of us are involved that way? If Brett's ever called to testify in court, the lawyers will tear him apart. People may shun Dillon. I could cause him to lose his business."

"Hon, people will always find things to talk about. Yes, there'll be some who will give you the cold shoulder. Dillon may get more business if it gets out—who knows with the people around here? But if the three of you decide that's what you want, then I can guarantee I will stand with you ."

"Why?"

Faith looked confused. "Because that's what families do for each other. They support each other, whether they agree with the other person's decisions or not. It's called love."

"Not in my family. Not in most of the families I know." She took a deep breath. "I'm afraid, Faith. I'm afraid what'll happen to us if I stay, but I'm afraid I'll lose them if I don't."

Faith caught her hand, something even her own mother hadn't done since she was a child. "Hon, it's time to put on your big girl panties. You have to stop living your life trying to please everyone else. I know it's tough—as women we're trained to put ourselves last. But there comes a time when you have to think of yourself. When you have to listen to your heart."

"What would you do? If you had to decide between Jackson and someone you loved just as much?"

"To be honest? I don't know. I doubt I'd have been brave enough to be with two men at the same time when I was your age. But times are different now. And you're not me."

"If Lilly came to you and told you she wanted to live with two guys, would you support her? If they came to visit, would you let the three of them sleep in the same bed under your roof?"

"I'm sure Jackson will have some issues with any boy she brings home, even once she's married. But it would be Lilly's decision to make. So if they made her happy, then yes, I'd hope I'd do the right thing by her. She's still my daughter, after all. The same with Dillon. And Brett, even though another woman carried him, I still think of him as my son. I will love them just as much no matter what you decide. I can't answer for Jackson, but I know he loves those boys too and I can't see him walking away from them."

"So how do I know I'm making the right decision?"

Faith considered the question for a few seconds. "Do they make you happy?"

"Yes." The last few weeks she'd been the happiest she'd ever been. They'd been a large part of that. It wasn't just the sex—although she wasn't about to trade that away—but the sense of teamwork as they mucked out the stalls and looked after their animals. The conversations were lively, filled with humour and respect. Even when they didn't agree on a topic, they could always find some common ground. Then there was that sense of contentment between them even when they were quiet They were not only her lovers, they were her friends too.

"Can you picture your life without them in it?"

She glanced at the empty house and realized that's what her life would be like without them. "No."

"Then stop running."

"But—"

"Brett is more relaxed than I've seen him in ages. Of all the people I know, that boy deserves to be happy." Faith clasped both of Nikki's hands. "He deserves to come home to a house that is filled with laughter and love."

Dillon was right, Nikki realized. His mother loved Brett as much as if she'd given birth to him. Blinking back tears, she squeezed Faith's hands, feeling the strength in them.

"And while Dillon has always been responsible when it came to his business, to looking after his men, there are times when he's been a bit of a wild child." Faith released Nikki's hands and hitched her purse on her shoulder. "Lord knows he's challenged us on occasion and sometimes we've had to get tough and lay down the law with him. But he's always come through." There was no bitterness or rancor in her voice, only warmth mixed with humor.

"Like when you grounded him ten years ago for sneaking out to see a concert?"

"Oh, honey, that was just one of a long list of boundaries he's tested." Faith's earthy chuckle had Nikki smiling. "It took quite a few doses of tough love to get some of life's lessons through his bullheadedness, I don't mind telling you. His intentions are always good, but he can be stubborn if he thinks his way is the only way of doin' things."

Like him not wanting to let her move back here, insisting she stay with him. Even though it meant moving out of his own bed. "He's a wonderful man. He's done so much for me for nothing in return."

"Thank you. He did turn out well, didn't he? They both did." Faith smiled then sighed. "I'm not saying you won't face challenges living with them both. You'll need to be tough with them. Not let them get away with not doing their chores around the house. You make sure they pull their weight. Let them know when you're not happy, and you have to make sure to listen to them if they're not. There are going to be a lot of compromises ahead. For all of you."

Nikki stared at her toes. "There's one more thing. I may not ever be able to have children. You may never have grandchildren, well, not Dillon's or Brett's, if they stay with me. And if we are in a permanent threesome, we'd never be approved to adopt."

"I'm so sorry, sweetie." Faith reached out and stroked her arm. "But you love them both, and they love you. In the end, that's all that matters."

"But they deserve their own children."

"Have you discussed it with them?"

"I have with Dillon. And Brett knows I probably can't carry a baby full-term." He'd known that from one of the first times the police had been dispatched to stop one of Wade's drunken tantrums, using her inabilities to blame her for his disappointment, his drunkeness.

"Did they ask you to stay with them before or after you told them?"

"After."

"Then that's their choice too, isn't it? And they've chosen you."

"But—"

"Honey, they're two grown men who know their own minds. I'd say they've given you their answer."

"You make it sound so easy."

Faith tsked. "Hon, falling in love is easy. *Staying* in love is the tough part."

Lord, she knew that already.

"I will tell you I know they both love you. It's plain on their faces when they look at you. So don't you dare walk away from them thinking you're not good enough or because you think others may not approve. If you walk away, make sure you know why you're walking. And the only acceptable reason I will accept is that you're walking because you don't love them enough to fight for them."

"But—"

"If you walk away, it would destroy Brett, and I have a feeling Dillon wouldn't fare so well either. If they don't make you happy then you have to leave, and I'll support your decision. But don't you dare run away from them because you're scared of what people might think, or because of what you *think* my boys might want in the future. Oh, and if you're worrying I'd be bugging you about makin' me a grandmother, don't forget I have four other children to give me lots of grandbabies." Her mouth twisted up at one side. "Hopefully they'll wait a few years before they do though. I'm not ready to start wearin' old lady shoes quite yet."

"I don't know, Faith. I need to—" Before she could finish her thought, the phone in the kitchen rang.

She excused herself and went to answer it, surprised to realize it was still working. If it hadn't been attached to the wall, Phil would probably have taken it too.

"Nik? I'm so glad you answered."

"Phil? Where are you?" Oh, crap, what this time? Didn't she have enough on her plate already?

"Austin. Look, the fuckin' cops here busted me on a totally bogus charge. They've thrown me in jail. Can you wire some money so I can post bail?"

"Bail?" He had the balls to call and ask for money after all he'd done? The acid in her stomach that had quieted weeks ago started roiling again. "Where do you expect me to get money, Phil? You cleaned out my bank account, remember?"

"Come on, Nik. I'm your brother. You have to help me out. We're family."

She looked at Faith, who watched her from the doorway. Family. *They support each other, whether they agree with the decisions or not. It's called love.*

She opened her mouth to agree, then closed it again.

It took quite a few doses of tough love to get some of life's lessons through his bullheadedness. Had Phil ever been told no by their parents? Maybe by their father, but their mother had always argued his side.

"You know what, Phil? I *am* going to help you. I'm going to help you learn to stand on your own two feet for once. You got yourself into this mess, Phillip Timothy Kimball, so you are going to accept the consequences. You're going to stay there, face the judge and plead guilty. You're going to do whatever sentence he gives you, and you're not going to phone me looking for money ever again. You're going to find a job, and you're going to pay back every cent you stole from me."

"You can't mean that—"

"Yeah, I do. It's called taking responsibility for your own actions, Phil. Mom and Dad kept bailing you out in high school." Would probably bail him out again now. Literally. "And when you got in trouble once they moved away, like a fool I took you in too, so you never learned about consequences. Well, guess what? You're all grown up now." She clutched the receiver, her palms sweaty. In her heart, she knew she was doing the right thing, but it took all her courage to say what she'd been thinking all these years.

"Nik, you gotta help me out here."

If he sounded more desperate instead of annoyed, she might have been tempted to help him. "No, Phil. When I took you in, you promised you'd help me with the horses, yet you didn't do a damned thing around here. I worked hard for that money. I scrimped and saved for every single penny, for every single bale of hay for the horses. I paid your doctor bills when you broke your hand in that bar fight, even though I needed the money to pay the next month's mortgage."

Good God, she'd never listed it off like this before. It astounded her that she'd let it go on so long without saying anything before. "You ate my food and watched my cable. I always found a way to excuse you because you're my brother, and I thought I was helping you. But the first time I turned my back, the first time I left you alone, you took everything from me and sold it so you could go gamble at the track or buy your next snort of coke. You didn't give a damn about whether I could pay for the roof over my head or feed my horses. Because everything has to be all about you and what you want, the hell with me and everyone else."

"So I made a couple bad decisions in a moment of weakness—"

"Moment of weakness?" Incredulous, she snorted at his gall. "From what the bank manager told me, you must have spent *months* forging those credit card applications in my name. Then you haunted the mailbox to make sure I didn't find them first. You knew exactly what you were doing. So do *not* tell me it was a spur-of-the-moment bad decision you made. You did the crime, Phil, so now you can frickin' well do the time."

She slammed the phone back on the hook, then covered her mouth with her hand. The enormity of what she'd just done, of how she'd turned her back on her own brother, knocked her breath from her as if she'd been hit between the shoulder blades with a shovel.

Faith put her arm around her shoulder and hugged her. "Good girl. I'm proud of you. I know how hard that must have been."

"My parents won't look at it the same way."

"Then they can bail him out. But promise me that if he comes back this way, you won't put up with any more of his nonsense. He'll never learn his lesson if everyone keeps running to his rescue." Faith hugged her again, then drew back and put her hands on her hips and frowned. "Now back to the matter between you and my boys. Are you seriously thinking of leaving them? Both of them?"

"I can't see any other way around it. If we all live together, they both stand to be ostracized, and who knows what people will say or do to me?"

"If you choose not to live with them, or don't choose one of them, then you're hurting not only yourself but *both* of them too. What would you prove by breaking their hearts and leaving all three of you unhappy? The question you need to be asking yourself is do they make you happy?"

She paused. "I know it's a tough decision and that you will face censure. But you're stronger than you think you are, Nicole. I also know you and my boys love each other and that's good enough for me." Giving her a stern look, Faith stepped back. "Now I'll get out of your hair and give you some room to think."

Nikki followed Faith to the front door. "Thank you for not… thank you for listening and not judging me."

Faith stepped onto the porch, then paused and looked over her shoulder as Nikki locked the door behind them. "A word of advice? Don't overthink things. Sometimes you can convince your head not to listen to your heart. Those are the decisions you regret for the rest of your life."

As Faith's car disappeared down the lane, Nikki stayed on the porch. She ran a hand along the rail of her porch as she stared at Dillon's house. They were there. Waiting.

They deserved an answer.

What would you prove by breaking their hearts and leaving all three of you unhappy?

But they'd get over it. They'd find someone who could give them the children they deserved.

They're two grown men who know their own minds. I'd say they've given you their answer. Was there an unspoken "so who are you to question their decisions" at the end of that statement? Still, it wasn't their decision how she'd run the rest of her life. She'd let others decide before.

She'd married straight out of school, not to the man she wanted to love for the rest of her life, but to please her parents who were scandalized at her pregnancy. She'd married Wade to provide her child with a father, a father who turned out to be irresponsible, a man who would have been a terrible father. She'd married Wade even though she hadn't loved him because that's what society dictated. She'd stayed married to him and continually tried to salvage her marriage long after she knew the marriage was a farce because she had let both her parents and Wade whittle away until she had no confidence left, made her feel responsible for his failures. Until she finally woke up and wrestled back control.

When both Wade and her parents predicted she'd be out on the streets having to earn her rent on her back, she'd found boarders for her stables and held onto the farm. She'd paid the mortgage and even had a good credit rating. Before Phil had gotten to it anyway.

Her gaze returned to Dillon's house where they stood on the back porch, watching her. She was too far to read their expressions but from the way they stood with crossed arms, she could read them enough to know they were worried but respecting her enough to give her time and distance to make her decision without trying to force their own opinions upon her. Something Wade and her parents had never done.

Did they make her happy?

The answer was a resounding yes.

She'd laughed more with Dillon, more than she had in the last ten years. He wouldn't let her sit around feeling sorry for herself. He'd poke and prod and get her moving, thinking of the future, not brooding over the past. And Brett? Brett kept them both grounded. He tethered Dillon's flights of fancy and stopped her imagination from going overboard, imagining the worst in situations with his practical approach. Between the two of them they had introduced her to a sensuality she'd never imagined existed inside her.

"Can you picture your life without them in it?" Faith had also asked.

No. She couldn't.

CHAPTER 24

Before she realized it, she'd stepped off the porch, grabbed Bashir's reins and swung herself into the saddle. The gelding sensed her urgency. His hooves pounded over the rocks and over the stream, his stride lengthening in a steady beat once they reached level ground. Rascal raced beside them, barking in excited yips at the chase.

As she approached Dillon and Brett stepped off the porch toward her, their faces grim. Worried. But not just about her.

"What's wrong? Has something happened?"

Brett nodded. "I just got a call from the station. Phil's been arrested by the Austin PD."

"I know. Phil called me looking for bail." She swung herself out of the saddle.

Cursing, Dillon grabbed the reins. "He had the balls to call you for a handout after what he did?"

Brett's hands had curled into fists but he didn't say anything.

Nikki stroked her hand along the jaw Brett had locked tight. "Don't worry. I said no."

His eyes closed as he dragged her against him. "Thank God. I was afraid you were going to ask me for a loan. I didn't know how I was going to tell you there was no way in hell I'd help bail him out."

"I'd have given her the money," Dillon said, his tone unusually dark. "Then I would have driven to Austin and beaten the living tar out of him."

She pulled away from Brett and threw her arms around Dillon's neck, giggling. "Thank you. But you don't have to do that now."

Though she knew there'd be tough times ahead, right here, right now, all was right with her world. And she was damned well going to enjoy the moment. "I told Phil to grow up. I'm through with putting up with his shit. With fixing all his problems."

"About damned time." Dillon kissed her forehead. "Come on, let's get the saddle off this fella and then go have some lunch."

Once they were in the barn and Dillon taking the saddle off Bashir's back, Brett asked, "Are you all right, Nik? When you ran out of here..."

"I'll admit, being seen by Tiny with both of you scared me, but I'm fine now." She laced her fingers with his. This was how it could be for the rest of her life. Dillon to her right, Brett to her left. Each supporting the other. All three of them. That's what love was about. It was respect and honor and commitment. "To tell the truth, I'm feeling better than I have in a very long time."

If she hadn't been watching carefully, she wouldn't have seen the subtle glance Brett gave Dillon. "You're not thinking of moving out on us?"

She could hear the careful control in Brett's voice. Knew the effort he was expending when his grip on her hand tightened.

"No, though I have to admit I thought about it." She held our her free hand for Dillon to take. "I've decided to stay here. If you'll have me."

Dillon stilled, doubt filling his eyes "With both of us?"

"Yes. All three of us."

Instead of whooping with joy the way she'd expected, he didn't move. "You ran out of here as fast as a jack rabbit with a coyote on his tail. What changed your mind?"

She glanced at Brett and saw the same cautiousness in his expression. Without meaning to, by dithering over her decision, she'd hurt them.

"Because I realized that I can't live without you. Either of you."

They shared another look. Without speaking, they set to work removing the rest of Bashir's tack. Brett's moves were deliberate and meticulous, as if he'd gone on high alert and needed the time to gather himself. Dillon shook out the saddle blanket and folded it with a precision she'd never seen from him before. The sense of peace that had enveloped her outside started to unravel.

"What's the matter? Don't you believe me?" She grabbed the blanket from his hands and tossed it onto the wall, not caring when it fell on the floor. "I thought you wanted this. The three of us."

Dillon rubbed his hands on his jeans then picked up a curry comb and started brushing Bashir. "We do, Nik. But— "

"—but we're not convinced you're going to stay with us," Brett finished for him. "That you're as committed to us as we are to you."

"We love you. Both of us. We're in for the long haul, no matter what happens." The comb Dillon wielded with precision stilled on Bashir's neck. When he looked at her, there was no trace of his usual optimism. "We're not going to push you into something you don't want, but we need a commitment from you, Nik."

Brett folded his arms across his chest. "We need to know that the first time someone makes some snide remark in the grocery store or when one of us tries to kiss you in public, you're not going to hightail it out on us again."

That's what she'd done, she couldn't deny it. While it hurt that they didn't believe her commitment to them both, she understood their hesitation. But how could she prove she meant what she said except over time?

"You could at least tell us what changed your mind," Dillon added.

That was something she could do. The tightness that had been building in her chest eased and she released her breath.

She walked over to Dillon and took the curry comb from him and tossed it into the tack room. "Remember how I said Phil called?"

"Yup." Both Dillon and Brett growled their identical responses.

"I told him he needed to start taking responsibility for his actions. Afterward, I realized I should follow my own advice."

"I don't follow." Dillon shook his head in confusion. "You're one of the most responsible people I know."

"Responsible for everyone else, yes. I paid the bills when Wade let them stack up. I took Phil in when he needed somewhere to stay. But I never took responsibility for my own happiness." She took another deep breath. "Did I ever tell you why I didn't leave Wade after we lost the baby?"

Dillon's expression softened, as did his voice. "I assumed you loved him."

She shook her head. "I didn't marry him because I loved him. I married because I was pregnant and didn't feel I had a choice. But I'm talking about later. When I found out he was screwing around on me. Even after I realized he'd been gaslighting me."

They both shook their heads.

"I stayed with him because I was a coward."

Brett grasped her hand, stroking his thumb over hers. "You

know you aren't, but why do you think you were a coward, Nik?"

"I married Wade because my parents said I had to marry him, or they'd kick me out into the streets. I was afraid of being homeless, especially pregnant and homeless. I convinced myself I loved Wade. I convinced myself we could make it work, but we hardly knew each other. I had all these dreams of us growing old together, and raising lots of babies. It wasn't until after we were married that I discovered he'd never had plans to have kids. He liked to drink and party all night with his buddies, while I preferred curling up on the couch reading or going out riding. Wade and I had nothing in common. Which we would have found out if I hadn't gotten pregnant."

She paused, remembering the blackness that had enveloped her during those weeks. Those months. Despair, hopelessness, and worse, her eventual resignation.

She took a deep breath and continued, "The week after I came home from the hospital, I told my parents I wanted to divorce Wade. I told them I wanted to move back home, to go to school and make something of myself. But they told me they'd never speak to me again if I did, that I wasn't welcome at home unless Wade and I were still together. So I stayed."

"You were what? Nineteen?" Dillon jumped in. "You had nowhere to go. You felt trapped."

"That's not cowardice," Brett agreed. "That's survival."

"No. I could have left him. I should have." Life could have been so different if she'd realized she'd had the power to change her life back then. If she'd taken charge of her own life instead of looking to others to tell her what to do. "Other women have survived a hell of a lot worse and gotten out. I could have gone out and looked for a job but I didn't because I was afraid of failing. I wanted to take night school courses but Wade'd bitch about it, and I got tired of arguing, so I gave in. Because I was afraid. I was afraid of being alone. I was afraid of my parents never speaking to me again. That's why I let

Phil come live with me too. Because I'd hoped they'd start talking to me again. I was afraid I'd never have anyone who cared."

That she'd convinced herself that Phil might have any sort of concern had been sheer desperation. And loneliness.

"When Tiny saw us this afternoon, I was afraid of being cut off from everyone again." She looked at Brett. "But you weren't worried at all."

Brett started to say something but she shook her head, needing to continue, needing to be heard.

"You'd decided that the three of us living together makes you happy, and you went for it. Even though you have to see Tiny every day. Even though he could make so much trouble for you on the job. But you weren't worried at all. I—"

"Nikki—" Brett broke in.

She stopped him again. "Please. I need to say this. I need to explain. I want to be strong for once. To make up my own mind, to make decisions that affect my life without checking with everyone I know to see if they'd approve. I want to stop trying to please everyone else before I please myself. I'm not going to let anyone ever tell me who I should or shouldn't love. Not again. So I'm not going to be a coward about our relationship anymore. I refuse to be."

She looked at Dillon. How had she gotten so lucky in finding him? In finding the Barnetts? She loved him. She loved them. Anyone else who questioned that love could go hang. Determined to never let fear drive her decisions again, she stood up straight. "Your mother told me I should listen to my heart instead of my head in this. My heart has known all along what I need to do. I love you, both of you, and I don't want a life without both of you in it. Forever. And I don't care who knows. You both can kiss me in the middle of Main Street at high noon if you want. I won't run away again. I promise."

A primitive intensity in his eyes, Brett disentangled his hand from her grasp. He dragged his fingers up her arm then along her shoulder. Time slowed as he cupped her head in his palms and captured her mouth with his. She grasped his biceps, dragging him closer, loving the feel of his strength beneath her fingers.

"You're promising that if someone were to walk in right now, you wouldn't panic? You wouldn't pull away?" His voice was tightly controlled, his cop mask on his face. But she realized that she could still read him, as hard as he tried to hide from her. The signs were all there. In the way he held his jaw at that slight angle, the way his hands tightened then relaxed. The way he clipped his words. He was afraid he'd lost her. Might lose her still.

"I'm not going anywhere. Honest."

From behind, cool, calloused hands encircled her waist. Dillon slipped his hands beneath the fabric of her tee and flattened over her belly, pulling her until his cock pressed hard against the small of her back.

Sandwiched between the two of them, she wondered how she could have considered walking away from them. From this. Their adulation. Their passion.

Glancing over her shoulder at Dillon, she smiled, hoping to see him return it. Though the erection pressed into her back left no doubt as to his passion, his eyes were dark, almost unreadable. She turned to face him, looping her arms around his neck. "You can change the name of the Double Bar to the Triple Bar or announce it in the *Sun-Times* if you want. I'm here for good."

Something flickered across his face. He couldn't control his emotions the way Brett could. He'd never had to. Hope. Perhaps. Relief. Maybe. Then his face cleared, and he stepped back.

"I think we need to agree upon some ground rules here."

Whatever his concern had been, he'd resolved it because his voice was firm, the business side of him rising to the surface.

"He's right. We need rules." Brett joined him in front of her, his arms folded across his chest.

"First off, the sleeping arrangements," Dillon announced. "We all sleep together. The bed's big enough. And our schedules will help out."

Brett nodded. "Agreed. And if need be we buy a bigger bed. I've seen ads for custom made mattresses that are bigger than a king. They cost more but it'll be worth it."

They both looked at her. "I can live with that. But if one of you starts snoring, the other two have the right to kick the other out."

They headed out of the barn and back to the house. As they walked, Dillon snickered. "Hey, Brett, if the snorer is gettin' kicked out, I guess that means you and me will be sleepin' together most nights, while Nik's in the guest bedroom sleepin' all alone."

"You guys don't snore, Dillon."

His mouth quirked at the edges, then spread into his trademark bright grin. "No, but you do."

With a gasp, she chased him onto the porch and into the kitchen. Laughing, he whirled and caught her about the waist, swinging her off her feet. By the time Brett made it into the kitchen, Dillon had stolen Nikki's breath with a deep kiss.

"Children, can we focus here?" Brett leaned against the counter until they broke apart. Once he had their attention, he resumed the negotiation. "Housework. Everyone pitches in. We rotate who cooks each day according to our schedule, and whoever cooks doesn't have to wash up. We each do our own laundry."

"Then Nikki'll never have to do laundry," Dillon said drily.

"Why's that?" Nikki asked.

"Because," he said, stepping forward and catching the bottom of her tee in his hands, lifting it over her head. "We're never going to give you a chance to wear clothes."

Seconds later, Dillon's pants were slung over the bench, his shirt and socks on top of the pile. He bent his head over one of her nipples, his tongue lashing it, his teeth nipping it, sending sharp tugs clear down to her pussy until she was panting. When she looked up, Brett had toed off his shoes, removed his shirt, and was in the middle of shucking his pants. Once he was completely naked, he faced her, his erection hard against his belly.

"So where do you think, Dillon? On the counter?" His suggestion rumbled from his chest, reminding her of a lion staking its territory. "Or on the table?"

Dillon straightened. The sight of her two hard-bodied lovers, their eyes—blue and brown—flashing with lust, their cocks hard and ready, stole her breath. They were hers. All hers.

"I have a hankering to take her in the rockin' chair out on the front porch."

Raising an eyebrow, she hooked her thumbs in her belt loops and sauntered to the hall door. "Remember how I promised I'd never run from you?"

"Yes," they replied at the same time.

"I lied." She raced down the hall, laughing when Brett cursed and Dillon groaned. "Catch me if you can, boys."

EPILOGUE

TWO YEARS LATER

THE CROWD GATHERED AROUND THE PICNIC TABLE THE ENTIRE Barnett family had set out for refreshments as Faith Barnett emerged from the kitchen. They parted as she carefully carried a huge chocolate slab cake with *Happy Birthday Ruth* written in white icing across the top.

Once the cake was settled on the table, Faith lit the two candles in the center, a 9 and a 5.

Dillon chuckled and murmured, "Good thing they didn't listen to Matty's suggestion about using 95 individual candles. They'd be having to call out the fire department."

His mother must have overheard because she turned to him with a raised eyebrow that every kid knew meant their mom wasn't happy.

"Busted," Nikki snickered. Which earned her a raised eyebrow from Faith. Which made Dillon laugh harder. Life with the two of them, Brett thought happily.

After they'd all serenaded Ruth with a rousing rendition of Happy Birthday and she'd blown out the candles, the other attendees surged to get in line for their slice. Brett held back, bending over Ruth to kiss her paper-thin skin on the cheek and wish her a happy birthday. She was ensconced in a massive emerald green wing-back chair Matty and Ethan had hauled from the front room. A throne fit for the queen, Matty—Matthew as he insisted he be called now he was in high school—had quipped at the time. Matty had the right of it, Brett decided as she accepted his kiss with a regal grace.

"If you're wonderin' if you'll be here helping me blow out the candles next year, I have every intention of livin' another year."

"I hope you will be, Grandma Ruth." The world would be dimmer without her in it. After being waved away with that same regality, he joined the line to claim his slice of cake.

Leaving Dillon and Nikki to talk to Lilly about college life, Brett settled on the edge of the porch with his plate. The cake had been professionally made, its cream cheese icing a tad too sweet, but he dug in, content to listen to the babble of the other attendees swirling around him.

His own plate in hand, Tiny ambled over, his new sheriff badge shining in the bright sunlight against his taupe Barnett Springs County uniform. "Mind if I pull up a seat?"

"Hitch your butt wherever you want."

After some shuffling to get himself comfortable, Tiny leaned against the post before tucking into the cake. After he'd finished it, he put his plate on the planks between them, twisted to face Brett, and eyed him. "So have you decided whether you're going to take that job at BSU or not?"

Barnett Springs University had offered Brett a teaching position in the Police Services unit. It would bring him a moderately bigger paycheck from his basic pay, though he'd miss the extra money from the overtime he racked up now. But it also meant no more shift work, which was a definite bonus and well worth the difference in pay.

Brett slowly nodded his head. This wasn't how he'd intended

to tell Tiny. He'd planned on having a more heart-to-heart conversation with the man who had been his mentor for so many years. "Yeah, I accepted their offer. I'll hand in my official resignation on Monday."

Tiny nodded approvingly. "Good. Those kids will learn what really happens on the job. Maybe you can send some of the better quality graduates our way, too."

"I'll see what I can do," Brett agreed, though he doubted he'd have any influence over anyone on that front. Besides, the county had precious few dollars to spend on new-hires.

Tiny aimed his chin toward where Dillon now stood talking with his father. "They're talking again, I see."

As amenable Faith had been to their unusual living arrangement, Jackson had been apoplectic. He'd refused their phone calls, blocked their texts, and even ordered Dillon off the family farm when he'd tried to reason with his father in person.

The final straw for Faith had been when he'd refused to allow them to come to Thanksgiving dinner. She'd packed up a suitcase and moved in with Ruth. Who had packed up her own things, and had Faith drive them back to the farm, where Ruth had informed her son that since she was the rightful owner of the ranch, she and Faith were taking over the house. Jackson, she decreed, could live in the stables or find somewhere else to stay for all she cared.

The news of the split had caused a flurry of worried calls, emails, and visits from Ethan, phone calls and a myriad of texts from Lilly, along with texts and video chats from Griffin, not to mention outraged calls from members of their church, and Faith's friends. Faith, however, was determined to act as if everything was fine and things would work out whether she reconciled with Jackson or not.

Neither Brett nor Nikki had been so convinced. Especially when Matty showed up at their place making them promise they wouldn't tell his father—who was now living in a crumbling bunk house at the far end of the property—that he'd visited them. The months of tension and battles between the older couple had tested not only Brett's resolve about the wisdom of the relationship but Nikki's as well. It had been enough that both he and Nikki had offered to move out. An offer Dillon had immediately and adamantly refused.

Through it all, Dillon had been the one with no doubts about their relationship, with the strength and determination to continue as they were, even if it meant having to give up his relationship with his father.

Faith had backed Dillon's position, encouraging them all to not let Jackson's mule-headedness break them apart. She admitted that their relationship had been just one of a myriad of issues between her and her husband, that Jackson needed to realize it was the twenty-first century and she was entitled to her own opinion, her own choices. Because apparently not only did he object to her endorsement of their relationship but Jackson had told Faith she was absolutely to not even think of buying goats to use for their milk so she could make money for herself.

To Brett, raising goats was a strange hill to take a stand on, but if that was Faith's stance, he'd back her one hundred percent. Though he suspected it was more about money and Jackson's tight control of the family accounts than the goats themselves.

Now, with Tiny's comment, Brett was surprised he hadn't discussed the latest turn of events with his friend then realized the other man had been spending most of his time on the campaign trail and neither man had had a chance to talk of much else. "About two months ago, Jackson showed up at our door, hat in hand. Literally. With no warning. He apologized to us all, said we were welcome back on the farm and then he left.

"From what I heard from Faith later, he'd shown up at the Circle Star with flowers for both Faith and Ruth, and tickets to a weekend cruise for two from Galveston, to be accompanied by whoever Faith chose. Then with his mother watching, got down on his knees and apologized." He suspected that the whole dropping down on his knees drama was either for Ruth's benefit or at her urging.

Tiny grunted. "And she took him back, just like that?"

"It took him a couple more tries and a lot of negotiation," Brett admitted. Faith had gone on the cruise, but with Ruth. Which Brett was pretty sure had not been Jackson's intention when he'd given her the tickets. "I'm not sure Faith is convinced yet that he really respects the idea that her opinions can be different than his. Or that she needs to have her own money." Though maybe the dozen goats in the pasture beyond were proof that she'd won on that front. He wasn't sure they'd make it either but he hoped they would. "But they're giving it a try."

"What changed his stance?"

Brett figured Ruth had finally kicked his butt hard enough to put some sense into him. Or Jackson had tired of living in a shack with outdoor plumbing, especially as winter approached. "Faith says it was because of a diary he found."

Tiny raised an eyebrow. "A diary?"

"Journal, diary, whatever," Brett granted. "Right before Faith walked out, they'd been in the middle of redoing their bedroom. Adding an ensuite. When they tore down a wall between their bedroom and what used to be Matty's room, they found a lockbox tucked into a hidden niche. It was filled with letters and journals from his great-grandparents' time." Or was it his great-great-grandparents? No, they were Ruth's grandparents, which made them Jackson's great-grandparents and Dillon's great-great grandparents. Whatever. He shook it off and continued, "The three who were in a relationship like ours. According to Faith, the diary revealed that Nate and Jackson had been in a relationship before they'd met Sarah, that it was a true threesome."

Tiny rocked back and stared over the throng. "Huh. So d'you think he sees you guys as the lesser of two evils?"

Brett could only shrug.

"Do you think he wonders about you two? If he wonders if you and Dillon are a couple and Nikki's your beard?" Tiny asked quietly.

He'd heard the rumors about his relationship with Dillon, but he didn't care what strangers thought. What went on in their house was no one else's business. But agreeing with Tiny meant Jackson was still an asshole, and a homophobe. Which Brett thought Dillon's father might be though he daren't voice it to anyone, not even Dillon.

"At this point, I don't give a damned fuck what he or anyone else thinks." Brett took a deep breath and tried to shrug off the rising irritation. "He tries to hide that he's uncomfortable sometimes," most times, "He's been polite enough when we visit, and our invitation to Sunday dinners has been reinstated. And why we're here today." Which had gone a long way to easing Nikki's concerns.

"This journal. Have you read it?"

"Nope."

The two men sat quietly for a long while, letting the crowd swell and ebb around them. Brett thought, not for the first time, about the contents of that diary. One day Dillon might find the book, or have it passed down to him and they'd read it for themselves but no matter what it revealed, it didn't matter to their lives now. Or maybe Jackson had burned it.

He realized Tiny was watching him more than the party on the lawn. "What?"

"Are *you* happy?" Tiny asked softly. "I mean, seriously happy sharing a woman you love with Barnett?"

That was a no-brainer. "Yeah, I am."

"I'm your friend, right? You know I'm always here for you."

"Yeah. I know." Brett shifted to face the other man. "What's going on? What's worrying you?"

Tiny returned to staring across the yard, but Brett suspected he wasn't actually seeing anything. There was a long pause before Tiny finally sighed, and said, "Maybe I should have said this two years ago but I'm worried that you've settled for second best with this relationship. I wonder if you're really sure this is what you want, what you deserve. Long term."

Ah. Was that thought what had kept Tiny more distant than usual these past years, not the political ambitions he'd claimed? As for the other man's worries, Brett didn't have to think about his answer for a second. "I am happy. I love Nikki, and this relationship, as unusual as it is, it's working for us. All of us." Not that there hadn't been the occasional bump—not including the stone mountain named Jackson Barnett—that they'd had to work through but they had.

Tiny gave a heavy sigh but still wouldn't look him in the eye.

"You don't believe me," Brett said.

Finally Tiny lifted his eyes to meet Brett's gaze. "I took you in after that big fight with Dillon, right? I protected you, let you work through everything you were going through back then."

"You did. And I appreciated it. I still do." Even more once he'd realized Tiny had only been four years older than him at the time. Taking on a messed-up kid had been a hell of a brave act to step into a such a fatherly role. Or maybe big brother role?

"I look at you sitting here," Tiny admitted, "and wonder if you're in this threesome because you're afraid of holding out for someone of your own. If you think sharing the woman you love is as much as you deserve. Because it isn't, you know. You're entitled to a woman, a partner, someone you don't have to share with anyone. You don't have to be afraid to admit you deserve more. You don't have to be afraid of..."

"Of being alone?" Brett finished quietly. Was the other man projecting his own needs onto Brett?

"No." Tiny huffed in frustration. "I don't think you're afraid of being alone. Look, I remember those first days after you ran away from the Barnetts, back in your senior year, how lost you were. But I also remember you telling me how you didn't feel you deserved anyone caring for you. For anyone to love you. That you were..." He shook his head. "You were still dealing with a lot of trauma carried from that bastard of your old man. I worry that maybe you feel this type of relationship, this need to share is all you deserve even now."

Yet he was only addressing this concern now? "I didn't settle for anything. I know it's unconventional but it works for us," he repeated. "Any one of us could walk away anytime we want." Didn't that thought send a shiver up his spine. "Believe me, we're happy in this relationship. I *am* happy in this relationship, Tiny."

"You say so."

Brett leaned forward. "What is bothering you, really? Is something going on with you that I should know about?"

Tiny scratched his jaw. "Maybe I haven't got my own head around your relationship. Maybe I can't imagine sharing a woman I loved with someone else, watching someone else making love to them without feeling jealous. Plus there's all that baggage your father laid on you. I worry about you thinking you aren't worthy of someone all your own."

"If you find the right person, the right people maybe, it's not an issue. Not for me. Not for Dillon either." Oh sure, there were times at the very start, before they'd agreed to the threesome, he'd definitely been jealous, but once they'd set the rules, once they'd figured out their boundaries, he'd not been jealous once. "I understand it's different, but it works for us.

"As for the trauma..." Brett took a deep breath and admitted, "I got counselling when I was in college." He'd had a few more sessions since he'd become a cop too, which Tiny should remember because he'd had mandated counselling as well. "I'll always have a form of PTSD thanks to my father, but I'm aware of what the triggers are now. I know how to deal with it, and so do Nikki and Dillon. They're my rocks."

Was that disbelief in Tiny's expression? He didn't mention that they'd found a group in Texas of others who lived in permanent threesomes, and a few online who offered advice. Tiny was his friend, but some things didn't need to be shared. "Believe me. I didn't *settle*. I'm happy as things are. I can't imagine my life without Dillon or Nikki in it."

Tiny searched his face for a long moment before nodding. "All right then." He pushed himself to a stand and hitched his trousers. "I guess I should go mingle with my constituents."

Brett stood up and held out his hand. "Congratulations on the win, Sheriff. You deserve it."

"Thanks, but we're gonna miss you on the force. If things don't work out at the college, come see me and I'll see what I can do to make you a better offer. Maybe even get you a promotion."

"Thanks." The offer was appreciated but Brett hoped he'd never have to take the sheriff up on it.

Alone for the first time that afternoon, Brett realized he hadn't seen Nikki since the cake had been distributed. He glanced around the yard and found Dillon still talking with his father, both men solemn. Then Jackson reached over and laid a hand on his son's shoulder. Brett decided to take that as a good sign that the father-son relationship was truly on the mend.

As his gaze continued across the lawn, he found Nikki chatting with Ruth, Faith, and several other women. Nikki caught his eye and smiled. With a word to the others, she left them and walked across the lawn toward him, a glass of wine in one hand and an old leather-bound book in the other.

Damn, he got hard just watching her approach, loving the glint of sun off her hair, the way her dress clung to her curves, how her lips curved a smile just for him, lips that had wrapped around his dick the night before. God, he loved her. No matter Tiny's concerns, he was more than just happy. He was fucking ecstatic about the direction his life had turned, with Nikki and Dillon both in it.

"Hey, you." She tilted her head to accept Brett's kiss on her cheek and held up the book. "Look what Ruth gave me."

"What is it?" He accepted the book and flipped through fragile pages as she hopped up to sit onto the porch beside him.

"It's her grandmother Sarah's diary. Nate wasn't the only one who kept a journal apparently." As Brett squinted at the tiny writing, Nikki inhaled his scent. She'd bought him that aftershave and he'd worn it every day since. To her that scent meant love and acceptance, safety and trust.

"Was it in that box they discovered during the demolition?"

"No, Ruth's mother gave it to her since she knew Ruth had a special relationship with her grandmother. Ruth wants me to have it now."

That Ruth had decided to pass a family journal on to her instead of Lilly had initially surprised her. After all, she wasn't officially a Barnett and to let a piece of Barnett history fall out of family hands just seemed wrong. Until Ruth had told who had originally owned it.

"Did she say what's in it?" He handed it back to her.

"Not really. She just said she thinks they had it a lot harder than we did. Then she said that there will be rough times ahead for us too," Nikki continued as she placed the book beside her, "both between us, and with outsiders, but she thinks we'll make it if we stay true to each other. If we trust each other."

Brett nodded, his hand brushing against her cheek. "I hope she's not right about rough times still being ahead of us, but she is right about us succeeding as long as we stay true to each other."

Someone whooped on the other side of the field, a triumphant shout that had everyone turning to look in that direction. Ethan apparently approved of something Griffin had just told him. Brett smiled as if he knew what was going on there too. The man missed nothing. Maybe it was part of his being a cop. She wondered if his students knew just how much they wouldn't be able to put past him as an instructor. Or maybe he was just happy to be back in the Barnett family fold.

He glanced down at her, swiped a hand over his mouth. "What? Do I have icing on my chin or something?"

"No. But now that you mention it, I wouldn't mind licking some icing off you later." She leaned against him, deliberately licked her lips, and watched the denim stretch over his erection. If they were at home, she had no doubt he'd be pulling her onto his lap, or she'd be clambering onto it herself.

Maybe he sensed what she was imagining because he wrapped his arm around her shoulders, pulling her against him to whisper into her ear, "Promises, promises." He loosened his grip and frowned. "Dillon's waving at us. Come on, let's go find out what he wants."

He jumped off the porch, turned around and swung her down in his arms, and set her on the ground. She paused to grab the journal, then hurried to catch up as he strode across the yard.

Dillon met them halfway across the lawn, scowling. "About time. I've been waving to you for ages."

"What's wrong?"

"Gram wants to see us. Like yesterday."

Nikki hesitated. "Us? As in me too?"

"You're family, Nik. I thought you'd figured that out by now," Dillon grumbled. "Come on, you do not want to keep Gram waiting."

Even before she'd started living with Dillon, Nikki had heard the legendary tales of what Ruth Barnett thought of people who kept her waiting. Being scolded by the old lady in front of all of their friends, and all Faith's and Ruth's friends too would be far too embarrassing.

She hurried to keep up as Dillon led them across the lawn where Faith, Jackson, Lilly, Ethan, Matty, Griffin and his partner Trent crowding Grandma Barnett who was still ensconced in the massive wing-back chair. A dozen of Ruth's friends, and a dozen of theirs, stayed in the background, cameras pointed in their direction.

Uh oh. This seemed ominous.

"Good, you're finally here," Grandma Barnett barked. She pointed to the small patch of lawn in front of her. "Stand right there. All three of you."

"What's going on?" Brett asked suspiciously, not moving, as if he was ready to bolt.

His question earned him an eye roll from Ruth, who harumphed in impatience. "Just get your scrawny butt over here and I'll explain."

Glancing around, Nikki noticed that Faith's lips were pursed together as she stared at the sky, the ground, and back to the sky. Beside her, Jackson looked stiff and unhappy, while Lilly, Ethan, and Griffin were grinning from ear to ear, and Matty fairly bounced in place.

"What's going on?" Nikki repeated Brett's question, as she slowly walked to where Ruth had directed them. She felt like she'd been called to the principal's office. Something that had never happened when she had been in high school, but she was sure it felt like this.

Her question earned her a glare from Ruth. Who continued glaring at them all until they stood facing her.

Brett muttered something under his breath that sounded suspiciously like "fucking firing line." She wasn't sure that was exactly what he'd said though. Maybe she was projecting how she felt.

Ruth clapped her hands, a quiet sound to garner attention though it probably didn't carry to those in the back, but she raised her voice to such a pitch that Nikki was certain the neighbours two miles away could hear her. "Today is my birthday, and I don't know how many more of them I'm going to have so I have some things to get off my chest."

She pointed a gnarled finger at Dillon, Nikki, and Brett, in turn. "You three certainly set the cat among the pigeons these past couple of years. But you—" the finger trained on Dillon "—stepped up. You held your ground even when your father—" the finger then trained on Jackson. Who cringed "—acted like a jackass and forgot his own family's heritage."

She dropped her hand and softened, smiling at Dillon. "I'm proud of you for standing up to your father, Dillon. And I'm proud of Nicole and Brett there too. It takes spine to go against society, but it takes more guts to stand up to your father. None of you crumbled. You supported each other against the whims of others."

Dillon clasped Nikki's hand and squeezed. "Thanks, Gram." On her other side, Brett clasped her hand too but stayed quiet.

Ruth swept her gaze across everyone before turning back to the three of them. "I know I'm supposed to be gettin' the presents today but I have a present for you three." She gestured to Faith who handed her a small silk pouch. "When my Grandmother Sarah died, she left me these because she knew I'd treasure them. Now I want you three to have them because I know you'll treasure them too."

She opened the pouch and poured three plain gold chains with gold bands into her palm. She gave one to each of them. "They're too thin and worn to wear, so I had Faith buy some chains so you can wear them that way if you want."

Nikki took the smaller one that Ruth handed her, and

twisted the ring to the light when she noticed something engraved on the inside.

"J.S.N. 1873," she read.

"Jackson. Sarah. Nathaniel," Dillon said, awe filling both his voice and his expression.

The original threesome. The bands were pitted and worn, thin in spots from years of use. And in her eyes, priceless. Nikki sniffed back the tears at the trust Ruth was showing them, showing her.

"Now, you three can't get married. Not in a church. Not in city hall. But in my eyes, with what you've put up with over the past two years and how you've stayed together, the commitment you've shown to each other, you're stronger together than a lot of married folks. The same as my grandparents were committed to each other. So I had these made for you."

Faith handed her another silk bag. This time Ruth held up three shining gold rings, along with another band with a large pear-shaped diamond. "Even got 'em engraved with your initials." She winked at Matty who nodded as his grin widened. "And if Matty here did his job right, he assures me we managed to get the sizes right for y'all."

Ruth ceremoniously handed Dillon the diamond ring, Brett the gold band, and Nikki the final two bands. "They're engraved just like my grandparents' rings."

Nikki glanced inside and saw a tiny DNB along with the year inscribed inside just as Ruth had promised.

Ruth caught her hand and clutched it between hers. "You stand up to these boys, d'you hear? I know Faith trained 'em to do dishes and their own laundry, and how to clean a house, so don't you let 'em treat you like a servant. Lord knows, it's hard enough livin' with one man, let alone two.

"You let them get away with anything and they'll have you doin' their bidding for as long as you'll give in." Her gaze slid to

Jackson. "It took Faith long enough to stand up to my son. Who should've known better."

Jackson groaned out a "Momma" which earned him a wagged finger and shake of his mother's head.

"Don't you *Momma* me, boy. I trained you better than how you've been behaving these last few years. I was damned ashamed that it took you so long to get your head out of your ass towards Faith and your sons."

Jackson heaved a long heavy sigh. "Sorry, Momma."

She narrowed her eyes at him. "Make sure your head stays out of your ass, Jackson. Otherwise I'll whup your ass even harder next time, you hear?"

"Yes, Momma," he responded, meeker than Nikki had ever seen him act before.

Those rheumy eyes narrowed so tight they were almost slits. "Even if I'm dead, I'll come back and haunt you, boy. Sure'n if I don't."

"Yes, Momma."

She raised her voice back to its original levels, addressing everyone. "These are my family, whether I gave birth to them or not, and they are continuing a tradition set by my grandparents. If you don't like how they're living, get your butt off my property right now. But if you leave, know that you won't ever be welcome on my land again."

Nikki wasn't surprised when one couple put down their drinks and walked away.

Ruth called to the women, "Should have expected you to just be here for the food, Lorna Murphy. Considering you refuse to talk to your grandson and his partner these days."

Clutching her bag to her chest, Lorna sped up, forcing her husband to rush after her.

Ruth narrowed her eyes at the rest. "Anyone else got a problem with my family?" Another survey of the crowd. "No? Good."

She looked back at the threesome in front of her. "You ain't gonna get a chance to say any words in front of a preacher or a judge so if you've got words to say, say 'em now."

"No pressure then," Dillon muttered.

After a glance between them ending with a shrug from Dillon, Brett lifted Nikki's hand and gently slid the diamond ring on her finger. "I wasn't prepared for this so I don't know what to say other than..." He swallowed. "I love you, Nikki. I promise I will be here for you always. I will love you and cherish you in sickness, and in health..." His voice broke. "I will do everything in my power to make sure you have no doubts about how much I love you every single day." He slanted a glance at Ruth. "And you have my permission to kick my butt anytime you feel I've got my head up my ass."

Laughter broke out around them as he bent down and kissed her, a long lingering kiss that stole her breath.

"My turn," Dillon said, taking her hand from Brett. He slid the plain gold wedding band so it nestled beside the diamond that sparkled in the sunlight, before looking up again, laughter in his dark eyes. He gestured with his chin toward Brett. "What he said. You have my permission to kick his butt anytime I've got my head up my ass too."

After scattered laughter and a quiet groan of "Dillon" from his mother, he shook his head, his expression growing somber. "Seriously, Nik, I love you, and the fact that you took a chance on me, on us, that you let us both love you, that you've endured what you have from people in the town, and from my own family."

Everyone's gaze focused on Jackson who hunched his shoulders and nodded.

"Gram's right, you've got spine." Dillon glanced at Brett. "We both need a woman with that type of strength. So we thank you for taking that chance on us. For trusting us. For loving us. And I'm right there with Brett about making sure that you never have to doubt that you're loved. Because you *are* loved. And always will be."

He lifted her hand and kissed her knuckles before kissing her on the mouth, leaning her backward over his arm as cheers arose around them.

Once again, by the time she straightened, Nikki was breathless, and painfully aware of everyone's gaze on her. Waiting for her to say something insightful.

Her mind totally blank, she glanced around and found Faith's unwavering, supportive gaze on her.

She slid their rings into place, and after a deep breath, stood in front of both Dillon and Brett, holding their hands. "A wise woman once told me not to overthink things. That sometimes you can convince your head not to listen to your heart. She told me that those decisions would be the ones I might regret for the rest of my life. If I hadn't listened to her, if I had listened to my head, I would not have you in my life today. I can't imagine that. I was terrified when Dillon suggested we live together, all three of us. But you've both proven to me that love can conquer fear. That your love keeps me safe, that you will always be with me, beside me, supporting me, comforting me, when life isn't fair. You both believe in me when I have trouble believing in myself. You both prove your love every single day. And I cannot imagine my life without either of you in it.

She blinked hard, unable to stop her tears from flowing down her cheeks. "I love you both. So much, so very, very much. I am so proud of you both. I want to be a better person for both of you. Because of both of you. If we could get married in front of a preacher, or a judge, I would. Without hesitation. But since we can't, know this. I love you, Dillon. I love you, Brett. I always will."

She leaned up on her toes and kissed first Brett then Dillon, then whispered to them both. "And I'll show you how much when we get home tonight."

ABOUT THE AUTHOR

Married to her college sweetheart, and the mother of two sons, and grandmother to three grandsons, Leah Braemel is the only woman in a houseful of men—even their dog and cat are male. She loves escaping the ever-multiplying dust bunnies by opening up her laptop to write about sexy heroes and the women who challenge them.

Sign up for Leah's newsletter by scanning the QR code or visiting her website

facebook.com/AuthorLeahBraemel
twitter.com/LeahBraemel
instagram.com/LeahBraemel
bookbub.com/authors/leah-braemel

www.ingramcontent.com/pod-product-compliance
Lightning Source LLC
Chambersburg PA
CBHW021647110726
47902CB00007B/1867